MURDER BETWEEN THE SHEETS

MURDER
BETWEEN
THE SHEETS

TED HOLMBERG

MURDER BETWEEN THE SHEETS

Vantage Press Inc.
419 Park Avenue South
New York, NY 10016

Interior design by Maria Fernandez

Jacket design by Molly M. Black

This is a work of fiction. Names, characters, places, and incidents are the products of the author's imagination or are used fictitiously. Any resemblance to actual events, locales, or persons, living or dead, is entirely coincidental.

Library of Congress Catalog Card Number: 2012907681

ISBN: 978-0-533-16598-8 (hardcover)
ISBN: 978-0-533-16600-8 (paperback)

10 9 8 7 6 5 4 3 2 1

To Susan

Through thick and thin—and then some

CHAPTER ONE

Squashed. Dead. The heavy-duty tires rolled over the crusty shell without as much as a bump. Ronald F. Perry IV felt a sense of satisfaction. He had spotted the crab trying to cross Pond Road as he topped the hill and had nailed it. Just about. His old bike moved faster than the crab. Not by much.

Some day he would get a new bicycle, one with more than the three speeds of his aged Raleigh. He loved the ancient bike, however, a gift of his childhood. His father had given him the Raleigh 35 years ago when Ron was 10. The same summer that a huge blue claw crab almost took his pinkie off with one bite. He had beaten the crab to pieces with an oar, a lovely oaken oar that had been around the Little Bay dock for years.

Perry treasured tradition, valued history, especially his own family history, his place in it and in Rhode Island and Providence Plantations. He always used the full name of his home state. An ancestor had owned one of the plantations before the Revolutionary War. Probably owned slaves as well. Tradition and family gave him strength and comfort. He pedaled harder, pushed the old bike up Society Hill on this early summer, sunny, hazy day.

Sunday morning rides served a purpose beyond exercise. It cleared his head, gave him time alone, time to consider his choices. Often, on Sunday mornings, he spent hours on the bike and walking the beach he would reach in twenty minutes or so. He topped the crest of Society Hill and rested for a moment. Then he coasted down and let his momentum carry him a yard or two up the next rising, deep in thought, pedaling hard.

No more crabs. Too bad. He still liked killing them. They reminded him of the people who scuttled around his world, from one hiding place to another, from office or factory to home, always hiding from life. Like members of the press-man's union. Miserable cretins. Now looking for more money to man his new German presses. He'd like to run over their state secretary, that wise guy Pat Doyle.

Some problems were tougher. Like Angela. Perry smiled when he recalled their time together. He considered it a fling. Angela didn't. Imagine someone like Angela believing a Perry would be serious about her. Still, she had been wonderful while it lasted. There was that picnic on the spit of beach jutting into the Atlantic where a Civil War fort eroded into the sand. Extending from one fading wall of the structure was a grassy slope where families gathered on weekends to fly kites, sail Frisbees, and toss softballs. Angela and he had eaten crispy KFC chicken breasts, a three-bean salad, and drunk a bottle of ice-cold Frascati.

"I'm not too heavy for you?" she had asked. She straddled him as he lay on the blanket.

"Feels good," he murmured.

"It will feel better," she answered as she leaned over and kissed him, softly at first and then harder, opening her mouth and his. Meanwhile she was moving her hips slowly around and around and then forward and backward as she monkeyed with the belt on his madras shorts.

"I'm not wearing anything under the dress," she said. A pretty dress, its yellow and red flowers complemented her olive complexion, her dark eyes and red lips. She might have been a gypsy. The dress flowed out like a tent, shielding what they were doing from the kids playing nearby. The kids, the Frisbees, the ball playing, all added to the spice. He could see Angela's breasts now as she leaned over him, nipples stiff.

"Don't you move," she murmured.

"God, Angela, remember where we are," he said. What would the world say—never mind his family—if they could see Ronald F. Perry IV under Angela Rosso while kids flew kites around them.

"Don't you like where you are?" she asked as he entered her. She continued to move her hips, faster now. He couldn't do a damn thing. Didn't want to. Delicious feelings flowed through him, reached to his toes, a shivering, shining moment. The colorful kites shimmered overhead.

"You owe me one, Mr. Publisher," she had whispered in his ear. He didn't remember whether he paid her back. Now she wanted to meet with him. He was afraid of what it might be about. From childhood he had been warned about those after his money. He could not imagine Angela as a blackmailer. She still owned a part of his heart.

The affair had flamed up and out during Perry's separation from his wife. He and Louise finally settled their differences—or at least learned to live with them. It made sense for Perry to go back to her. A Perry always did what made sense. What

3

was right. For a Perry, they were always, or nearly always, the same. Louise was too good for him, of course. Cool and sweet at the same time. Caring. Smart. Appropriate.

So Angela and he had said goodbye in a tacky out-of-the-way Italian restaurant when he delivered the boxes of possessions Angela had left in his apartment during the separation from Louise. Toothbrushes. Panties and bras. Lavender water. He loved lavender. Slippers. They almost laughed. They almost cried.

"There's a tear in the corner of my eye," Angela said. He closed her car door and watched her drive away. He never told Louise about Angela. He hoped he didn't have to now. That was more than a year ago and now Angela wanted to talk. Had reconciliation with her husband failed? Was she alone and needing help? She didn't say. It probably wasn't good. He looked forward to seeing her maddeningly.

Admit it, he had probably loved her as much as he could anyone. The sex, of course. More than that, her honesty and intelligence. If she came from a different, better family he might actually have stayed with her. He wiped that daydream from his thoughts. While she fit nicely into his bed, she couldn't fit into the rest of his life.

He reached the top of another hill finally, took a deep breath, put his feet on the cracking tarmac and looked out to the Bay, silver streaked in the morning sunlight. The marshes, the fields, the shingled houses all remained as they were in his childhood. Sea birds floated on the wind. Soon the beach would be swarming with tiny newborn horseshoe crabs, those leftovers from prehistoric times, scuttling to reach the safety of the waves while gulls foraged the rich pickings. Ron Perry rooted for the gulls.

Perry loved it here, his house near the water managed by his appreciated and appropriate Louise, his Boston whaler resting by his dock, his son and daughter on hand. Everything in its place. So what if his daughter was too headstrong for her own good? He could handle that. Meanwhile, he let all three sleep in late this morning.

At the top of another hill, he looked down to watch a crab finishing his scuttle across the road. Too far along for Perry to crush. He thought of the Mob scuttling around this state, his state, trying to find hiding places. He couldn't take them seriously. Wished he could deal with them just as he did the crabs, under his tires. Perry was used to the threats he received, seldom any from the wise guys. They knew better. This time, maybe they didn't. He couldn't be sure.

"You should go to the police," his wife said after he received the first letter. He laughed it off.

As to the newspaper's mounting debt, there was always one way out, a simple one. Sell the company. Offers for a newspaper that dominated its state were always out there. He couldn't imagine a sale, however. Provincial and parochial and even bigoted he might be, but Ronald F. Perry IV believed in his family's mission as trustee of the newspaper. Just as important, he took very seriously that he was a last bastion of the Families, the six families that since the beginning had run the state, from the slave trade through the Industrial Revolution. *The Bulletin* favored the Families with gentle, positive coverage whether members were running banks or companies or schools. Especially when they ran for office. One of them was in the United States Senate.

So he had to get those presses running, with all the color advertising revenue they would bring in. Hold onto the paper, no matter what, as the twentieth century wound down to its troubled end. Hold on in spite of warnings about something called the Internet. Ron Perry loved his newspaper as much as life itself.

And he would meet with Angela and settle with her one way or another. God, he had been foolish. Still, she had been wonderful in bed. And even better everywhere else. He couldn't forget that. Perhaps she did want advice and not money.

For a moment, he sensed he was being followed, shadowed, watched. Not that he had seen anyone. It was a suspicion he had felt several times lately. Damn foolishness, of course. He didn't have the time or energy to take the feeling seriously. Hell, he had better things to do than worry about shadows.

Far from being a romantic, Perry still took a long, long look at the view this day and then settled onto the seat of his Raleigh to coast down the road for the rest of his Sunday morning ride. This Sunday, he needed that walk on the beach.

One thing for sure, Bill Hasner would be up when Perry got back, and they would have a serious talk. His old college roommate would have to be put in his place. Hasner needed to be reminded who was boss. Not crushed. But squeezed real hard. Perry looked forward to that.

The publisher, who carried 240 pounds on his more than six foot frame, promised himself regularly he would reduce the poundage. He was grateful to coast down the next hill fast. He wasn't wearing a helmet. He hated the damn things. Laws mandating them were one more symbol of the way the government was interfering in everything. Louise insisted he wear one when she caught him about to go biking. Not today, though.

Down the hill he rode, the wind whistling past his ears. He let the bike go because at the bottom of the hill he would begin another climb, a push for Perry. So as he started up the incline he was pumping hard to keep as much momentum going as he could. He heard the growl of a motor behind him. Well, a stray vehicle or two occasionally shared the road on

Sunday morning. Maybe it was that old Yankee, Cy Bitgood, in his pickup. Or that screwy Jim Gleason on his way to fish. He seemed to be around all the damn time.

The car or truck, or whatever it was, slowed down behind him. Ron Perry pulled over to the side of the road as much as he could without swerving into the marsh grass. Nothing passed him by and the sound persisted. What the hell was going on?

Perry tried to turn his head to see behind him, but he never quite made it. Suddenly, there was a stabbing pain. Stars, a blinding flash. Darkness closing in, his head bursting. Even in fading consciousness, he knew he had been attacked, sensed someone trying to kill him. Everything turned black and then blinding white. He was falling over the handlebars. How angry Louise would be when she found out he wasn't wearing a helmet.

CHAPTER TWO

The telephone rang at 12:47. Lieutenant Donna Pacheco of the State Police had finished Sunday dinner with her husband and three kids. Early because the kids were going to visit their aunt. Al had cooked. He always did. And she had told him how wonderful it was. She always did. It wasn't, of course. Never was. Baked cod this time. In the traditional Portuguese fashion with sausage and tomatoes.

The kids, Sarah, Al Junior, and Mary, were clearing the table. Sarah left the sink to answer the phone while Mary went on drying. Al Junior smiled and stalled and smiled some more. Donna sat at the table with Al and looked forward to an afternoon nap. She was tired. A silly case involving stolen cars and a murdered capo had kept her busy all week. She looked forward to a nap. Sarah called in to her mother from the living room and beckoned. She wrinkled her nose with all the exquisite distaste only someone 15 can manage.

The hope of a nap disappeared as soon as Donna heard the gruff voice on the receiver she took from her daughter. It was her boss, Colonel James T. "Rocky" Rockingham of the State Police. She felt her shoulders straighten, coming to attention, as soon as she heard the gravelly baritone.

"Sorry to bother you on Sunday afternoon," he said, almost apologetic. Not quite. "We've got a hot one. You know who Ron Perry is?"

She let the apology pass. She sure wasn't going to say it didn't matter. Not anymore. It happened too often for that. She let her boss wait a minute. Donna loved playing this kind of cat and mouse game with Rocky.

"Publisher of *The Bulletin*," she answered finally.

"He's dead."

"How?"

"A kid on his way to go fishing found Perry around eleven on Pond Road in Little Bay. Perry had been riding his bike."

"So why are you calling me?" She didn't add: On a Sunday?

"Perry's head was smashed in. An accident. Probably."

"Probably?"

"You heard me."

"No helmet?" A stupid question. No matter. It wouldn't be the first or last she asked.

"No helmet. Chief constable of Little Bay's on it. Hasn't notified the family yet. I've sent the medical examiner to the scene, but Josh isn't there yet. Get down there as fast as you can. You won't have any trouble taking charge. The constable doesn't want it. I don't have to tell you this one's as sensitive as a root canal . . ."

"Meaning?"

"Aside from Perry being publisher of the biggest paper in the state, his family's even bigger."

"Ouch."

"Right. Check in as soon as you can."

"Exactly where am I going again?"

"Pond Road in Little Bay. You'll find it."

"Where are you?"

"I'm out on Block Island. There isn't a ferry for two hours. Maybe. Our helicopter isn't working, as usual. I'll join you as soon as I can if I'm needed. Good luck."

"Thanks."

Donna put the phone on its receiver, walked back into the kitchen, looked at Al, and shrugged. He had heard the conversation and knew the routine.

"I was hoping we could grab a nap together," he said, raising an eyebrow. As subtle as a TV commercial. "Remember, my sister's going to take the kids to the movies."

"Afternoon delight?" She whispered and gave a rueful laugh.

Al looked hopeful, half a smile on his round face. "I hoped."

"Gotta go," Donna said. She stood over his chair, touched his shoulder, gave it a squeeze.

"Damn." His smile faded.

One more reason she loved him. Sweet and understanding. They had been sweethearts since high school. She had the career, he had a job. And he said he loved to cook. Donna liked nothing to do with the house. Her salary and benefits made up for the ungodly hours. He got the kids off to school and Al's work as a maintenance man at the state prison was a lenient and flexible 9 to 5. Everyone at the prison knew his wife was a top state cop and a tough one, a favorite of the legendary Colonel 'Rocky' Rockingham. It made it easier for Al. He liked that.

Donna had cracked a couple of high profile cases that established her reputation. She was smart enough to lean on the newspaper editor in her home town of Arctic. Now the Colonel depended on her. Thinking ahead as always, Donna knew that this was one more big case that might advance her reputation and career. And Matt Borg, of the *Arctic Valley Daily News*, might help her again. She knew he had worked at *The Bulletin*. Donna always tried to think a step or two ahead. She had learned that from her uncle Thomas, a parish priest who taught her chess. The Pacheco's were a big family.

She was in and out of the shower in a hurry. No time to wash her hair. Stopped to look herself over in the mirror. Pretty good. Still almost flat where she should be, still almost perky where it mattered.

"Carries a lot of sail for a small schooner." She remembered Borg saying that about someone. So did Donna. She slipped into a sports bra, just in case she had to chase someone. Then a pink shirt, blue slacks, and a warm blue jacket she slung over her shoulder. Black sports shoes. Small town informal.

"Know when you'll be back?" Al's smile drooped.

"I'll call," Donna said as she turned to kiss Sarah and Mary and Al Junior. As always, she felt guilty and even guiltier because she looked forward to the chase, the charge from solving the puzzle of a crime, the chance to show people how smart a Portuguese girl from Arctic could be. She'd tried to explain it to Al more than once. He didn't get it. Al didn't get a lot of things she said these days. She had given up.

"I'll make some sun tea," said Al. He loved to pop a handful of tea bags into a big jar of water and let the sun heat it. Al believed it to be truly special. Donna never admitted she couldn't tell the difference from a cup of the regular stuff.

"Great," she said. "Hope the sun is hot enough."

"It will be," Al said. Always an optimist.

Donna kissed her son, who looked up with big, soft brown eyes like his father's. She gave a peck to her older daughter, who was as independent and stubborn as herself and still simmered because she wasn't allowed to visit the mall today with her friends. Teenagers! Mary, the youngest, smiled up at her mother.

The ancient orange two-door Datsun was waiting in the driveway behind the family station wagon. It was small even for someone her size. Still, she squeezed her five feet into it. She loved the feeling of almost wearing the small car. It was an admitted indulgence, especially with the engine Al had practically remade and souped-up for her. She let it roar to the end of the street, shifting up three times, and was on her way to Little Bay.

CHAPTER THREE

Donna Pacheco had never even been in Little Bay. It was a town on the East Side of Narragansett Bay. She lived and worked on the West Side of the Bay. Rhode Island, the tiniest of states, remained fiercely provincial. Donna visited the other side of the Bay almost exclusively for Newport, with its restaurants, old mansions and occasional music festivals.

Little Bay was up island from Newport, which sat at the south tip of Aquidneck. It was one of the small villages, once devoted to farming, where summer folks and natives combined to keep their town free of fast food and flashier folks from New York and their like. Mostly old Brown professors and Yankees, Donna thought. There were occasional homes almost as big as Newport's smaller mansions. Most, though, were modest, older farm houses with modernized kitchens and bathrooms. Donna had seen pictures of them in the Home section of *The Bulletin*. A lot of granite and marble counters inside but the same shingle exteriors that had been in fashion a hundred years ago. Maybe more.

Donna sped along the interstate through the mill city of Fall River, took in the signs for the mill outlets where she sometimes shopped, then drove the state highway south until she reached the exit for Little Bay. She stopped at a gas station where a rusty sign with faded letters spelled out NAN'S. It was 1:30.

"Pond Street? Down the road apiece and turn left," the huge attendant, with a wart on the left side of her nose, told Donna. The voice came from deep within her massive chest. You believed it.

"Is it marked?" Donna asked, looking up from her little orange car. She liked asking directions. Often she found out more than which way to drive.

"You a reporter?"

"I'm Lieutenant Donna Pacheco of the State Police." She reached up to the woman who had filled her tank and dug a hand deep into her big paw to avoid it being squeezed, a trick an old politician had showed her. "You Nan?"

"Yup. Glad you're not one of those nosey parkers. Pond Road ain't marked. It's down the road apiece. In about two miles, you'll see a little restaurant, the Bide a While on the right. Turn left soon as you pass it. That's Pond Road."

"Thanks." Donna didn't admit she was a nosey parker herself, by inclination as well as profession.

"You here about Mr. Perry?"

"Yep," said Donna, wondering what would come next.

"Good luck." The woman trundled back into the station. She didn't waddle in spite of her breadth. Instead she moved with the heavy but impressive tread of a large animal, a bear, sure of itself.

Donna noted that if the woman knew about the death so fast she might know a lot more. She'd stop at Nan's again.

Now she followed Nan's directions onto Pond Road until finally she reached a police car and a few people standing around in a cluster: four men with their arms folded, two women gesturing as they talked. All of them wore sneakers. Sunday morning walkers.

Donna headed for a tall cop, separate from the others, with a big belly and a red face. Was everyone in this place huge? Still, she noted his uniform was sharply pressed and his belt, a healthy leather, shone right down to the tip of the cordovan holster. Sharp. Maybe it wouldn't be too bad after all. She showed him her badge and waited.

"Glad to see you, I'm Chief Constable Fred Glasgow." He led her along the road past the police car and the cluster of people. If he was in the panic Rocky suggested Glasgow was hiding it well. "I've tried to keep the scene as clean as I could and these folks have been helpful. Tommy Wilson found Mr. Perry around eleven. Tommy was goin' fishin'. He's a good boy and a smart one even though he's only thirteen. So he went to the next house, Cy Bitgood's, and told him what he'd found and Cy called me. Got me at St. Gregory's Church where I was makin' sure the parkin' lot emptied out OK after Mass. I sent Tommy home, figured his mother might want him for lunch."

"Tommy all alone?" Donna puffed. She took two steps to every one of the Chief Constable's and he had trouble keeping up. Like all good cops, she liked to hear everything twice.

"Yup. I got over here right away," he continued with his story, unhurried. "Called the Rescue in Newport. The paramedics came, said Mr. Perry was dead. By the road so we'd better wait for the medical examiner and detectives. Leave the body where it was. Could be a hit and run. The paramedics said Perry might have fallen backwards to cause the wound on his head. I called the Newport State Police barracks just in case. They had their people puttin' down a fracas by some college kids on Thames

Street, said they'd send somebody soon as they could. I guess you're the somebody.

"Looks like it." Donna didn't want to interrupt or rush him.

"Anyway, when I first came over Cy and Tommy were standin' by, like I said. A couple of people takin' Sunday walks were here too. Rubbernecking." He nodded at the cluster, its attention focused on them, and went on. "I asked Cy to keep the spectators away and took another look at the body. Couldn't tell much. A head wound in the back. I didn't get too close.

"Here's Cy—Cyrus Bitgood. Lives down the road in that farmhouse. Meet Lieutenant Pacheco. Cy's in charge of the town cemetery. Town official, so to speak."

"Thanks for all you've done," said Donna, wondering what someone in charge of a town cemetery did. Dig graves? "Everything pretty much as you found it?"

"Ayeh," said Bitgood, tall and spindly with a lantern jaw slung low. His blue eyes hid under thick, bushy eyebrows and behind cheekbones built like mountain ridges. He looked so old Donna wouldn't even try to guess his age.

"Nobody touched anything, right?" asked Donna. This guy wasn't going to volunteer much, if anything. A real Yankee, she thought to herself and immediately regretted the stereotyping. Actually, he looked more like her uncle, an ancient Portuguese fisherman out of New Bedford with hands so scarred and beaten he could have been a boxer.

"Not far as I know," said Bitgood.

"You live in that house down the road there, do you?"

"Ayeh," agreed Bitgood.

"Hear anything this morning?"

"Nothin' special," said Bitgood. "Some catbirds and a thrush."

"Guess they wouldn't know much about this death," said Donna, getting into the spirit of the thing.

"Can't say what birds know," said Bitgood. "Keep it to themselves." Was that a smile lifting the droopy corners of his mouth?

"What have you done so far?" asked Donna, turning to Glasgow. "Notified the family?"

"Not yet," said Glasgow. "Didn't know whether you'd want to do that, in charge of the investigation and all." No seeming resentment. "His wife and two daughters should be in their summer house about five minutes from here."

"Let me take a look and then we'll go see them. You can show me where they live. Somebody from the state police barracks should be arriving. With what's available of the crime team. They ought to be here already, even on a Sunday. The M.E., too. What have you got in the way of a backup?"

"Nobody. Normally, I have two full-time deputies. One is on vacation this weekend, and the other one lost his mother Friday so he's in Boston where she lived. There's the telephone operator at our station and that's it. My wife, actually. Here's the body."

He sounded annoyed. He should be, thought Donna. So was she. If she could shower and leave her family and get here in an hour or less the Medical Examiner should be able to do even better. Sunday or no Sunday. Good thing the Rescue Squad had been here to certify the death.

Donna stopped to take in the whole scene. The road was barely two lanes, less than 15 feet wide. She stood in the dip. After it, the road began to climb up a gentle slope. The landscape rolled deeply enough to hide the gully.

She pulled the blanket from the body. Bodies didn't bother her much except if they were kids. Or beaten women. Ronald Perry had been neither. A big guy, looked over six feet, more than 200 pounds for sure. Wound on the back of his head, blood matter on his thin brown hair. Arms under him. As though he fell forward, not backward as the paramedics had said. His bicycle rested to the right, partly off the road. There were no marks anywhere around the scene that Donna could see.

She bent over to be sure. Bent further to look at his face, squashed against the ground. No fear on it from what she could see. Self-satisfaction? Maybe. Maybe the guy always wore the complacent mask, hiding something else. Died wearing it.

"Lying on his stomach," said Glasgow, repeating what she saw. Didn't say anything about the arms. "Head wound must have killed him."

"No helmet?" she asked.

"Not many folks wear them out here," said Glasgow. "Tell you the truth I don't enforce that law much."

"What do you think?"

"Don't know what to think," said Glasgow. "Seems to me he would have fallen forward if he was leaning over the handle-bars to chug up the hill. Funny if he fell back he landed on his stomach."

Potbelly or not, Glasgow was no fool.

"I guess," said Donna. "He's a big guy though. Maybe he fell backward and didn't have time to react."

Glasgow didn't say anything. Donna didn't believe it herself.

"You didn't hear a car this morning, did you?" Donna turned to Bitgood, who had trailed them. His blue eyes were active.

"Not so I would have noticed," he said. "Wasn't payin' much attention. Just havin' my mornin' water and readin' the paper."

"Your morning water?"

"That's right," said Bitgood. "Cup of hot water. Better'n coffee or tea. Healthier. Cheaper too."

Tired of playing straight woman, Donna turned to the two State Police, who had arrived and left their car. She recognized them but didn't remember the names. Young, strong, looking just the way State Police should, hats squared on their heads. She hoped they had a brain between them. They recognized her.

"Nice to see you," she said, didn't add that it was about time. "You know the deal. Keep the area secure. Nothing moves until the M.E. gets here. If you see anything make sure you note it."

She turned and began a walk around the scene. The road was paved. No tire prints. No sign of any marks she could see. Let the crime scene people do their job. The two state cops stood to the side. They'd relax once she was gone. Or maybe not. They looked new.

"The wife hasn't called about her husband?" Donna asked Glasgow.

"Nope. Just checked with the station before you got here."

"Funny, don't you think?"

"Folks who live in big houses can be funny," he said. He wasn't smiling.

"Well, let's go to the big house and talk to Mrs. Perry," she said. She turned to the State Police duo. "The Chief Constable and I will be back within an hour or I'll call your car. You can reach us through the Constable's car. You've got that number." They nodded, standing very straight, hands at their sides.

"Ready to go?" she asked Glasgow.

"Nope," he said. "But we better."

She hadn't told the state cops they were going to see the Perry family. Neither had Glasgow. Less said the better. Glasgow opened the door of his Mercury Marquis for her. It wasn't locked. Ah, the country, thought Donna. Then the Constable pointed the car down Pond Road. No siren. Sunday in Little Bay.

CHAPTER FOUR

The Perry house looked the way Donna expected or hoped it would, looming in the distance from between dunes and tall rushes. Like the mansion in the old movie she had seen on TV, the one that burned down. *Rebecca*, that was the movie's name. Glasgow said the family called it Isle de l'Espoire. Donna didn't know what that meant but it sounded right as it rolled off the Constable's tongue. Isle de l'Espoire. She repeated it in her head.

Glasgow turned off Pond Road and pointed his Mercury down a dirt path. Underbrush and scrawny pine gave way to wetlands, the Bay's fingers reaching up between patches of sea grass and brush on either side of the road. The house disappeared for a while. Then, Isle de l'Espoire loomed large straight ahead.

"Area used to be an island," said Glasgow. That explained the Isle, thought Donna. She smiled to herself. Wow, a real detective.

Stone and dominating, Isle de l'Espoire stood on ground higher than the land around it. Brick chimneys at either end, perfectly balanced, the entrance door solid and massive, framed by flowering dogwoods, white against gray. Mandalay, was that the name of the mansion that burned in the movie? Maybe. To the right of the house was a tennis court, clay with a droopy net. On the other side of the house was a three-car garage.

Two stone steps, granite slabs actually, led up to the door. A couple of bicycles rested on a block of stone about a foot and a half high, down the path. Both were women's. Obviously, the Perrys were a bicycle family.

"That's what the ladies used to mount their horses," Glasgow said as he saw Donna looking at the stone block. "And the older gentleman too, of course."

"Of course," said Donna and grinned at herself as she led the way up the steps and grasped the large, brass knocker centered in the door. In the form of a horse head, it felt cold in her hand, heavy and as solid as old money. She raised it and then let it fall of its own weight.

"Yes?" said the woman who answered the door. She stood very straight so she looked taller than she was, a straight line from toe to top. Blondish hair. Hazel eyes wide apart. Solid, not fat. Composed with a half-smile like those on old Greek busts Donna had seen in the RISD Museum, content and comfortable with herself. She was wearing a bulky blue cashmere sweater and white linen shorts that showed off her good legs. Blue espadrilles. It could be cool out here by the Bay, thought Donna, glad she had worn a casual yet good cotton blazer and slacks. This woman would notice such things.

"Mrs. Perry, this is Lieutenant Pacheco of the State Police," said Glasgow. "May we come in?" Donna noticed the change in his grammar. Easy to underestimate a fat country cop. "We'd like to talk to you."

"Of course," said Louise Perry and smiled. "I hope we haven't broken any laws."

They followed her into a room that had to take up almost the entire first floor. Baronial and shabby genteel. On the walls were old paintings of ships and the seashore and an occasional lake. A grand piano was at one end before a fireplace. Heavy stuffed chairs and a sofa faced a huge fireplace at the other. In between was more overstuffed and frayed furniture and a couple of game tables. They hardly filled the great room. Enough space left for dancing. Bigger than the whole house Donna grew up in.

French doors opened onto a patio of slate slabs facing the water. A table with wrought iron legs supporting a marble top was set with a white tablecloth.

"Would you like to join me outside?" Not waiting for an answer, Mrs. Perry led them through the open doors. She was used to being followed. "I was just about to have my coffee. My husband Ron will be home soon from his bike ride. Should be home already as a matter of fact. Now what is this about, Constable?"

"I'm afraid your husband is what we've come about," said Glasgow.

"My God, I hope he hasn't fallen and hurt himself," Louise Perry said, seating herself. "I keep telling him to wear his helmet." She paused. "He hasn't hit some youngster, has he?"

"It's not that," said Glasgow very slowly, stretching it out. He pursed his lips, looked down towards Louise Perry's blue shoes, swallowed, looked up again into her eyes. All of it in seconds.

Donna was glad he was carrying the ball. She watched Mrs. Perry while fighting off her own insecurity. Louise Perry's family and people like her owned the mills where the Pacheco family had worked, Donna's parents and grandparents and cousins and all the rest. The tradition of separation and presumed superiority lingered on. And not just the tradition. The Pacheco's went to public or Catholic schools, the Perrys to private schools and Ivy League colleges. Is that where they learned to sit so straight?

Louise Perry waited. The realization of something awful seemed to grow in her. She centered herself squarely in her chair with her hands clasped on her thighs, feet planted solidly on the floor, as though bracing for what was to come. She wasn't going to ask, she wasn't going to rush toward the inevitable. She would wait. The news would wait.

"Mr. Perry has met with an accident," said Glasgow. He paused, his eyes still focused on her. "Your husband is dead, Mrs. Perry. We're sorry."

Louise Perry didn't say anything for a long moment. Her eyes grew wider and somehow bluer, her hands clasped in front of her face as though in prayer. Her jaw clenched. In my family someone would have been screaming or weeping, Donna thought. Better or worse? Who knew? Different, that's for sure.

"How could that be?" Mrs. Perry hissed, squeezing the words out between tight lips. "He was just on Pond Road. Was he hit by a car? He couldn't just have fallen off that bike. Are you sure it's Ron?"

"No question about that. We're not sure exactly what happened," said Donna. It was time for her to step in. "We're trying to figure it out ourselves."

"Who are you again?" Mrs. Perry asked, turning to Donna. Her jaw was working, finally settled in a firm line.

"I'm Lieutenant Donna Pacheco of the State Police." Why else would I be here in this house, she thought, talking to a Perry.

"Why would you be here if Ron just fell off his bike?" Louise Perry asked, no fool. Not someone who would be impressed by the state police.

"To give the Constable here any help he might need and to try to answer questions like the ones you just asked."

"So you suspect it could be something other than an accident?" Louise was quick as well as contained. Her jaw muscles worked, clenched.

"We don't know much for sure," said Donna. "Do you mind if we ask you a few questions?"

"Of course not," she said, then paused, her strong jaw moved forward. She pushed an errant strand of hair behind an ear. Well, at least she does that just like the rest of us, Donna observed. "God, what will I tell the children?"

The news, the loss, would not hit Louise Perry until later. Donna guessed. Right now the woman was in shock. Yet she still functioned. Later she might come apart. Perhaps not. Louise Perry looked tough. Quite tough. She folded, unfolded, and then folded her hands on her lap once more.

"So this morning was normal," said Donna, making it less a question than an opportunity for Louise Perry to tell them about the way the day began.

First Louise Perry swallowed hard. Took a breath. The heel of her right foot raised slightly from the floor, her right knee jiggled nervously, before it settled firmly in place again. Her hands, stubby for someone so statuesque, remained firmly together.

"Ron always gets up first," Louise Perry began. "He's a morning person. I'm not much good in the morning. So he was up about 9, which is late for him, perhaps because we were out last night for dinner with Bill Hasner, who's staying with us. I heard Ron moving around but he tries to keep as quiet as he can. That's about it . . ."

Donna and Glasgow waited. If Louise Perry, now less than imperturbable, went on something useful might emerge.

"So I got up around 10:30," she finally continued. "Amanda and Muffy weren't up until later. You know how teenagers are. They hit the tennis ball for a while and then took a shower. They're getting dressed now, I hope. I think that Bill went out for a drive—his car isn't in front. Maybe he went looking for a Starbucks. He won't have any luck, there isn't one around here. Genevieve, our maid, is off for the day so I tidied up the kitchen a little because the girls aren't as neat as they should be and made toast and more coffee. I was about to come out here and have it. Then I heard you at the door."

She sounded almost indignant before stopping abruptly. Her eyes tightened, she swallowed, visibly regained her composure.

"Was your husband upset about anything?" asked Donna. "Anything bothering him especially? Anybody?"

"There are always pressures and problems in business, Lieutenant. Especially in our business, as I think you can imagine. There are people who just don't like newspaper publishers and Ron's been under enormous pressure because we're opening a new production center today.

"It's why he looked forward to these bike rides on Sunday morning so much. It was a chance to clear his mind for a couple of hours. He said he got most of his good ideas and solutions to problems while he pedaled his old Raleigh. He loved that stupid old thing."

Louise Perry gulped and swallowed again. Donna could see her straining to hold herself together. Her head dropped. Glasgow got up. He would be sensitive to the richest and most powerful family in his town. So would she if she were in his shoes, a local cop, thought Donna. She was pretty careful herself. That's one of the reasons the Colonel sent her here. It was time to leave, but not quite yet.

"Will your daughters be down soon?" Donna asked. Just to get away from talking about Ron Perry. Perhaps Louise Perry picked that up.

"Don't worry about me," Louise Perry said. "I'll be all right. Where is Ron now?" A tidy question. Constable Glasgow told her that her husband's body would be taken to the medical examiner's office in Providence and he would keep her informed. In the awkward pause that followed, they heard the front door open and in burst a big, ruddy man with a smile on his face. Sweatshirt with BROWN across the front. Chinos. He tramped directly onto the patio. At home.

"What's up, Louise?" he said, after a moment, looking at Glasgow and Donna. Waiting for an explanation. Not saying anything. Cool, thought Donna. People in this house don't give anything away. Never have, thought Donna, which is why they have houses like this.

"This is Bill Hasner," Louise Perry said. She waved a hand in his direction, reached out to touch a shoulder.

"I'm afraid we've have bad news for Mrs. Perry." Constable Glasgow stepped in and introduced and identified himself and Donna Pacheco before turning back to Louise Perry. "Once again, we're sorry to bring you the bad news." Donna saw Louise Perry's shoulders slump.

"Maybe we can step outside for a moment," Glasgow said to Hasner. The door was left open as they descended the stone stairs to stand together by the car in which Hasner had arrived. Donna followed.

"I can't believe it," Hasner said when he was told about Ron Perry. He leaned against his own classic, racing green Jaguar. Took a deep breath. Folded his arms. Distracted, obviously thinking about something else, he stared at Constable Glasgow with empty eyes. "No one saw anything or heard anything?"

"Not a thing," said Glasgow. "You were out driving this morning. Looking for a Starbucks, Mrs. Perry said." His English was better, Donna noticed.

"Not really. Louise must have been kidding. I took a drive down to East Beach. It was a beautiful morning and I didn't want to wake anyone up. Didn't see Louise. I thought I might even watch the horseshoe crabs or take a walk. I had some papers, work stuff, with me and ended up reading them instead."

"You didn't see anyone then?" Donna asked.

"Not a soul. Just some baby horseshoe crabs, dodging gulls, preserving life," Hasner said. He smiled a sad smile. Winsome, thought Donna. Then he swallowed hard. "Ron and I were roommates at Brown. He was my best friend. I owed him everything, my job at *The Bulletin*, everything. I'm finding it hard to believe he's gone."

"He's gone," said Donna. "It's good that you're here for Mrs. Perry. Anything unusual happen last night, by the way?"

"Not really. We had a few drinks here and then went down to The Fish Place, a restaurant, not much more than a shack really, by the water. The fish is fresh every day and the cook, an old fisherman, doesn't spoil it with fancy sauces. Just some butter in a pan."

"Discuss anything special?"

"Not much," he said. "A little business. I'm executive vice president of Ron's company. We were going to get to more serious stuff today. Maybe I better get inside if you haven't anything more for me." Hasner showed a nice ability to be brisk as well as friendly, a good combination in an executive, or anyone else. Smooth, thought Donna.

"One more thing," said Donna. "Did you drive to East Beach on Pond Road?"

"Best way to go," said Bill Hasner.

"And you didn't see Mr. Perry?"

"No, that's usually the last part of Ron's ride."

"You knew that, did you?"

"We all kidded him about how regular he was, a creature of habit, really."

"So you didn't drive back that way?" said Donna. Still friendly-like.

"Not really. Pond Road circles along the Bay shore and then comes back up this way," said Hasner. "That's the way I came back. Full circle, you might say."

"Thanks," said Donna. "I'm sure we'll be seeing you again."

"I look forward to being of any help I can," said Hasner. Still smiling his helpful smile.

"Great car," said Glasgow, cocking an eyebrow at Donna, as Hasner left his Jaguar. "Must be pretty old to have the steering wheel on the right that way. Now the British make the Jaguars with the wheel on the left for the market over here."

"Old enough, but I love it," said Hasner as he climbed the steps to the Perry front door. "Goodbye."

Donna took one last look at the house as she got into Glasgow's Mercury. Through the front door as it closed, did she see Hasner reach his arms out to Louise Perry? Maybe the Jaguar wasn't all he loved. And that steering wheel on the right would have made it easy to swing a club at someone on a bike alongside his car.

CHAPTER FIVE

Donna and Glasgow exchanged not a word as the Constable drove back the five minutes to where the Medical Examiner was still stooped over the body.

"About time he got here," Donna said to Glasgow as they got out of the Mercury walked toward the corpse of Ronald F. Perry IV. Donna stopped before she reached it. "Where does Tommy Wilson live? I better go talk to him after I check in with the M.E."

"On Beach Street right on the water. His parents are over-age-in-grade hippies." Glasgow gave away his military background. "Just go back up Pond Street and take your first left. It's a dirt road that curves down to the water."

"I see we've got the first team on board," said the M.E., Josh Chambers, as she approached him. Sarcastic? Donna couldn't tell. Told herself to forget it. Chambers was bent over the body, didn't look up. "Before you ask, unofficially you can see the blow that killed him. I'll know more later."

"Soon I hope." She gave him a look.

"Soon as I can." He shook his head at her. His sour, knowing look indicated he understood the crack about his being late, knew Donna's reputation for being sharp, appreciated the fact she was the Colonel's favored investigator.

Donna slid into her car and wheeled the Datsun into a U-turn. She hadn't gone far before she turned left onto the dirt road she figured was Beach Street. No sign. She didn't expect one. Didn't go very far on Beach.

Tommy Wilson looked about the same size as Donna's son, Al Junior, who was thirteen. Stringy and lanky, tanned, blue eyes, patch of dirty blonde hair. The kid sat on the steps of the porch of a big fishing shack. Behind him were the white plastic chairs that never seem to wear out. Dirty. The shack had one floor, flat roof, weathered shingles. It backed onto an inlet of the bay. Tommy's worn and stained shorts almost reached his dirty white sneakers. No socks. His T-shirt saluted Manny Ramirez of the Red Sox. He was reading a book. Donna parked her car between lobster pots in the front yard. A few grass blades grew between the weeds.

"Hi," said Donna. "You must be Tommy Wilson. Parents home?"

"Who's asking?" He got to his feet. Shorts drooped from his waist to his hipbone.

"My name is Donna Pacheco and I'm a lieutenant with the State Police. I'm looking into the death of Ronald Perry. I'd like to talk to you for a few minutes."

"Got identification?"

Donna pulled her ID from her wallet and damned those TV shows that taught kids all the tricks. Then again, maybe not, thinking of her kids. Better safe than sorry.

"Thanks," said the kid, now grinning, showing the space a front tooth once filled. "My parents are always after me to be careful with people who say they're cops. It was kind of fun to make you pull out your wallet and stuff. Cool car. Datsun, right?" He closed the book. Donna saw it was *Catcher in the Rye.*

"Thanks about the car. Not many guys your age would know it's a Datsun. Now that the company's called Nissan. Mind if we talk for a while?" Donna took it for granted the parents weren't home. No car, no lights, no movement. Most of the time she'd follow procedure and ask permission to talk to a kid. This time she'd take a chance. Figured she could get away with it. A big shot dead and all that.

"Like the book?" She had seen it in her own Sarah's book pile.

"Not much. The kids a whiner, a sissie. Everything going for him and he complains and complains. I felt like sluggin' him."

"You look like more of a stand-up guy."

Tommy Wilson shrugged, gave her a half-smile. He still hadn't said whether his parents were home. Donna hoped her son could perform as well.

"I really like the way you handled everything today, Tommy. You did the right thing from beginning to the end. I'm going to tell my boss, the Colonel of the State Police about it. He'll be impressed. You were a big help."

"Thanks," said Tommy, the smile wider, his face red under the tan, his shrug extending to his arms. "I watch *Law and Order* and the other police stuff even though my folks don't like those shows. They call the cops storm troopers."

"Well, you can see I'm no storm trooper." Donna smiled, reached out a hand to pat his head, stopped herself. The kid's too old for that. So was Al Junior for that matter, as he kept telling her. "Could you go over once more what happened? Just so I've got it straight?"

"No problem. I was on my way to go fishin', just walkin' down a hill and saw Mr. Perry lyin' just off the road. Wasn't movin'. I shouted at him and he still didn't move. I knew from *Law and Order* not to touch him. So I ran over to old Mr. Bitgood's place and he called Constable Glasgow. Then we waited for him to arrive."

"You really tell the story well, Tommy."

"Well, I had to tell it a couple of times. To the Constable."

"You didn't see anyone else, a car or a truck or anything?" Donna sat down beside him, leaned her elbows on her knees, relaxed. Watched a gull glide by on a puff of wind. She noticed Tommy glancing over at her. Up and down. Stopping at her chest. The blush returned to his face. Men! Even thirteen-year-olds!

"Like I told the Constable, not a thing."

"You out most Sundays, Tommy?

"Yep. Never gets too crowded down on Eastern Beach." Maybe the kid knew more than he thought.

"Alone on the road most always, I guess, it being Sunday and all?"

Tommy Wilson thought about it for a minute, chewed a nail on his left hand and watched a crab emerge from a clump of grass near her car. It looked around and fled into the rushes. Donna felt like slapping the kid's hand away from his mouth. She smiled instead.

"Sometimes I see Mr. Gleason or Frankie Levesque's truck. Mr. Gleason fishes down the beach like me. Frankie delivers the Sunday papers."

"Who's Mr. Gleason?"

"Some guy who lives down here. Around most of the time. Maybe he works nights."

"Not around last Sunday, eh?"

"I didn't see him." Worked on the nail again. Like her Al Junior. Wouldn't have any left if he kept that up. Donna still wanted to grab Tommy's hand and pull it from his mouth. Resisted. He gave it up, studied it, and went on, "Sometimes there's a guy from the Perry house drivin' around."

"Same guy all the time ?"

"Yep. A guy in a great old Jag. It's English, you know."

"I know. Those same guys around all the time, on Sundays mostly?"

"Sunday's mostly when I go fishin'. Never saw them when I was out durin' the week. Except maybe for Mister Gleason."

"See Gleason much?" She had to be careful not to lead him.

"Seems to be. Can't say. I guess I wasn't payin' attention much."

"You've been great, Tommy." Then she established herself once more. "When are your parents coming home, by the way?"

"Is that a little trick, Lieutenant, to see if they're home now?" The kid laughed, shook his head, blushed again.

"Maybe." Donna laughed with him, got up, watched another crab come out, look around and scuttle away.

"Who knows," said Tommy. "My mom's a painter and my pop sells T-shirts he tie-dyes." Did Tommy shake his head? "They're in Providence demonstrating."

"Know what the demonstration's about?"

"Beats me," said the kid.

"Anyway I hope they're very proud of you," said Donna as the kid got up to say goodbye. Nice. She took a last look at the kid and his house and wondered how the Wilsons had found the fishing shack. Maybe it found them.

It had been a good chat with the boy. He knew more than he thought. Like most everyone. At least three people rode along Pond Street on Sundays. Who besides Bill Hasner was out this Sunday she'd have to find out.

CHAPTER SIX

Monday morning at an afternoon newspaper can be a grind. Especially on a small daily newspaper with no Sunday edition. Especially in a mill town buried in the center of Rhode Island. So Matt Borg was ready when he bowled into *The Arctic Valley Times* this Monday morning.

Obituaries pile up over the weekend. In early summer, there are more than ever. Not much seems to be going on besides dying. Everyone's at the beach or having a picnic. Or kicking the bucket. Politicians aren't in full swing yet. You'd better have stories in the works if you're an editor or there won't be much to put in your Monday paper.

Worse than that, over the weekend old computers and presses have time to consider their age and are cranky on Monday mornings. Like most people. So it is on Monday morning at *The Arctic Valley Times*.

"You got a call from Lieutenant Donna Pacheco of the State Police," called out Bob D'Orio, the advertising manager. "And the air conditioning is off down here."

'Down here' was the advertising department on the first floor. As usual, D'Orio was the first to arrive in that department. As usual he let editor and publisher Matt Borg know about it.

"Can you call the air conditioning people?" Borg asked him, knowing the answer.

"Have already," said D'Orio, smile as bright as his white shirt, red and blue tie firmly centered as always. "Said they'd try to get here this morning."

"Thanks, Bob." Borg climbed the stairs toward the news department, on the second floor of the old tenement. Politicians would eagerly climb a flight of stairs to spin their stories. But you couldn't take a chance on advertisers toting their money up the steps. So news was upstairs and advertising down, alongside the composing room and circulation.

"If it's hot in here, get the salespeople out on the road. It's where they belong anyway," Borg shouted over his shoulder. Running up and down the stairs all day kept Borg in shape. He hated it.

Matt Borg found himself at *The Arctic Valley Times* because three little old ladies had invited him to tea six years before to explain that they would have to shut down their paper unless someone bought it. Borg felt obliged to try and save the paper for no good reason he could sensibly explain. Maybe he was just a sucker for freedom of the press. Any excuse would do. The three sisters insisted on an outrageous price and that Borg keep a treasured picture of their father on the wall of the newsroom. The price was negotiated, but the old man still looked down on reporters, thanks to his daughters and Borg. Glowered is more like it—from between mutton chops.

He hadn't minded the old man then. That was when Jane had been alive. When they had shared a dream. Now she was gone. And the dream with her. In the dream's place was an emptiness that often filled with a dark anger he tried hard to contain. Mostly he succeeded. Not always. He tried to cover the anger with sarcasm and a black humor that was often poisonous. Often he didn't like himself. The newspaper lived on. Barely. But he loved escaping into its bustle, into knowing what happened as it happened. He loved escaping into reality and out of his memories.

Hazel, behind the desk facing the door, didn't look up as Borg galloped into the newsroom. She scribbled notes furiously, on the phone taking obituaries from undertakers who charged survivors for the service. You had to get births, weddings, and deaths right in a community paper. You hatch 'em, match 'em and dispatch 'em. Not easy. Brothers that demanded that estranged sisters be omitted from the obituaries submitted by funeral parlors, bereaved old women insisted that prison records of murdered sons be left out. It went on and on.

"Good morning," said Borg. "Anything?"

"Mrs. Daly doesn't want her late husband's first wife to be mentioned in his obit."

"Can you handle it?"

"Of course," said Hazel. Seldom did a complaint reach Borg. Hazel knew her job and the communities the daily newspaper served. She knew what mattered in an obit and what didn't. A hundred years of journalism school couldn't give you that. More than fifty years of Hazel's life in The Valley could.

"You won't believe this." Aimee Solante tailed him into his office, a small room with yellow walls, darkened by ink seeping up from the press in the basement, and a window that looked out on Main Street. Plaques and awards, equally yellow or dusty, hung on the walls. A picture of Borg's dead wife Jane rested on the desk.

Borg slapped his briefcase on his desk and turned to face Aimee. The managing editor, 27, short and sturdy, pretended to be tougher than she was.

"Try me," said Borg, trying to keep a straight face but smiling anyway. He was 15 years older than Aimee and admired her unflagging enthusiasm and the romanticism she hid beneath a patina of cynicism. In other words, a typical young journalist. She was a bright spot in his life.

"We're loaded," said Aimee. "First of all, your old boss is dead . . ."

"What the hell happened? Ron Perry is younger than me." That must be what Donna Pacheco of the State Police called about. Sundays he avoided the local news if possible. He'd get to Donna as soon as he could. Today's paper came first.

"Perry fell off his bike or was pushed or something. It's on the first page of his paper. Want it on ours?"

"How about a box? AP should give you that."

"Your Indians have put a deposit on a strip of land by the state highway. Want to build a casino . . ."

"How do you know?"

"The Chief called this morning. Wanted you, but you weren't here, so he talked to me. He'd like you to call when you have a chance."

Chief Roger Crandall led the Quonsets who had tried for years to build a casino on their own threadbare reservation near the Atlantic Ocean. Nothing doing. The state Lottery might have suffered and the Mob's bookies would have taken a hit. So would the other Indian casinos operating just across the state line. Moralists enthusiastically joined the battle to protect the state from the sin of gambling. Big money weighed in.

"The Chief actually said they'll try to build a casino?" Borg had heard the rumors.

"Yup," said Aimee. "He figures he can get this town to support him, with our paper's help, and then take it statewide to get an OK through a referendum."

"It won't happen," said Borg. "Even if everyone in this town wants it, *The Bulletin* will browbeat the state legislators and gambling interests and other casinos will do the same."

"*The Bulletin* hasn't got the story?"

"Not a squeak."

"You might as well tell me what else you've got before I sit down." He had pulled his chair out from under the desk and hesitated. Maybe Aimee would need him out in the newsroom.

"Mostly garbage. The folks in the Natick area are complaining about the smell from the sewage treatment plant and we're getting reaction from the town manager. I live near there and it does stink."

"I'm sure you'll see it gets a good play. What else?"

"Oh yeah, two cops out in Clinton are accused of making dirty movies. They're suspended."

"How'd you get that?" Borg stood up straighter. Crossed his arms.

Aimee relaxed, sat down in the chair facing Borg him, looked up, put her pen to her lips, clicked it against her front teeth a couple of times and smiled. She loved to surprise him.

"Cowboy Carl told us, who else?" she said, referring to a former cop still furious about his dismissal five years before. "The Chief of Police won't comment. We've got a copy of the suspension order and one of the cops is ratting on the other. We also have the Deputy Chief confirming."

"Tell me more." Borg almost laughed at the look of satisfaction on Aimee's face.

"Two Clinton cops were blackmailing the wife of a part-time cop over there into appearing in their movies. They used the old quarry during the day and a room at the Hilltop Motel by night."

"I wondered how that motel stayed in business. Not bad for a Monday," said Borg. "Both the casino and the dirty movies have legs so you better be following them up. Make damn sure of your verification."

"You bet. Want to read the casino piece and the dirty movies story before they go?"

"Maybe I better. Maybe the Perry stuff, too. Busy day. Get out of here, get the sheets downstairs and put her to bed." Without noticing, Borg used sheets as the slang for pages. Putting the paper to bed began back when type was set on metal "beds" or tables before being made into the blankets that would be put on the presses and printed.

"Bye," said Amy over her shoulder. Then she was gone.

Borg skimmed the newspapers on his desk, noted that *The Bulletin* had credited its dead leader with all the progress in journalism since Gutenberg invented the press. He turned to the previous week's advertising lineage report (not bad) and circulation figures (not good). The phone rang. It was 7:36. What could a reader be pissed about already?

"Matt Borg," he answered, then heard the familiar voice of Lieutenant Donna Pacheco.

"I thought you'd be at work by now. You heard the news about Perry?"

"Yup. How'd it happen?" Doesn't hurt to confirm.

"He was riding his bike near his summer place in Little Bay and died of a head wound."

"So?"

"The head wound was in the back of his head," said Donna.

"So?" He paused, thought, waited.

"Some people are saying he'd hit the front of his head because he'd fall forward off the bike. Not the back."

"Can't the Medical Examiner settle that?"

"We don't have any of the answers yet," said Donna. "The family is saying it must be murder even though the Medical Examiner doesn't know anything yet, the cowardly jerk. The wound on the back of Perry's head makes it tough to imagine he fell the way we found him. Not impossible, though. You can make a case that he fell backward because he was pedaling up the hill."

"Sounds like he could have fallen forward and hit his forehead," said Borg. "Now that I think about it."

"You knew him, didn't you?"

"Not well. He was a power behind the throne during the last days of Ace Adams's stint as publisher. Ron was the younger son of the Perry family. He was up in New Hampshire working for a small daily and then suddenly he was back here again as Ace's assistant and then he became boss shortly after I left."

"Seen him much since you left *The Bulletin*? Leave on good terms?"

"What? Am I a suspect?" Borg laughed. "Yeah, I saw him a couple of times. Our parting was kind of funny. When I was leaving his office after telling him I was going, he stood up and shook my hand and looked down at his shoes as he always did and said, 'Good luck . . . but not much.' And I said, 'Thanks, but not much.' And I left."

"Not very warm," Donna said.

Borg could imagine Donna's eyes, dark and piercing, focused on his face, maybe looking for something he hadn't said. She wouldn't find much. Especially over the phone. One more reason to talk to people face to face.

"Warm was not what I'd use to describe him," Borg said. "Not a bad guy I guess. For a publisher. I guess that's the best that can be said about any of us."

"You should know. Anyway, I'm calling for a favor."

"As always," from Borg.

Unfazed, Donna went on, "I need some background on the newspaper and on the Perrys and on the people around them. Maybe on the Indians. You're connected with them too, aren't you?"

"I'm an honorary Quonset if you must know. So don't be picking on my people."

"The Perry family received threats from some of the tribe back when *The Bulletin* fought the casino so hard. I'm on my way down to the barracks in Eastwick to meet with Colonel Rockingham. Can I stop on my way? Say about 11?"

"If you're still driving that yellow Datsun, park it in front of our building. It will add some class."

"It's orange." Donna cackled as she hung up. Triumphantly? It sounded like it. Borg was amused. He had helped her with a couple of tough cases, guiding her through the social and historical mazes of the small state. She was Hazel's cousin, after all, and local to Arctic. And his paper was local most of all. Besides, he liked her. Before anyone else could ring him, he placed a call.

"Chief Crandall," came the answer at the other end, in a voice buried deep below bass.

"So you're going to try for a casino in Arctic," Borg said. "It'll be a long shot."

"The guys behind us will put up the money. They're betting we can get the town to support us and we can get a statewide referendum."

"The guys" owned casinos in Vegas and Atlantic City. Borg hoped the Indians knew what they were doing, playing games with guys who invented the games.

"Anyway," the Chief continued, "we've put down a deposit on the land and I hope we can count on your help."

"Champion of the underdog and lost causes, that's me," Borg said. "Is that why you made me an honorary member of your tribe? That and my ability with the bow and arrow?"

"Sure, sure. By the way, you heard about the publisher of *The Bulletin*?"

"Yep. What do you think?"

"Not much. If he was murdered I hope they don't blame us. I didn't like the guy. We didn't kill him though. Think it will change the newspaper's attitude towards us?"

"The newspaper won't change. Still, unless he was murdered with a tomahawk you're in the clear." Actually, Borg didn't know that for sure. He'd ask Donna Pacheco.

CHAPTER SEVEN

"**T**he editor in his den," Donna said. "How ya' doin'?" She was wearing tan slacks, a blazer and a blue shirt that fell open as she bent forward to take his hastily offered hand. He could see wisps of her blue bra. She knew that, of course.

Donna Pacheco had marched past Hazel and barely grazed her knuckles on Borg's open door before she sat before him. She looked a lot better than the new syndicated column Borg had been reading. It was supposedly written by a teenage rock star and offered advice to those her age who had not achieved the wisdom conferred by two hit albums and surgically enhanced breasts.

"Hello and please come right in," Borg said, chuckling. "Don't be shy."

"I'm not and you know it," she said.

"Indeed."

"Let's cut to the chase. I don't have a lot of time."

"Glad I do and have nothing to do but help the law and its ace detective. What's up?"

"OK. So I need your help. This Ron Perry thing is going to be a buster. The family is after the Governor and the Governor is after my boss, Colonel Rockingham, and the Colonel is after me. I need you to tell me who's who."

Colonel Rockingham of the state police was all business. So was Donna. Unless it served her purpose not to be. Pretty and she knew it. Used it when it helped her. A legal pad materialized on her lap, a ball point pen served as a pointer in her right hand. Both from the big bag she carried. Hazel had left her desk and peeked into Borg's office. She shook her head as a grin raised the corners of her mouth. She wasn't used to anyone barging past her and into Borg's office. Not even a cousin in the state police. Donna, however, charmed even her older cousin.

"All right then," said Borg. What choice did he have?

"You got first dibs on everything, OK?" said Donna, as though offering a gift. *The Arctic Valley Times* always got dibs on any story in the Valley and anything Borg heard first. Which was plenty. Donna didn't wait for his nod. "Here's where we are. We don't know whether Perry was murdered or not. We hope not. It would be neater and easier. The medical examiner isn't worth a hill of beans. He's seen all the TV programs about guys who solve cases in the lab. So he's stalling with his findings . . ."

"He must be telling you something . . ."

"He says the wound in the back of Perry's head could have been caused by a fall or a blow. Tiny bits of stuff in the wound could have been picked up from the road. They could also be from a club. Says he's taking a closer look right now. If you can believe the boob. He also thinks the body could have fallen backward or forward. How's that for a help?"

"What's his name? Butler or something? Doesn't he have political ambitions?"

"Yeah, yeah, probably. Doesn't everybody in this state? Anyway, if Perry was murdered, we really don't have a clue. Wife's always first on the list of suspects. But Perry was happily married, I guess. You never know about that, though . . ."

"No, you don't . . ."

Donna got up from her chair, walked around Borg's desk, stood behind him looking out the window on the main street of Arctic. Borg swung his chair around. Close quarters. He looked up. Borg knew how proud Donna was. Asking for help pained her. Almost as smart as she thought she was, he could see her almost squirming to admit the world of the Perrys was beyond her.

She sighed. "The sanitation guys haven't cleared the street of sand and salt from the last snow," she said. She shook her head, walked back to sit down.

She rested her elbows on the arms of the chair, grimaced. "This Bill Hasner guy gets to be boss of *The Bulletin*, I guess . . ."

"My guess, too," said Borg.

"He's doing all right, in other words. The family thinks the Mafia killed their boy because of the last series the paper did about laundering money. They even think the Indians may have done it because Perry fought the casino so hard . . ."

"So you've got the Mafia and the Indians. And maybe even Hasner. Anyone in the state you've left out?" Borg smiled at Donna. She didn't smile back. She leaned even further forward in her chair. He noticed her knuckles whiten as they gripped the pen and the arm of the chair.

She took a breath, cackled. "Wait 'till you hear the rest." Still kept her sense of humor, anyway. A good thing.

Borg had helped Donna in another murder case involving Mayor Toby Fragnoli of Providence. The Mayor had washed clean—at least of murder. He was accurately described as colorful but devious, at least by those who didn't like him. *The Bulletin* and its publisher were first in that line.

"The Mafia doesn't usually kill civilians," Borg said. "You know that better than me. The Indians stopped killing pale faces a long time ago. You may have to look someplace else if you want to find a murderer."

"Maybe." Donna rested her chin on her palms, knuckles less white. "That's why I could use your help." She didn't mention "again." "With *The Bulletin* and with the Mob. And with the Indians."

"From what I gather, there are guys in the Mob these days who talk up a storm without any help from you or me. You know that."

"I do. But half the guys turning state's evidence are lying." Donna paused, looked down. "You know the old Don, don't you? That's what the Colonel says, anyway. And you must know some of your fellow Quonsets pretty well. Like Chief Crandall."

"Donna, I also have a business to run here." He put his hands on his desk, palms down, hunched his shoulders as if ready to rise. "It's far from big enough for me to have somebody else run it while I play detective."

"You might win a Pugilist Prize or something . . ." She cackled again, kidding him.

"That's a Pulitzer and you know it," he said, "And nobody gets Pulitzers for crime stories anymore. Newspapers devote forests of trees to special sections that reveal social problems everyone knows about already . . ."

"OK, OK already. You'll get a scoop and I know you like that. And come on, you do enjoy snooping around. It's what you do."

Borg laughed out loud. Donna didn't know a Pulitzer from a palooka or made believe she didn't. But the street smart cop knew people, including him. He had served as mentor from the moment she joined the State Police. That was the day her cousin Hazel had brought Donna to meet him. The new and pretty state cop was smart enough to ask his advice, a ploy few men could resist. Borg took his hands off the desk. What the hell else was he doing with his life?

"No promises. Let's hear what you want . . ."

"Talk to Pastorini for me," she said, referring to the old Don. She held a hand up before he could reply. "I'd like the skinny on *The Bulletin* and Hasner. You knew Carolyn Perry. Do you know any of the other Perrys?"

"Hold on, Donna," Borg said. Just bringing up the murdered Carolyn Perry still brought him pain. "Why don't you just ask me to solve your case?"

"It sure would save me the trouble." She laughed her way into another cackle, then looked down, faking forlorn. Hunched her shoulders. He couldn't resist the move even though he recognized it as more theatrical than honest. Donna was about as fragile as a Sherman tank. A small one and like any tank, she could be outgunned.

"Let me think about it," he said finally. She looked up, smiled. He knew she knew he was ensnared. She knew too that once into solving a puzzle, he wouldn't stop searching for the answers. He was focusing on it already.

"Wait a minute. I do know Mrs. John Black. She's a Perry and once helped me with a magazine about Italy. I can call her. She might remember me. She knows everything about the Families."

"Is she the widow of John Rodman Black? Wasn't he the richest baby in the world or something? What's the Families?"

"The Families, six of them, used to run the state. Some people think they still do. The Perrys are one, the Blacks another. About the Colonel: Did he put you up to this?"

"Yep, but I wanted to see you anyway." She got up to leave. "You're glad to see me too, aren't you?"

"I am," he admitted. Collaborating on a previous murder investigation had been fun and circulation had improved with his columns about it. And, he admitted, it was a relief occasionally to get away from *The Arctic Valley Times* and its problems, the dwindling base of advertising, the fewer readers as a transient population lost interest in local affairs. Thank goodness, some still cared.

"Still seeing Alex?" she said as she reached the door.

"Yep," he said. She smiled at him over her shoulder as she walked out the door. He appreciated the look and the walk and she knew it.

She hadn't pushed the Indians too hard. Good thing. After all, the Quonset people had to stick together. Even honorary Quonsets like himself.

CHAPTER EIGHT

Patrick Doyle arrived on the heels of Donna Pacheco. Noticed her heels, of course. Noticed other assets, too. Didn't knock.

"Best looking cop in the state of Rhode Island and Providence Plantations," he said as he sauntered into Borg's office. "The older I get the more I appreciate butts."

"We've had this conversation before. Watch out you don't get arrested for what you're thinking, you hound."

"If I got arrested for what I was thinking I'd spend my life in prison instead of helping you."

"Helping me to pay your damn pressmen more than they're worth," said Borg with a laugh. Patrick Doyle (he was called Pat and Paddy and even Patsy by his friends and much worse by his enemies) was state secretary of the pressman's union, which provided manning (there were no female pressmen) for all six of the state's daily newspapers. Four for Borg's paper. The secretary of the craft union was a continuing job. Presidents came and presidents went. Secretary Doyle stayed on.

Patrick Doyle wasn't more than five nine, wiry and stocky at the same time, a tough and ready Irishman with salt and pepper hair and a moustache to match, up from working the presses himself. He ran marathons. Cocky, too.

He was shrewd and the best friend both newspapers and pressmen had in the state. A publisher, if he played his cards right and Doyle trusted him, always knew what would really matter in negotiations and what was window dressing with shouting to support it. You never lied to Pat Doyle.

Borg enjoyed their twice a year catch-up lunches. They were friendly adversaries; both wanted to keep newspapers operating. Both knew the pressmen were a dying breed. Newspapers too, probably, as the century neared its end. Neither whispered the thought aloud.

"Let me check the newsroom and I'm ready for lunch," Borg told him, leaving Doyle in his office reading *The Wall Street Journal* he had collected off Borg's desk. Borg read the casino and dirty movie stories from Aimee, made a few changes, told her where he would be, and returned to his office. He called circulation and ordered a printing of a few hundred extra papers. It should be a good day.

They drove in Borg's vintage black Caprice Classic to a local restaurant which had declined ever since the couple who started it had gone to Florida and left their son in charge. It still advertised in *The Arctic Valley Times*, reason enough for Borg to eat there. Soup and salad always. After Borg and Doyle had eaten and bemoaned the rising cost of medical insurance, Borg brought up Perry.

"Funny guy," said Doyle. "Never looked you right in the eye. Did you know he had an uncle who did the same thing, a guy nicknamed Shifty? Wasn't a bad guy. Didn't trust him worth a damn."

"Did you trust Ron Perry?"

"Not much. He never got mad no matter how we put it to him. I don't trust a guy who never gets mad. Remember I'm Irish . . ."

"As though anyone could forget . . ."

"Anyway, Perry always looked to me like he had a hidden agenda. Not that we all don't. Just seemed all hidden agenda. Not much else."

"You wouldn't want to kill him, would you Patrick?" Borg laughed. He ordered a cup of tea and Doyle ordered another cup of coffee and chatted up the waitress, his blue eyes all over her. She didn't seem to mind. He turned back to Borg and joined him in a lingering chuckle.

"I heard this morning there was something funny about Perry's death. I wouldn't kill him, no." Doyle hesitated.

"You know someone who might?"

"It's always money, right? Or sex?" Doyle smiled his crooked smile, the smile that attracted women and warned those in his way. In neither category, Borg waited. Not long.

"What would you say if I told you *The Bulletin* might be for sale?"

"Not much," said Borg.

Now Pat grinned, sipped his coffee. Borg dipped his tea bag, admired his own wrist action, regular as a metronome. Pat finally added, "These days every newspaper is for sale. Yours too, I'll bet."

"Not so you'd notice. But what I always say is even this jacket I'm wearing is available if someone came in here and offered me enough."

"All right, all right. But what if I told you Ron Perry was dead set against selling *The Bulletin*, wouldn't listen to his family or his friends about it," said Pat. "Dug his heels in."

"Doesn't surprise me, I guess," Borg said. "Say what you will about Perry, he loved his family paper . . ."

"More than anything. Anyway, Perry's death means *The Bulletin* is a step closer to being sold."

"And you know this, how, Pat?"

"Never mind how I know. You learn a lot in negotiations. And our guys pick up a lot in the halls . . . ."

"Just talk?"

"This is golden, Matt. If he has anything to say, Hasner will sell it . . ."

"And the family will go along?" Borg studied his tea. "There have to be some of them who would like to preserve *The Bulletin* as a family paper?"

"Not many," said Doyle. "The cousins will get some real cash instead of lousy dividends. Offers are on the table and Hasner'll come out of it a very rich man."

"Perry was his best friend."

"I'm just telling you what I know, Matt. The relationships you figure out. I'm just a pressman."

"How about Mrs. Perry?"

"A class act, all the way."

Both men paused. Borg digesting, lunch and information. Doyle watching.

"Some corporation coming in would sure as hell hurt you, my friend," said Borg.

"Damn right. Better the devil you know and all that stuff. Well, I hope this helps you."

"Don't like Hasner much, do you?"

"Not a newspaper guy, Matt, not a newspaper guy. Bean counter all the way."

"Maybe I should be more of one, Pat, and less of an old reporter."

"Maybe not. Don't change, Matt. You're one of the few newspaper guys left."

"Thanks, I think. And I hope you remember that in our next negotiations."

"Don't count on it, but I hope this background makes it easier for you and the sweet cop, too." He winked. "I'm available if she wants to talk to me. Just remember, nothing came from me . . ."

"Not even your share of the lunch, I'll bet?"

"You got it," he said as he rose from his chair. "I'll hit the men's room while you get the check . . ."

"And chat up the waitress?"

"You bet. See you outside."

CHAPTER NINE

I n the smallest of all states, the past lingered as part of the present. In families, in buildings, in business. Even the memory of slavery lingered in its full name, Rhode Island and Providence Plantations. People stayed in the same places. Borg was reminded of that every time he drove back to his newspaper.

The big old Victorian houses where mill owners and super-intendents once lived still stood on Main Street in Arctic. Row houses or cottages, almost all duplexes, had provided places for the workers closer to the mills. Many descendents still lived in them, took pride in the yellow and purple flowers that filled the small front gardens. Portuguese and French Canadians dominated Arctic, a reminder of the days when mill owners imported workers by the ship or trainload, each group from a different country.

Tales persisted of soccer games between towns that turned into furious fights, enriched by ethnic animosity. Even now, police chiefs and new patrolmen were chosen on the basis of where their antecedents came from. Donna Pacheco's career had begun on the Arctic police force when an uncle, a Medeiros, was president of the Town Council. When a Catholic in Arctic left his church, it meant he went across the street, the French Catholic Church being on one side, the Portuguese on the other.

The old row houses and tenements had once emptied out on Sundays after Mass when everyone took off for the seaside amusement park in trolley cars. Now everyone stayed home and watched TV or went to the mall. The same people lived in one or two of the big houses too. They played golf or went to the country club. Most of the big old Victorians had been converted into apartments and were shedding their paint.

Borg left Doyle in the parking lot of *The Times*, where he had parked his car, noticing that the pressman cast an appraising eye at the waitress who came out of the back of the breakfast joint that shared a parking lot with *The Times*. Patrick Doyle probably dined out a lot.

Desks in the advertising department were empty and only the Managing Editor remained on the second floor where she edited copy and prepared pages for the next day. Borg looked over her shoulder at a feature page almost finished and retreated to his office. Only a couple of messages on his desk. Then the phone rang.

"Some woman named Lorelei Smollens," said Suzie, the receptionist. "Says she's from *The Bulletin*. Want it?"

"Why not?" said Borg. Lorelei Smollens didn't waste any time.

"I'd like to pick your brain," she said as soon as he picked up the phone. A newcomer to the state, Smollens had a reputation for being direct, too direct sometimes. Borg knew that weakness. Had it himself. She combined it with a devious nature. Hoped he didn't have that. Disarmed by her blunt, seemingly honest way, you were then sandbagged by a question she sneaked in.

Lorelie Smollens had worked for Borg when he was Sunday Managing Editor of *The Bulletin*. She loved to embarrass what many called her betters, stopping just short of getting canned. Arcane practices of the elite clubs in the state were a subject she specialized in, especially when they punished women. Borg remembered the fuss when she found out that the University Club wouldn't allow women to enter by the front door. The Club did now. Her piece had kicked up a fuss, which Borg had enjoyed even though he had taken some heat from Ron Perry, then newly installed as assistant to the publisher of the paper. As an editor he was amused by Smollens, as a possible subject he was wary. He didn't trust her.

"What's up?" he said. "You can't be calling me for any story *The Bulletin* will print."

"I'm doing a freelance piece for a New York magazine about the Perry death," she said. "And I'm trying to get some background about the guy and how he ran the newspaper and what will happen now."

"Lorelei, you work there," he said. "I haven't been at *The Bulletin* for more than five years. You want to talk to some of the people there now."

"They won't say a word," she said. I can't imagine why, Borg thought to himself.

"I'll only take a minute."

"I'm busy but go ahead," he said. You can't believe in freedom of press and then not talk to reporters.

"I guess you know that the paper may be sold."

"No, I didn't," he lied. "What's going on?"

"The Perry family, cousins and all, want the money. The paper never paid great dividends and there are a lot of relatives, most of them greedy. I hear Bill Hasner wanted to sell but Perry wouldn't go along. Now that Perry's gone maybe the paper will go too. I hear a big Texas outfit is after it."

"Jesus, I wouldn't have thought of that," he said. Leave it to Lorelei to sow a little information in the hopes of harvesting more. "Is it a new offer?"

"From what I hear it first came in here a few weeks ago, was turned down, and is in play again."

"Where'd you hear that?"

"The guys at the New York magazine I'm talking to say it's around down there. One more family newspaper bites the dust." So Doyle's tip was solid, the word was out, *The Bulletin* was in play.

Lorelei pressed on. "How well did Perry and Hasner get along?"

"Listen, I didn't have much to do with them socially. Played tennis with Perry once down at his estate in Dexter but I didn't really know him well. As far as I know, he and Hasner were best friends, roommates in college. Hasner came to the paper with Perry and was his right arm. I had no idea he wanted to sell the paper and Perry didn't. Are you sure about that?"

"Yes, I am. Can I get a quote from you on Perry?"

"Not on your life. Listen if you quote anything I've said I'll never give you another goddamn bit of information."

"How was he to work for?"

"You heard me, Lorelei. No more. Now I've got to get back to work. Good luck with the piece." God, reporters were a pain. Especially good ones. Especially reporters like Lorelei Smollens who always seemed to have a grudge. Stay out of my hair.

The story was percolating, that much was obvious, if the pressmen knew and Lorelei was pursuing it. Why not? It would be a good story if the newspaper, in the same family for almost 150 years, were sold. He'd better write something for the next day's edition of his own paper. Not much better than Lorelie, he thought to himself. Probably not, he answered, as he went to work.

CHAPTER TEN

Borg was on his way out the door—a little late—to drive to seaside Galilee to buy flounder fresh off the boat for dinner. The phone rang as he passed the front desk. Suzie flagged him.

"Want to take a call?"

"Who?"

"Lieutenant Pacheco."

"OK, I'll take it at Bob D'Orio's desk." The advertising manager's alcove was strategically near the front door so no possible advertiser could get past him without a greeting from D'Orio. Borg glanced down at the ad layout on D'Orio's desk as D'Orio slid the phone to him.

"I'm in the Colonel's office down in South County," Donna said. "Can I see you on my way back to Providence? I'll even buy dinner. And here, Colonel Rockingham wants to talk to you."

"Matt, how are you?" asked the head of state police. He didn't wait for an answer. "We could use your help on this one. The family is driving me nuts. Donna will explain. I'd appreciate any help you can give her."

The Colonel was a good cop and a better politician. He didn't have to mention that he had once helped a friend of Borg's through a scrape with the police. A kid had been nabbed with beer in his car. The Colonel made it go away. Still, Borg wanted Rocky to know the debt was about paid off, maybe even beginning to go in the other direction.

"Glad to help," said Borg. "I hope you remind your guys about it if one of our reporters is after a story."

"Confirmed," said the Colonel. "This whole thing may be nothing. Not a thing. We want to make sure we touch all the bases."

Trust Rocky not to say much over the phone, which was probably recording every word. Trust him also to make sure he put on tape that he was doing everything he could to pursue the case. Maybe he actually would tell his state police to give Borg's young reporters a break. Borg wasn't counting on that. He still agreed to meet Donna at the Sail Loft, a restaurant on Greenwich Bay. He could use whatever she told him to stay ahead of what *The Bulletin* would be reporting. The flounder was put on hold.

It was about six, still light, when he found a table by the rail at the Sail Loft. The restaurant was in an old building where once sails were made and on its seaside deck were ten or more tables. Borg could look down on the waters of Greenwich Bay and out at the boats in the slips of the marina. Many were 40-footers, Sea Rays and the like.

From the nearest boat a heavyset man looked back while nursing a tall drink. He seemed familiar but Borg couldn't place him. Maybe he had seen him before in the same boat. Few of the powerboats went out to sea. Many owners couldn't afford the couple of hundred dollars in fuel it took to move them. Mortgages were as easy to get on boats as on houses so the owners sat, preened, cased the women at the dockside restaurant and hoped they could score before being foreclosed.

Then Borg realized why the seafarer was smiling at him. It was Peeps Parilli, one of Mayor Toby Fragnoli's cronies or, more accurately, bodyguards. Peeps was an honest thug, loyal to the mayor and an opera fan. You never knew about people. Borg smiled back and waved. Peeps smiled even more broadly as Donna arrived.

"Does that guy own that beautiful boat?" she said as she sat down.

"Don't you recognize Peeps Parelli? He sure as hell doesn't recognize you or he wouldn't be giving you the eye."

"Hey Peeps." She waved. The pseudo sailor then recognized Donna, gave her a faint grin and fled into the cabin of the Sea Ray. Donna turned to Borg. "He can't own that thing."

"Who knows?" said Borg. "He owns it or the Mayor owns it or the mob owns it or, most probably, the bank owns it," said Borg. "Still, Peeps looks right at home, captain of all he surveys. And he seems to go for you, Donna." Borg grinned, enjoying the scene and Donna's discomfort, perhaps more than he should. She did look cute as a button.

"Not my type," said Donna. "I couldn't go for anyone who blow dries his chest and wears more gold than me. And what about that undershirt. I didn't know men still wore those things with the silly straps. Don't they know about T-shirts?"

"Maybe it's the style," said Borg. "Maybe it's a gift from the Mayor."

"The Mayor is one of the things that Rocky wanted me to talk to you about," she said, after ordering a vodka and tonic. "I'm officially off-duty."

"You're never off duty, Donna, and we both know it. Maybe Peeps doesn't."

The mobster had regained the deck, regained his composure, resumed his bravado, and now eyed Donna with appreciation. She did full justice to the blue silk blouse and tan slacks she wore. The blouse was unbuttoned to a deep V and a white necklace of small shells set off her tan and matched her small earrings. She ordered a Caesar salad with shrimp. Borg chose the chowder and scrod.

"Will you look at that guy?" said Borg. "I think he wants us to come aboard. Or at least he wants you to come aboard."

"Maybe he remembers the last time I cuffed him," she said.

"Must have liked it," said Borg.

"Must have a snoot full is more like it." Donna waved back to Peeps and then turned away and toward Borg.

"Now I need to talk to you."

"Nice to see you too," Borg said.

"I've got some questions. This is off the record, right?"

"I hate it when people say that. It doesn't mean much. Still, if you say so, sure."

"Well," and she paused, "the Perry family, or Mrs. Perry at least, has been calling the Colonel. And she's been calling the Governor. She's sure her husband was murdered. So is this guy, Bill Hasner."

"Was he?"

"The trouble is we don't know. I told you the medical examiner was no help. Neither are the forensic guys. So we'll probably never know for sure."

"By the way, I hear that *The Bulletin* is for sale. Bill Hasner wanted to sell and Ron Perry didn't."

"Big disagreement?" Donna toyed with the lettuce on her plate. There wasn't much else. Borg dug into his clam chowder dredging for a clam. Found potatoes instead. Sipped his pinot grigio. Enjoyed the fishy breeze coming off the bay at low tide. Waited. Donna finally put her fork down. It clattered with her determination.

"Don't know how serious the disagreement was. Perry held all the cards after all." He gave up his search for clams, chewed on an oyster cracker.

"Sounds like you might have a lot to talk to Mrs. Black about."

He sighed and resumed his search for a clam. Finally asked, "Any other requests? Would you like to write the questions down?"

"Sorry," said Donna. "Sometimes I know I'm too pushy." She picked up her fork. Stabbed a piece of lettuce. Hard. Apology was not something she took to.

"It's what the Colonel wanted you to do," Borg said. "Too cute to ask himself. Or not cute enough."

Donna sighed, looked at her plate, then straightened her shoulders and, mouth tight, almost spit out the words, "Well, how about it?"

"Your boss knows they'll talk to me?"

"Yep."

Borg stirred his chowder. He had again given up on the finding a clam. They had probably swum away with the anchovies from the Caesar salad.

"What are the questions?"

"Is the Don sure none of his people were involved in the death of Perry? Let him know the Colonel will get his answers."

"OK, I'll do this, but just for you, Donna. You can tell the Colonel that." They were also good questions for him at ask. Most of all, they indicated the Colonel was not writing off Ron Perry's murder as a possibility. A column was taking shape in Borg's head.

"You'll get great columns out of it also," said Donna, almost reading his mind. "Don't kid me, Borg. The Don and Anne Black wouldn't talk to you if there wasn't something going on here."

"Maybe and maybe not. What have you got so far, by the way?"

"Off the record again, three guys drove around Little Bay on Sundays. Bill Hasner, when he stayed with the Perry's, a Frankie Levesque, who was Perry's driver and lived in Little Bay, and a guy named Jim Gleason . . ."

"That Gleason sounds familiar. I can't nail it right now but maybe it will come to me. Anyway, let's get out of here. I've got a busy day tomorrow."

Borg had paid the check and they were almost beyond the awning that covered the dock and marked the end of the restaurant when Peeps shouted his invitation: "Come on aboard. It's a great boat." Donna stopped in her tracks, surprising Borg.

"I've never been on a Ray that big," said Donna. "Let's take a look." Borg had forgotten that Donna's husband, Al, was a fisherman.

Peeps took Donna firmly by the waist with both hands and lifted her onto the Sea Ray, leaving one of his arms snugly in place as she landed on deck. Borg hopped on by himself. Peeps' hand had dropped from Donna's waist to a hip when Borg faced them so he saw exactly what happened. With a quick twist of her right wrist, Donna grabbed the big middle finger of Peeps' left hand and twisted until it almost touched the back of his hand. Peeps' face went white, grimaced, but he didn't say a word as he released his hold on Donna.

"Nice boat," she said. "Bet it's pretty busy during the summer. Do much fishin'?"

"Not much," said Peeps, still grinning but massaging his left hand with his right. It had to hurt. "Mostly just cocktail cruises, like the Mayor calls them . . ."

"So he owns it, does he?" Borg wondered why the Mayor hadn't sold it yet. Maybe he had and the new owners hadn't taken possession.

"Yeah, he does, and you'd be surprised at some of the people he's had on it."

"Like who?" said Donna.

"Some of the Red Sox and even a big shot from the paper." Peeps, deep in his cups, couldn't resist showing off to a pretty woman, even one who had almost broken his finger.

"You mean *The Bulletin?*"

"You bet." Peeps swaggered a little. "He wasn't alone neither."

"You were on board too, Peeps?"

"You bet. Serving drinks. And the big shot had a babe with him too. Not a kid. A few years on her but a knockout. Blonde. Great legs."

"Come on, Peeps, I can't believe that," said Donna.

"No shhh . . . kidding."

"What was his name, then?"

"Haskell or something like that. Really."

"Hasner?"

"That's it."

"And the woman? Was it his wife?"

"You got to be kidding. Didn't catch her last name. He called her Lulu or something." All of a sudden, Peeps opened his eyes wide, swallowed, realized what he had said, shut up.

"Louise?" Donna sniffed an opening.

"I dunno . . . forgot," said Peeps. Huffing and puffing, face red.

"How long ago was that?" asked Donna.

"Don't remember," Peeps gulped, swallowed. "Maybe it wasn't even him. Like a tour?"

Peeps's tour had been drained of enthusiasm. Even the look at the lush main cabin of the 52-foot cruiser was cursory. Peeps didn't offer them a drink. Donna managed to climb out of the boat and onto the dock without help. Walking back to their cars, her step had a bounce.

"Enjoyed that, didn't you?" said Borg. "Feel better now?"

"Damn straight." Donna's grin stretched her face. "Know anything about a Hasner girlfriend?"

"Not until now. You?"

"Not until now. Talk to you tomorrow. I've got to get home to my hubby and kids." Donna still smiled as she slid into her little orange Datsun. Borg remembered Louise Perry's legs. Great? Pretty close.

CHAPTER ELEVEN

Borg was on his way to see the boss of organized crime in New England about the death of a newspaper publisher. He still wasn't quite sure why except that Donna Pacheco had asked him to and the head of the state cops had reinforced her request. Then again, Borg liked the Don; he had a weakness for scoundrels and knaves. And Raymond Pastorini might know something about the death of Ron Perry. Maybe more than something. Borg loved digging into things and into people.

When Borg called earlier he had been surprised that Pastorini agreed to see him this same day. So he spent the morning and early afternoon cramming his day's work into fewer hours than the work deserved. First there had been a seemingly endless discussion of how many new honor boxes *The Arctic Valley Daily Times* needed—only five it was decided, the rest could be repaired.

Then there were the porn movies the two Clinton cops had been making—a reporter would try to get copies to make sure they actually existed, to see what it was all about and, undoubtedly, for the prurient pleasure of the staff as well.

A possible addition to the advertising department resulted in heated exchanges between the advertising director and managing editor as hiring a new salesman precluded a new reporter. Neither side got their wish.

All the while, organized crime had occupied one compartment of Borg's mind. As he drove up Federal Hill to see the accepted crime boss of New England, Borg reviewed the curious relationship he had with the Don.

Years before, when he lived on University Hill, where the local Ivy League college was planted, he noticed while walking to work at *The Bulletin* an especially neat garden. On his way home he saw someone weeding it, on his knees. Borg couldn't miss the slicked black hair and black trousers and white undershirt, a shirt kids today called a wife-beater, the same kind that Peeps Parelli wore much later on the fancy boat.

Borg admired the garden and said so and after that there were regular chats. He realized very soon that the gardener was Raymond Pastorini and that he knew a lot more about growing flowers than Borg. For several years they compared notes about shrubs and weeds and bugs and more. Was it surprising that a crime boss lived in such an average middle-class neighborhood? Maybe not. He had to live someplace. And Borg went right on talking to him until he left *The Bulletin* and moved from the neighborhood.

Under an arch Borg drove onto The Hill, which is what everyone called this section of the city. This Hill was directly across the city from University Hill. No school of higher learning lived here. Instead, Victorian houses, big gingerbread concoctions painted vivid colors, shared space with Italian restaurants, delis, and food markets. Gentrification and an agreeable Mayor had added an occasional small park. An arch with a pineapple at its center welcomed visitors to the area.

Borg continued two blocks before parking in the first available space. Directly across the street was a small storefront with a weathered sign over the door, ACME VENDING MACHINES. The Don's office. Behind a small desk sat a woman no longer young with a lot of hair piled on top of her head like a pagoda. In the late sunshine splashing through the window it gleamed blonde enough to look milk white. Glasses perched on the tip of her nose. She worked at a computer. When she looked up she smiled. The glasses dropped from her nose to dangle by a cord and nestle finally in the V-neck of her straining red blouse.

"Mr. Borg?" she asked, and as he nodded, said, "Mr. Pastorini is expecting you." She picked up the phone.

It wasn't the movies. No gangsters flipping coins. Even the vending machines against a wall looked harmless. Maybe there was muscle across the street or next door but this felt like a typical small business office with a secretary who was nicer than most.

Borg remembered a story from years before about the Don, when he was serving his only prison term—for tax fraud or some such charge. There had been a serious riot in the state penitentiary and the convicts rampaged for two days. Pastorini worked in the prison hospital ward. The rioting prisoners, many of them murderers, tore through the halls until they reached the clinic and looked through the window to see Pastorini reading a magazine. He didn't look up and they didn't look further. The clinic was the only area in the prison left unscathed. Borg knew because he visited the institution shortly after the riot to see the convicts who staffed the prison newspaper. They had tossed the IBM typewriters out of their third floor offices.

The Bulletin had provided the IBMs for the convicts when they produced a magazine for the paper under Borg's direction. Not purely a good deed, of course. *The Bulletin* was getting rid of the IBMs anyway. After the riot, the cons wanted replacements for their typewriters. Borg refused. No surprise. No more were on hand. Then he stopped by the clinic to say hello to Pastorini, who kept a window box of flowers in the prison. It was blooming. Pansies. That was ten years ago. Now the bosomy blonde guarded Pastorini.

"Good morning, Mister Borg," the Don said as he emerged from his office. "It's nice to see you."

Don Pastorini wore a Calvinist smile, guarded and thin-lipped, under a hawk-like Roman nose that looked bigger because of his high forehead. His hair was jet-black, parted in the middle and slicked straight back. Under heavy black eyebrows were the darkest eyes Borg had ever seen. Yet the face had a yellow, sickly tinge to it. Pastorini wore a black suit, nicely, not obtrusively tailored—no wasp waist for him—and a white on white shirt, blue and green paisley tie and wingtip black shoes that shined well enough to reflect the sun coming through the window. He was a serious man. His eyes could turn to black ice in an instant.

"Let's take a walk," he said, smiling that thin-lipped smile. It wasn't cold exactly. It wasn't warm either. Both knew the office was surely bugged.

"It's a beautiful day, isn't it?" the Don asked as they walked along the street and crossed over to a small park with a bocce ball court. Overhead puffy clouds scudded by, peach faces to the sun, dark bottoms to the earth.

Those who passed nodded respectfully, and the Don always nodded back. He walked very straight, his head almost leaning backward so that he seemed to be looking down his hawklike nose at the world, not in contempt, but from a distance. You didn't notice he wasn't tall.

When they reached a bench by the bocce court, the old men who were playing looked over. Their nods were almost bows. The two wearing battered hats doffed them. Pastorini raised his right hand. It was all done so quietly, like a whisper on the soft spring air, you might have missed it if you weren't watching. Plane trees shaded the bench. Nearby patches of pansies, yellow and purple, bloomed.

"You come here to talk about your garden?" Pastorini had a slight accent, the accent of Sicily where men like him had dispensed justice in the fierce hill country for centuries.

"I come on an errand," said Borg, as courtly as Pastorini.

"From my good friend, Colonel Rockingham." It wasn't a question. It was Pastorini's business to know what was happening in law enforcement.

"What do you think of the death of Mr. Perry?" said Borg.

"Not much. Not anything. I did not know him. He did not know me."

"What about the series his paper just ran about the Mafia?"

"It was as true as most newspaper stories."

"It didn't bother you?"

"That *The Bulletin* discovered drugs are being sold in this state? That there is gambling? That there is prostitution? It did not surprise me. Did it surprise you?" The question was rhetorical.

Pastorini smiled again and nodded at a particularly good pitch by one of the bocce players. The player looked over and smiled back.

"Don Pastorini," Borg finally said, "Maybe the best way is to come directly to the point. The Perry death may be murder and the family is blaming the Mafia."

Pastorini watched the bocce game. Silent. His expression hadn't changed. Finally he turned toward Borg, looking at him directly with those fierce black eyes, the slight smile still on his lips. One of his hands was in his jacket pocket, the other hung at his side. Not in a fist, just loose and easy. But it quivered. Slightly. You could read a man by his eyes and by his hands Borg always told young reporters.

"If there is a Mafia do you think it would spend time killing publishers who sold their newspapers by printing stories about it? Even if the stories were true or meaningful, which most are not, my friend. You are too intelligent to believe that. Meanwhile, how is your garden and how is your paper doing?"

"Struggling but all right. Don Pastorini, are you saying you had nothing to do with the death?"

"You are a blunt man, Mister Borg. I forgive you because we are fellow gardeners and I suspect you are honest and honorable. I had nothing to do with the death of Mr. Perry. That is what I am saying. Are not most murders about love or money? That is what I've heard. And we Italians aren't the only ones who seek revenge. Do not overlook revenge, my friend. By the way, you must be patient with your newspaper as with your garden. Perhaps good things will come your way. Perhaps more restaurant and automobile advertising. I know you are struggling."

He paused, shaking his head at a bad roll of a bocce ball. The player who rolled looked at the Don and shrugged. The Don smiled. His promise about the advertising was a surprise to Borg. On second thought it shouldn't have been. Favors were a way of doing business in Rhode Island—and in the mob. A promise from the Don was always good. Perhaps the *Times* would get a lift in auto and restaurant advertising. It would help. When the Don spoke again, it was little more than a whisper. Borg noticed again, as he had before, that Pastorini did not contract his words. The result was a courtly English, simple and precise.

"I extend my very late condolences on the death of your wife. I imagine you pay less attention to your garden now."

Pastorini turned to Borg after a moment and nodded. As he rose from the bench, he stumbled very slightly and quickly recovered to stand as straight as the barrel of a rifle. Not without a grimace. Nothing more about Perry would be said, Borg knew. Still, he was satisfied that the Mob had not killed Perry. Pastorini was the last of his kind. He had kept relative crime peace in Rhode Island for decades, a man of weight who was as good as his word. Not a man to make an enemy. Not if you valued your life. Because his words, however gentle, could kill, could order death. Yet he remembered that Borg's wife had killed herself four years before.

Pastorini's son wore flak jackets and jeans and was an obvious choice to become Don after his father. Or try to. But no one would call him Don, thought Borg, and old men on the bocce court would not doff their hats.

CHAPTER TWELVE

"The Don must know more about Perry and his death than he's saying." Donna sighed. Borg had called her at the East Bay state police barracks and passed along most of his conversation with Don Pastorini.

"He always knows more than he says." Borg chuckled. "Just like you."

"Like you, too," Donna shot back. "What's going on with the Colonel and him anyway?"

"Nothing for sure."

"Tell me what's not for sure."

"These guys have been opponents for a long time. Maybe some kind of symbiosis has developed . . ."

"What's that?" Donna was annoyed. He could hear it in her voice. She hated not to know something. Anything. And she soaked up what she learned like a sponge. Borg loved to rag her about words, felt ashamed of himself later. Sometimes.

"Not anything dirty, Donna, so don't worry about that." He paused. "I mean maybe they've developed some kind of relationship. Maybe they trust each other in a strange way . . ."

"Wait a minute. The head of the state police and the boss of organized crime? That's dirty enough. Come on, now. You don't really believe that."

"I'm not sure what I believe," said Borg, believing that. "Let me tell you what I've heard from people who ought to know."

"And you're not going to tell me who they are, right?"

"Right. Here goes. I've heard that your Colonel and the Don have a gentleman's agreement of sorts. Nothing they ever spelled out, nothing even whispered . . ."

"God, you men and your gentlemen's agreements. Who keeps track of the darn things? And what are you talking about?"

"Hey, don't jump at me. What I've heard is that the Mob based here does almost all of its dirty work outside this state's borders. I've heard that even the safecrackers in Westerly don't work the town. They go over into Connecticut. Same with the crooks in Providence and Pawtucket. They work mostly in Massachusetts."

"You're kidding. Do you believe that?" Donna was sputtering. "Do you expect me to?" Borg savored the moment. Still, he couldn't blame her. Complain as she might about what her boss put her through, he knew she respected the Colonel. Almost worshipped him. Just short of idolatry, as the poem put it.

"I told you I don't know what to believe—or not believe. Maybe you should check the records." He paused for a moment, thought about it, "Come on, you must have heard something about this, a rumor, something?"

"I don't pay much attention to rumors." Cutie pie, Donna, recovering. Dumb as a fox. He'd play along. Why not?

"Anyway, it's just a rumor. Back to the Colonel's question, the Don says his guys didn't have anything to do with murdering Perry . . ."

"If Perry was murdered," Donna interrupted. "You believe him?"

"If he was murdered. And I believe him."

"Well, for the record I don't believe anything you just said about my boss and the Don. Not a word, got it?" Donna leaped into another question: "What do you know about Perry and his personal life? And about his wife?"

"Here's another rumor, Donna." He paused, not sure he liked sharing the personal stuff he was about to. " I've heard that the Perrys were separated for almost a year."

"Know the reason?"

"Nope. Most of us knew he was married, had kids, and his best friend was his buddy at the paper, Bill Hasner. They roomed together at Brown and that's about it."

"That's it?"

"What else do you want to know? I know his secretary is as faithful to the Perrys as her days are long. You won't get much from her. Ditto Mrs. Perry and Hasner."

"Listen, you smart ass and simple country editor, if this is a murder, we need to know as much as we can about the victim. The dirt, in other words. Come on, there must be someone who hated the guy enough to kill him. Or to diss him, at least."

"Donna, I don't want to get involved in dissing dirt, as you put it. Least of all about a guy who was always straight with me."

"You have the damn strangest code or whatever you call it. Anyway, I'll tell the Colonel what the Don said to you and, one more thing. . . ."

"No, I don't know any more dirt about your boss."

"Not that," said Donna. This time there was a pause. "A guy named Pat Doyle asked me to lunch. Said he has some information that might be useful. Says he knows you."

Borg hesitated. He wanted to get started writing something about the proposed Indian casino and its possible effects on Arctic and the entire Valley area. He had hoped this telephone conversation would be short and sweet. It was turning out to be neither. Which is what he should have expected with Donna on the other end.

"He's the state secretary of the Pressman's Union . . ."

"Yeah, he told me that."

"And he's a hound . . ."

"I figured as much."

"And the last time you were in my office he came in afterwards and admired your assets very much indeed as you were leaving."

"Think he may know something?"

"He just might. He knows what he wants, that's for sure." Borg did his best to resist a leer. Succeeded he hoped. "Going to see him?"

"Yep. Tomorrow at the Lakeside."

"Take care of yourself."

"Always do. Ask Peeps Parelli."

CHAPTER THIRTEEN

Lakeside Restaurant perched on the side of Spectacle Lake, right outside of Providence. Donna reached it by taking a pleasant street that wound through a nice residential neighborhood of green and brown lawns that suddenly opened onto a parking lot. Packed as always.

Donna knew it for years as one of those places where people met. The food was adequate, the service the same. The view of the lake from the bright front room was as good as can be expected of a body of water lined by houses very much like her own. No vacation houses here. People lived in them year round. There were a lot of booths in the dimly lit back room.

Roberto, the head waiter, knew everyone in Rhode Island and Providence Plantations. Then again, there were fewer than a million people in the state with the longest name and Roberto had a good memory. He looked as though he had been born into his tuxedo and hadn't changed in the twenty-five years Donna had eaten at the Lakeside, beginning as a kid with her parents. The servings were mountainous, especially for Sunday brunch. At night the clientele changed, from the family friendly bright lights of the front room to the dark and much cozier atmosphere of the back.

"Good evening, Lieutenant," said Roberto as Donna entered the Lakeside. Roberto was not a stranger to the police. "Mr. Doyle is waiting for you." She followed him into the section of booths until they reached what seemed the darkest section of the restaurant. The man who stood to greet her was not much taller than Donna. In her high heels she stretched almost five feet four.

"Thanks for coming," he said. Big smile, hair of salt and pepper, brown sports jacket, blue silk tie on a blue and white striped shirt. A small perfectly centered moustache added a touch of the debonair. Blue eyes picked up the sparkle from the candle on the table. In spite of herself, Donna smiled. The guy knew how to set a scene.

"I hope this is important," she said. "I just left my husband and three kids to see you." Putting that on the record to start with. She wore her careful blue suit, white blouse buttoned up and a little bit baggy. Hard to hide the fact that she was full bodied, as the TV commercials said. Glad she had used lipstick a little less red than usual.

"I think so," said Doyle. "And I'm sorry to take you away from your kids. I know how that is. Got two of my own. Would you like a glass of wine? I'm drinking chablis."

"No thanks," she said. Who drank chablis anymore? Nobody. Even she knew that. Doyle wasn't quite as smooth as he thought he was. "I don't drink on duty." Put that in your pipe in this dark little corner of the Lakeside, Mr. Doyle.

"I understand," he said. Smiled again. His eyes never drifted down from her face to her blouse. God, he was good, hound or not. "Would you like to order something?"

"Not really," said Donna. "I really would like to hear what you have." She was aware of his arms on the table, his hands stretched toward her beyond his half, as he leaned forward. She kept hers clasped behind her glass of water and bread plate. Wall of modesty? Perhaps.

"I'm Irish," he said. She didn't say anything. "So I've got a story to tell." He waited again. She wouldn't give him anything to start with.

"It's about another Irishman, about an Irish family as a matter of fact." He smiled. Waited once more. She looked him over, gave him her cop stare. Undaunted, he uncorked another cocky grin. She swallowed a smile. He swallowed a sip of wine. She noticed he held the glass of white wine by the bowl. Borg had told her he held a white wine glass by the stem so the warmth of his hand wouldn't warm the chilled wine. Now she held her glass that way and noticed when others didn't. One more lesson for a little girl from the mill town of Arctic.

"Anyway, the Perrys did a job on Gleason's father and grandfather," Doyle went on. "The father—everyone called him Jimmy Junior—killed himself. Our own Gleason is still madder than hell."

"Tell me about him."

"The story goes back a while, back to the beginning of the century or before."

"Keep it short. Please."

"That's hard for me. You know how it is. Or maybe you don't, you being all business I guess." Was he slipping into a brogue?

"OK, OK, whatever . . ."

"The story begins in Pawtucket with a guy named Jimmy Gleason, a bartender who became a politician and then went into trolley cars. Jimmy, an Irish lad and a good Catholic, found out where the big new Catholic cemetery was going to be located, out near Stony Point on the Bay. He got the rights to a trolley line from the city to Stony Point. No flies on our Jimmy. That didn't sit well with the Families, that a Mick finagled the trolley line. They had pretty much controlled railroads and the trolleys for a long time."

"Is this getting to Perry?" Donna was enjoying this more than she should. And the story might be worth the listening. You never knew. She noticed her clasped hands had loosened up, her fingers spread out. She tightened them up again. Donna knew herself well enough to admit she enjoyed a bit of flirtation. Always had. Even used it in her work as a cop. She was also tough enough to know the limits. She hoped. She watched Patsy as he warmed to his story.

"To go on, in those days cemeteries were a big deal. People went to them on Sundays and had picnics and spent the day, the kids playing and the women talking and the men drinking. So Gleason's little trolley line did all right. It was a different world. You can see it in some of Randall Ransom's old paintings, men in those straw hats, boaters I guess you call them, women in dresses even when they went swimming. They all looked happy though. In Ransom's paintings at least."

Donna's interest in art was limited. Borg would know what Doyle was talking about. She didn't and didn't care.

"Then our Jimmy boy came up with an even better idea than trolley rides to the cemetery. An amusement park at Stony Point. Gleason brought the people there in his trolleys and made money from the rides."

"Cute." Was that a foot she felt edging toward hers under the table? She tucked her feet under the bench. Gave him a look but she felt her face flush. He didn't seem to notice, went on . . .

"Aye, you might say. Gleason did well. Ran through his money as fast as he made it, though. Generous as well, the damn fool. Anyway, along came Henry Ford and his cars. Hard times for trolley cars followed. Amusement parks built by the water at the end of trolley lines weren't the place anymore.

"To make it even worse, the Gleasons, Jimmy and Jimmy Junior, got mad at *The Bulletin*. Thought the Irish and the Catholics didn't get a fair break in that Yankee paper. They didn't, of course. Still, I'm a prejudiced witness, being of Irish persuasion myself. So the Gleasons started a paper, *The Tribune*. Well, the old Yankees knew more than how to clip coupons. They could also clip wings . . ."

"Clipped coupons?"

"Clipped coupons on their bonds is how I understand it. Just collect money from their investments in other words. Didn't have to do a damn thing . . ."

"Gotcha. Never heard that before."

"Not many people have," said Doyle. Sympathetic to a fault. His fingers, surprisingly long and slender, slid the bread plate away to the side. They almost touched Donna's hands. She withdrew them toward herself, folded them. She was beginning to feel as though she was back in Catholic high school. And a little bit tingly, she admitted.

"Anyway, the Perrys ran *The Tribune* into the ground. Lowered their ad rates and price of the paper. The rest of the Gleason stuff collapsed. Overextended, I guess you'd call it. The amusement park was bleeding money and so was the trolley line. All that was left was the land under the amusement park. Gleason thought he could sell it to the state for an airport. The WASPs had the legislature in their pocket. The state bought another place. The Gleasons went broke, lost everything."

"I don't mean to be rude but . . ."

"I understand," said Doyle. He leaned forward, not smiling now. Gave her his understanding look. His hands reached out across the table. Donna put hers in her lap.

"The Gleasons never forgot. They're Irish, after all. Do you know who works on the presses at night at *The Bulletin*?"

"A Gleason?"

"Right on the button, my dear. The last of the Gleasons."

"Why would he be working there? For the Perrys, of all people. Why would they want him?"

Now Doyle laughed out loud. Took a sip of his wine. Leaned back. Touched his moustache. Donna listened. If the Doyle tale was true, it sounded as though the current Gleason had a motive, all right.

"Because this is Rhode Island and the Pressman's Union controls who works in the press room of *The Bulletin*. And the pressmen are among the best paid workers in the state. Maybe the best."

"So the Perrys have nothing to say about it."

"Not so long as Gleason does his job. I don't even know if they know he works for them."

"Bet they do," said Donna.

"No bet. They've never said a word. Maybe they like one of the Gleasons manning their presses."

"And how does he feel?"

"You'll have to ask him."

"I will." This guy had the bluest eyes she had ever seen outside of Paul Newman. "Where does he live, by the way?"

"Little Bay. Surprised?"

"Not so you'd notice," said Donna. "One more thing. Why are you telling me all this? About one of your own pressmen, I mean."

"Because he's a pain in the neck and because I like you." Doyle leaned forward again. Donna was glad she had her hands in her lap. His foot reached the toe of her open shoe, gently rubbed it.

"Now will you join me in a glass of wine?"

"Gotta go," she said. She smiled as she darted up from her seat. "Thanks."

"No problem," she heard Doyle say as she headed for the door. She could sense him watching her walk past Roberto. Gave an extra sway to her hips. Take that, Patsy Doyle. It's all you'll ever get from me. She smiled. She had enjoyed the byplay more than she wanted to admit to herself.

CHAPTER FOURTEEN

Borg had just finished an editorial supporting the Indian casino in Arctic when there was a knock at his door. The managing editor didn't wait for an invitation to come in, she slumped into a chair, armed with her usual sheaf of papers in one hand and pen in the other.

"What's going on?" Aimee Solante was angry. "Closed door? You got secrets?"

"Never from you, Aimee. Once in a while I like a little privacy, though. Even a few minutes to think. That's why there's a door to this office."

"Forget it," she said. "Listen, we have something new on the Indians and on the porn. Want to hear about it or do you want me to close the door so you can hide in your office and think deep thoughts?"

"Whoa, not so fast," said Borg. "Aren't you getting a little big for your britches? You must have something good and juicy or you wouldn't be giving me this guff."

"God, you're the only one in the world who still uses words

like guff." She looked down at the papers now on her lap, tapped her front teeth with the ball point pen and grinned. She had something.

"Here's what we know about the Indians. Their money is coming from Bonanza Gaming, a Nevada outfit that manages a number of Indian casinos around the country. They've hired a lobbyist and have put up some money for advertising and promotion."

"Good. Where'd you get it?"

"The lobbyist is from here in Arctic. Lives up on High School Hill."

"Move it along. What about the porn?"

"Here's the story I get. The two cops were on the night shift and they surprised a couple in a car down by the quarry."

"That a local lover's lane?"

"Right on. Anyway, she was giving him oral sex." Aimee paused, obviously uncomfortable talking about it with her male boss. Put on her tough face, tight lips creased at the corners to show disapproval. "The two cops are sleaze bags and the couple scared to death. They're both married."

"Was she hooking?" Borg felt a little uncomfortable himself.

"Who knows? Maybe it was true love. Anyway, the cops say they'll forget it but first they want her to take off her clothes. And they pull out a camera. Well, Lucy—that's her name, Lucy Baker—is no virgin but she doesn't want her naked picture flashed around either. The guy, her boyfriend, pleads with her and gives her a hundred bucks to satisfy her modesty."

"The guy's a bigger sleaze than the cops."

"Listen, it's a sleaze convention at the quarry. Anyway, Lucy gets into it. I guess drugs were involved and it's hot stuff. She's good-looking woman and a natural, if you'll forgive the editorializing."

"A woman of many talents."

"You might say. Anyway, the cops get to thinking. The first thing you know they're paying Patsy and making hard-core movies. Short stuff they call loops. Not very good. Still, there's a market for almost any of that stuff, I guess."

"You're getting an education in the porn world, Aimee."

"It's not something I expected in this job," she said. "The nuns at St. Mary's would be disappointed in me."

Borg chuckled, surprised again by how almost everything out in the larger world sooner or later intruded in the small Arctic Valley.

"American free enterprise," he said finally. "What brought down our fledgling Larry Flynts?"

"Who's that?"

"The publisher of *Hustler*, a girlie magazine. Into movies too."

"Porn?"

"You bet. What else?"

"The police chief got a copy of one of the tapes with a note. He would have brushed it under the table but his mail is opened by his secretary, who just happens to be a member of the choir at St. Mary's."

"Never trust your secretary."

"Not if she's a member of the church choir. Anyway, she hits the ceiling. One way or another, Cowboy Carl finds out. And so do we."

"So what have we got besides today's story that the two cops were suspended and the possibility of a minor league porn ring? And who do you think sent the tape to the chief?"

"Don't know. Obviously someone after the two cops. Or after the woman. Maybe the Mob . . ."

"What?"

"Yeah. You know they control porn here and almost everywhere else. And they don't like amateurs horning in . . ."

"I thought the Don doesn't like the porn trade . . ."

"The Don's son does and he's making moves. If you don't mind me saying so, I think you romanticize that old guy. He's not Robin Hood."

"Neither was Robin Hood . . ."

"All right, all right." Aimee waved her sheaf of papers, went on. "Anyway, we've got a copy of the tape." She smiled, tapped her teeth with the pen once more.

"You're kidding?" Borg leaned back in his chair and chuckled. Even the Don couldn't control his family. And maybe he did like the Don a bit too much.

"You know how cops are. They all had to see it once it got around the station house. Copies were made. And our pal, Cowboy Carl, got his hands on one. I'm not sure what we can do with it."

"Aside from arousing our young reporters. And our sports editor. I'm sure he's seen it already."

"Twice that I know about. My idea is we try to get to the two cops this afternoon or tonight. Probably won't talk. Still, you never know."

"Good work. Should you try to talk to the woman?"

"Why? Because I'm a woman?"

"Good a reason as any. But you're also smarter and a better and more experienced journalist than our reporters. I'll nose around, too."

Borg looked out the window, watched a woman across Main Street walking two huge black and white Great Danes. Where would they crap, he wondered? Not a spot of grass or even weeds anywhere. He was glad they were across the street.

His thoughts jumped to what Aimee had said about the Don's son. So the Don's hold on things was weakening. Something to keep in mind. He swiveled back to his desk to consider a syndicated column about losing weight from a female race car driver who had posed for *Playboy* but had yet to win a lap. The phone rang. Donna.

"Free tonight?"

"I guess. What's up?"

"A guy named Jimmy Gleason doesn't want to see me at his workplace," she said. "His family was ruined by the Perrys. He's a pressman at *The Bulletin*, gets off around midnight and says he could meet you and me at the Last Call Diner. You know the one on wheels that they roll into the park in front of City Hall every night."

"I lived on their hotdogs when I was on the lobster shift at *The Bulletin*. Hey, what am I doing there? This guy a suspect?"

"Maybe," said Donna. "And you could help me understand what he says about the paper. You might get a good column. Also, Gleason suggested it. He insisted. He knows you left *The Bulletin* and figures you don't like them much."

"Couldn't you just bring him in?"

"Yeah but he wouldn't talk as much. I'd rather start this way. He says his foreman thought it might be a good idea for you to be along."

"Patsy Doyle?"

"Close. His brother, Mike. So you'll come?"

"Curiosity killed the cat," said Borg. "However, it's the life-blood of my profession. See you at midnight."

Not before a telephone call alerted him to the danger of finding pirates in London.

CHAPTER FIFTEEN

"**I** have to fly to London tomorrow to find some pirates." Alex Cord was calling from California. A casting director for movies and TV, she might become the love of his life. He might even become the love of hers. Meanwhile, their lives and jobs and locations kept them apart most of the time.

"Well, London should be fun, anyway," Borg said. He had reached his town house a few minutes before, had his feet up, and was sipping a glass of cold pinot gris, munching on peanuts and watching someone maneuver a good sized sloop into Greenwich Bay, helped by a sweet breeze. The sun sparkled on modest whitecaps and across the mouth of the Bay in the state park trees waved to each other in the wind.

"No fun with this director. He's a real jerk. Only wants pirates with English accents in spite of the fact that the star is from Wyoming."

"How do you find pirates in London, anyway? Sail up and down the Thames in a schooner and throw out a net?"

"At a casting call like everywhere else, wise guy."

"Why are you doing it if you dislike this guy so much? And why do you dislike him, by the way?"

"He's a sleaze, always touching and pawing, especially after a few drinks, and you know he'll have a few drinks flying over. I'm doing it for the producer, a good guy who gave me some jobs when I was getting started. The movie will be hash. They're making it on the cheap, might even use pirate ships from a theme park. And this guy wants English pirates. I'll insist we have dinner at the Ivy anyway."

"I hope you remember me over a Scotch . . ." Was that jealousy raising its ugly head? He cast it aside. You either trusted someone or you didn't. Or so he told himself.

"Of course I will . . ."

"Where does that leave next weekend?" He tried to keep it light. Yet Borg looked forward to seeing her more than he admitted, even to himself. Maybe he better start admitting it.

"Not bad, actually," said Alex. "We'll fly back to New York on Friday and I can grab a shuttle up." He could hear voices in the background. Sounded like actors reading for a part. Alex had a two room office with one of the rooms equipped with camera and taping equipment. Two assistants helped out, one for the equipment, the other for secretarial work. The door between the offices was almost always open. Borg had been surprised at how plain it was when he visited six months before.

"Get a reservation early." Borg hoped he didn't sound too anxious. Then again, screw pride. "Those flights up here get filled up in the spring and summer. But you know that. And please don't bring any pirates."

"Not a one. You have enough there already. What's new with you?"

"Some fun, actually, and some not so fun. There may be an Indian casino in Arctic, we're looking into a small-time porno ring in Clinton and the publisher of *The Bulletin* died over the weekend."

"I saw something about the publisher in the state-by-state roundup in *USA Today*. A biking accident, wasn't it? By the way, how does *USA Today* sum up a whole state in one paragraph every day? I could see Rhode Island. But Texas? That takes some arrogance, if you ask me."

"You, more than most, must know that newspaper editors are superior beings. Maybe *USA Today* feels that what happens in most states every day isn't worth more than a graph. Maybe they're right. Anyway, the State Police are not so sure the bicycle accident was an accident. The wife is screaming murder to the head of State Police."

"Do you think it's murder?"

"I'm beginning to wonder." He took a sip of wine, watched the sloop hit a dock hard. Someone wasn't as good a sailor as he thought. "Lots of motive around and there seems to be a lot of hanky-panky going on."

"God, I hope you're not going to get involved. And especially not with that little cop from Arctic, whatever her name is."

"You know damn well it's Donna Pacheco and I may help a little. I have to fill the time some way while you're flying all over the world with lecherous directors."

"Well, don't fill it with hanky panky I warn you, or I will take sweet revenge. I have pirates to back me up, remember. And make sure you don't fill next weekend with anything but me."

"Love you, too."

Matt Borg hung up feeling a little bit guilty that he had not said anything about meeting Donna later to talk to Gleason. Alex and he had been seeing each other for more than a year in spite of the problems of a long-distance relationship. More than that, she worked in the sexual hothouse of Hollywood and he was far from sequestered. Still, it had worked in its own quirky, curious way and, in relationships, whatever worked, worked. Would it work forever? Who knew? Not since Jane had he felt this way about anyone. That's all he knew for now. And that was enough. The black hole in him might be healing. Or so he hoped.

In any event, he put it all aside and made a salad of lettuce, tomatoes, onion, and chicken, put his feet up to watch a History Channel special about Egypt's pharaohs—and promptly fell asleep.

It was just after 11:00 p.m. when the TV woke him up as the History Channel began its daily reprise of World War II. He knew Hitler would lose so he grabbed a fast shower, put on a yellow polo shirt, khaki slacks, and Docksiders, and headed down the stairs to his Caprice Classic. First he grabbed a blue sweater. Spring nights could be cool.

CHAPTER SIXTEEN

When did American office buildings start leaving their lights on at night? Borg didn't remember. He did recall years ago driving into Tokyo from the airport late one evening and seeing offices in every building still shining brightly, a symbol then of the hardworking Japanese and how they were outworking and outperforming their soft American competitors.

All of those lights and all of that work didn't help the Japanese much when their economy went dark. Borg hoped the lights he saw this night, lights that outlined the downtown Providence skyline, helped to ward off economic disaster. Then again, Providence had seen it all before, boom and bust, the hub of a mill economy, then a jewelry center. Locomotives had been manufactured here and automobiles and once a movie or two before everything moved south and west, the textiles to the Carolinas and still sliding south, the cars to Detroit and now moving right out of the country and the movies to California and some of those trying out Vancouver.

Providence was on the rebound with events like its Water Fire, with its bonfires cradled in metal baskets in the middle of the river, with its walks along the river banks, with the whole river newly exposed, the river once blanketed by concrete. Gondolas glided along its waters and most everyone agreed they were better than traffic. Largely responsible for the face-lift was the colorful, charismatic, and mildly corrupt mayor, Toby Fragnoli, a favorite of Borg, who felt that all politicians were somewhat bent and at least Toby gave good value for chicanery.

There was no trouble finding a place to park. Downtown Providence on a late Tuesday night was quiet and dark, the tall buildings forming a skyline. One of them was the bank where a treasure trove of gold had once been stored to supply the state's jewelry industry. In front of City Hall, with its man-sard roof of green copper sheath, was a wide street and then a park. The street was not only for traffic. It also served as a place in which crowds gathered for political events or patriotic celebrations—which also inevitably became political events. Mayor Toby Fragnoli was awfully good at those, able to carry a crowd along with him as he painted verbal pictures of a great city—his city—in the making.

Now, though, at midnight, the plaza was quiet. A cool spring breeze carried an occasional whitecap of paper across the street until it flowed up against a curb. The conversations of the few men gathered around the Last Call Diner were muted. The Last Call wasn't really a diner, just a dirty white wagon with a peaked shingle roof that looked like a small shack on wheels. One side opened up to a counter and a short order kitchen. You could order anything just so long as it was a hotdog or burger or Polish sausage or a doughnut. You could drink anything as long as it was coffee or a Coke. Pete Petroukis from behind his counter treated everyone the same—with contempt. He and his place were an institution so his ugly temper was accepted or laughed at. Which made him just a little bit uglier.

Borg had to look twice to see Donna at the side of the diner. She was in a black sweater and slacks and a black jacket, standing in the shadows, a white cardboard cup of coffee in her hand the only accent in the dark.

"Undercover?" he asked as he joined her.

"Whenever I can be," she said as she emptied the coffee into a garbage can by the trailer, crushed the cardboard cup and tossed it as well. "Know what this guy looks like?"

"I think I see him right now coming across the street."

"In the jeans and black T-shirt? Looks in pretty good shape."

"Most pressmen are. It sure isn't because of the amount of hard work they do."

"Spoken like a real boss."

"I didn't know you were a defender of union workers," he said.

"Maybe I am and maybe not." She bristled. Out of sorts.

Borg shut up. No use upsetting Donna. There were lots of things he didn't know about her. About everyone, as a matter of fact. He knew he had to keep reminding himself that assuming made an ass of you and me. He knew he could be a wise ass without portfolio.

With that the man in the black T-shirt was at the diner. Donna stepped out of the shadows to identify herself. Gleason took half a step back. He adjusted fast. How quickly men adjust to a pretty woman, whether a police lieutenant or not. Borg joined them and the three walked around the diner into the darkness behind it.

"Now, what's this all about?" The look on Gleason's face lurked between a smirk and a sneer. He had the good looks of the black Irish, dark hair and eyes and very white skin. Still, he was a sour man. You could almost smell him, like a pickle.

"I'm looking into the death of Ronald Perry and we thought you might be of some help," said Donna.

"You trust this guy?" he pointed at Borg.

"As much as I trust anybody," said Donna. "You wanted him here."

"Pat Doyle thought it would be a good idea. A witness or something. Not that I give a damn," said Gleason. "Anything I know about the Perrys you can broadcast to the world. You know about what the bastard's family did to my grandfather and father. Ruined us."

"Then why do you work for him?" Donna hugged herself, stopped. A cold breeze swirled around the trailer but she hated showing any weakness.

"For one thing, the job pays better than any other I could get." His mouth turned mean. "For another, I work nights so my days are free. And it gave me a chance to watch the son of a bitch, to maybe nail him."

And to damage his presses if given the chance, thought Borg.

"So you watched him?" Donna rubbed her hands together, put them on her hips, her right one hooked under her sweater in her belt. Borg knew her gun, a standard .38 Smith and Wesson, was on her right hip.

"Damn right. I live down in Little Bay. You probably know that. So I know a helluva lot about the proper Mr. Ronald Perry."

"Like that he takes a bike ride on Sunday morning?"

"Everyone in Little Bay knows that." He smirked. "Most of us also knew your fancy Mr. Perry had somethin' goin' with a babe named Angela a while back and it didn't end so good."

"You know Angela's last name?" Donna had taken a small notebook from a jacket pocket.

"Angela Rosso," said Gleason. "Hot. A lot hotter'n that vanilla wife of his. He couldn't get enough of her."

"You know that how?"

"Not that it's anythin' to you but frankly, I don't give a damn. I'm union and they can't touch me for talkin'. I saw the Rosso woman and Perry together . . ."

"Following Perry, were you?"

"Just hangin' out." He grinned, gave notice he knew more than he was saying. A wise guy ready to muddy Perry any way he could.

"I hang out in the garage on my breaks," Gleason added. "I listen to the guys who come into the pressroom. You hear a lot. Like Bill Hasner and Perry arguing about sellin' the company if the presses don't work. Maybe even if they do. Last Friday night they almost got into a fight when the presses broke down. It was fun for me to watch the bastards."

"They ever hit each other?" Donna asked it quietly.

"Wusses. Both of them. Just talkers. One night Hasner was screaming about all the money down the drain with Perry's damn toy presses. I thought they might actually go at it. But Mike Doyle, that's my foreman, grabbed Hasner and Frankie Levesque grabbed Perry or it might have been fun. They finally cooled off. And we got the presses runnin' again. Guys in the pressroom talk, you know. We think it's a question of time before the place is sold."

"Mike Doyle related to Pat, the union secretary?" From Donna.

"Brother." Gleason snickered. "Good jobs stay in the family in this state."

"What about this Angela?" said Donna.

"You gotta know that Perry and his wife lived apart for a while," said Gleason. "That's when he got involved with Angela. Pretty hot and heavy for a while."

"Ever see her around?"

"Maybe the guy you should be talkin' to is Frankie Levesque. He was Perry's driver. He would know more about his personal life than anyone. Just don't tell him I told you that."

"We'd find him at the paper during the day?" asked Donna.

"Or at his mother's garage out in Little Bay. Big Nan's is what it's called."

"I've met her," said Donna. "She gave me directions on Sunday. So it's her son?"

"Yep."

"Anybody else you hear might have a grudge against Perry?"

"How about the boys up on the Hill?" Donna could see Gleason was getting into his tale, finding someone to share it with. Fancy tales would follow.

"Don't kid with me," said Donna. "Why would they want to kill a newspaper publisher? They don't do that and you know it."

"Try this on for size. Angela is a Rosso. Or married to one. The husband is connected. They don't take lightly to their wives screwing around."

"I wouldn't think those guys would want to get anywhere near a newspaper," said Borg.

"Let me tell you somethin', smart guy. When my family was runnin' *The Tribune* and *The Bulletin* was tryin' to run us out of business, the real war was between the distributors, the guys deliverin' the papers. And there were whole sections of the city and state we couldn't get a paper into. Tires were slashed, windshields were broken, drivers were scared to death."

"I never heard that before," said Borg.

"Where would you hear it? At *The Bulletin*? No way. All I know is that after a while you couldn't get a *Tribune* on The Hill or a lot of other places. And you never saw an ad for an Italian restaurant in our pages."

"Why would that have anything to do with what happened to Perry?"

"Maybe, just maybe, the last series in the paper turned up a little bit too much about where the mob money is goin', into businesses like car dealerships and real estate development. Maybe the boys felt they weren't gettin' the respect they deserved for past favors."

"That sounds nuts, Jim," said Borg.

"Yeah. Well, maybe Angela was the last straw. And any more nuts than the way the mob helped elect Kennedy and then turned on him because it felt betrayed? Like Sinatra felt when Jack wouldn't stay at his house in California?"

"By the way," said Donna. "Ever see Louise Perry around while you were hanging out in Little Bay?"

"Not much. Maybe at Mom's with Hasner for lunch. He was at the house some."

It was starting to rain, to spit really. Soft but steady.

"Listen, I've got to go," said Gleason. "I got to say that if Perry was killed, more power to whoever did it. I hope you never catch him."

"You wouldn't be the guy who did it, would you?" Donna looked hard at Gleason. Finally he flinched, looked down.

"Not me," he said. "Not me."

"Mind if I ask where you were Sunday morning last?"

"Not a bit. At Mass in St. Gregory's in Little Bay."

"We'll talk again," said Donna.

"Whatever . . ."

And he was gone, jogging lightly into the darkness. Borg and Donna walked across the street to the shelter of a bus stop's canopy.

"What do you think?" she asked him.

"I don't know what to think. You think you know something and then you turn over a rock and there's a lot more you than you imagined. Not that everything Gleason said may be true. Then again, maybe it is. You know Pastorini said his people weren't involved."

"Pastorini might have lied."

Borg grimaced, shook his head almost imperceptively. Even in the dark Donna caught it.

"Or maybe he's getting old and doesn't know what all his boys, or his son, are doing," she said. "Like a cup of coffee?'

Borg had heard a lot. He needed time to digest it before he wanted to say much more.

"I don't think so, Donna. I've got a paper to get out tomorrow and I'd like to think about this stuff. Let me take a rain check. What's up with you?"

"I'm going to try to talk to Frankie Levesque tomorrow down in Little Bay. I'll stop by the gas station and talk to Nan, too. And to anyone else down there I think can help. I'll call you afterwards. Thanks for coming tonight and thanks for talking to the Don."

"Wouldn't have missed it. Want me to walk you to your car?"

"I've got an umbrella and my Smith and Wesson. I'm just in the mood for some wise guy to stop me tonight."

"Better him than me," he said as she walked away.

CHAPTER SEVENTEEN

I t was still drizzling the next morning as Donna Pacheco drove to Little Bay. In and out of the light rain. As though each cloud had a mind of its own. One minute she'd have the windshield wipers on and the next they would be smearing the glass, the rainfall gone. A little like the case she was on. One moment a clear view and then the spit and smear. Just like life: You never really knew anything about anyone. If you thought you did you were fooling yourself. She once believed this state was different. It was so small that almost everyone knew everyone else. Knew a little of the truth and all of the lies. No one knew the difference, of course. No one ever knew that anywhere. She'd like to talk about that with Borg sometime.

Donna stopped herself. There was a time she'd shared any thoughts she had with her husband, Al. And stuff about her work. Somehow that had ended. She forgot when. Al didn't like talking about life and different people and how they lived. The Red Sox and family and town gossip were his thing. She hated the feeling that she and her sweetheart since junior high school were growing apart. Hated it and couldn't help it. God, even Patsy Doyle had seemed interesting. Where was this going? She drove the thoughts from her mind or tried to. Focused on the driving and the case.

Knowing the way to Little Bay made it easier than it had been just last Sunday and she was soon on her way past Fall River and on Route 24 down and into Little Bay. On the left was Big Nan's. The gas station looked even more bedraggled in the rain, its rusting signs hanging crooked alongside the window at the front of the station. The signs advertised Coke and Marlboro. Rust stains dripped down the once white siding of the building. Donna pulled past the pump and parked. She ran through the drizzle to the front door and then had to push hard to open it. Moisture stuck it, she guessed.

"The sleuth is back," said Nan. "I figured you would be—if you were any good. Are you any good?"

"We'll see," said Donna.

Nan sat in an ancient stuffed armchair of faded blue facing the door. Behind her were shelves of crackers and bread and Kenyon's pancake flour. In no particular order and they all looked dusty. Alongside the shelves was a small refrigerator. Through its glass door she could see a shelf of milk and orange juice. And three shelves of soda. To Donna's left was the counter, about six feet long, with what looked like an original huge cash register resting on top of it, its brass parts still shiny, sharing shelf space with open-boxed displays of beef jerky and chewing gum. The contents of the display cabinet beneath the counter looked as unsavory as they were obscure. Dirty old cans of tomato soup, even a box or two of wooden matches. Off in the corner was a woodstove. To the side of the counter was a TV set tuned to the business channel. It was a 38-inch color Sony with a DVD player sitting on top. Nan clicked it off.

"Market's up," Nan continued. "Gives the experts on the TV a chance to push their favorite stocks and scams." She smiled. "Have a seat."

"I'm looking for some help—and I'd like to talk to your son, Mrs. Levesque." Donna sat down in a wooden chair whose right arm was a small desk, obviously from some old schoolhouse.

"Figured you would," said Nan. "And you can call me Nan or Big Nan. Everybody does."

"Tell me about the Perrys."

"Not much small talk, eh? You city people are always in a hurry. Not much to tell you. Like most married couples, seemed to have good days and bad ones. Had more money than most of us. Ron Perry was good to my Frank most of the time . . ."

"Most of the time?"

"He could be mean. Nothing serious. Most bosses are mean, I guess. Frankie didn't mind."

Donna, born and bred in Arctic, population 16,734 by latest count, had never been called city folks before. She'd try to remember to tell Borg. Stopped herself. She meant tell her husband. She buried a worry.

"Sorry if I'm rushing things," she said, finally. "Maybe it's 'cause I'm wet from the rain." She took a breath. "Do you think Ron Perry's death was an accident?"

"A man falls off his bike and hits the back of his head hard enough to kill him? Stranger things have happened, I guess. I hear Mrs. Perry doesn't think so."

"Where'd you hear that?"

"It's all over town. Some folks say it's even on the radio talk shows."

Big Nan probably knew more than the talk shows. How to open this tough old quahog?

"So you know Mrs. Perry?" Donna asked.

"Didn't say that. Know her better than she knows me, if you know what I mean. Heard what she's saying, though."

"What do you think about her?

"She's all right. Gets her nose in the air once in a while."

"Any problems in the marriage?"

"You married?" she asked and when there was a nod of the head she went on: "Then you know there are problems in every marriage. Solvin' them is what matters. Or ignoring them. Or both. Or not."

"I hear the Perrys were separated for a while. Know why?"

"If I did I wouldn't tell you." Donna didn't believe Big Nan for a minute. Gave her a look and waited. Not in vain.

"Let me tell you about a fella we have around here," said Nan. "Name of Stephen. Happily married I guess. Still, he's a hound. Would nail a snake if it stood still. Says he loves his wife. Says she's a wonderful woman, but not much good between the sheets, if you know what I mean. His excuse, I guess. Been married thirty-five years. Happily? I don't know." She paused, smiled. "It's lasted."

"And that was true of the Perrys?"

"Didn't say that . . ." The phone rang. Nan picked it up from the small table by her side, listened, answered, "I'm open until six tonight, Ned. See you."

"I'd like to talk to your son if he's around," Donna said

Big Nan hesitated, lips twisted, shook her head, hesitated a minute before turning back to Donna. "I'll call him over but take it easy. He's a good boy, but Frank Junior gets rattled easy. He's next door in the house. I wouldn't want anyone takin' advantage of my Frankie, by the way."

She went to the door, opened it, shouted "Frankie" into the drizzle, and returned to her chair. Donna noticed again how gracefully the big woman moved. Smooth. Nan stayed standing until Frankie opened the door and the outline of her body waited in the pillows.

Frankie was dressed like a Catholic high school kid, in a white shirt with its sleeves rolled up, black slacks and sneakers. Like her thirteen-year old son, Donna thought. Frankie, however, looked to be in his forties, a bit over six feet tall, with the pudgy, round face of a simply drawn cartoon or the happy symbol that some people used in their notes. A thatch of blonde hair and wide, innocent blue eyes over a smile of gapped teeth.

"Give your mama a kiss," said Nan and he went over and kissed her cheek and hugged her shoulder. Donna could see her powerful arm reaching out from Nan's short-sleeve shirt as his mother touched Frankie's hand and went around his waist. A big hand, Donna noticed. Big and callused. Frankie remained standing beside her. He had his mother's wide shoulders. "Lieutenant Pacheco of the State Police wants to ask you a few questions about Mr. Perry."

"He was my boss," said Frankie Levesque.

"Did you know him long?" asked Donna. Best to go slow with Frankie.

"Frankie drove Mr. Perry everywhere. I never had an accident. Mr. Perry liked to have a clean car."

"Ron Perry and my son met when they were kids and the Perry's summered here, like now," said Nan. "They would fish and go crabbin' together . . ."

"Mr. Perry hated crabs," said Frankie. "Hated them . . ."

Big Nan interrupted. "There weren't an awful lot of other kids around. Later Ron got him a job at *The Bulletin*. Frankie had been working at the Ford dealership in Fall River."

"Frankie worked for Mr. Ahr," said Frankie. "First he cleaned all the cars on the lot. Then he cleaned the loan cars. Frankie loved cleanin' cars. Then he cleaned the rental cars. They were awful dirty. Kids left gum and food. Frankie cleaned them good even if it took all day. Mr. Ahr said Frankie was the best car washer he ever had."

"Ron Perry finally got Frankie a job in the circulation department at *The Bulletin*," said Nan. "Doing odd jobs and driving. Then when the publisher's driver retired he gave Frankie the job."

"Frankie never had an accident," said Frankie. "Even in the snow or ice. Mr. Perry would get mad if we slid . . ."

"Frankie took care of that car like a baby," said Nan. "He was on call to Mr. Perry day and night. Perry got full value and more for what he paid my Frankie."

"Did you ever drive an Angela Rosso in the car?" asked Donna. She had thrown in the name just to see the reaction. She could feel Nan freeze.

"Frankie not talk about anyone in the car." Frankie said it very slowly.

"It's OK now," said Donna. "I'm trying to find out if anyone hurt Mr. Perry."

"OK?" Frankie asked his mother, who gave him an unhappy nod. "Miss Angela was nice. Very pretty. Frankie drove her sometimes. To The Spaghetti Place. That's on The Hill."

"With Mr. Perry?"

"No one without Mr. Perry. Unless Mr. Perry said so."

"She seem like a nice lady?"

"Yes. She was pretty. I helped her get out of the car. Pretty legs. Like you."

Donna looked him over. So he knew what pretty meant and he knew that described Angela. And he had watched Angela get out of the car. Skirt riding up? His mother saw Donna looking at her son.

"Frankie couldn't know much," said Nan. "There was a glass window between driver and passengers in the Lincoln, a dark one, wasn't there Frankie?"

"Not always up. I watched the road. Frankie never had an accident."

Donna searched his face. It took him a few seconds before he could put a thought into words and it showed. Of course, Frankie could use the mirror to watch his passengers in the back seat. Especially a pretty woman. Could this guy have a crush on Angela Rosso? And his boss would have talked to him at least once in a while. Could he know more than he was saying? Nan Levesque broke in.

"The Lieutenant knows what a good driver you are, Frankie. Is that all, Lieutenant? Frankie has to run some errands for me, don't you Frankie?"

"To the grocery store, Mom?" His mother wanted no more conversation. She put an arm around her son's waist and pulled him closer. What's stronger than a mother's love? Only the hate Donna had witnessed in a dozen murders.

"That's a good boy," said Nan, still gripping her son by the waist. She wasn't going to let him say much more. "Is that all, then, Lieutenant?"

"I suppose so. Thanks for the time and thank you, Frankie."

"Frankie never had an accident," said Frankie with a smile. "Even in my truck."

"Drive that around on Sundays much?"

"Deliver the Sunday paper," said Frankie, puffed up a little.

"Last Sunday, too?"

"Yes, I did."

"See Mr. Perry?"

"Nope. Frankie never saw him at all."

"Better be going on those errands," said his mother and walked him to the door.

As Donna ran through the rain to her car, she watched Frankie carefully steer the old Post Office truck out of the gas station. Its steering wheel on the right side would help deliver newspapers. Or make it easier to club someone on a bicycle while still driving. Old as it was, the truck, painted blue, shone even in the rain. Clean and sparkling. Donna whistled as she started her Datsun. Maybe she was getting somewhere.

CHAPTER EIGHTEEN

I t was almost noon and the drizzle persisted. In spite of a morning forecast predicting sunshine. Donna had hoped for clearing, had set herself a busy day of interviews. Next she'd pay a visit to Cyrus Bitgood, the man in the house nearest to the death scene. And then stop to see the widow again.

Bitgood's place looked the way it should, an old farmhouse with cedar siding long since turned a dusky silver with a barn off behind it. In front was parked a Plymouth, a faded blue, so old it had a sailing ship on its hood. Bitgood answered the door wearing worn brown and baggy corduroy trousers held up by red suspenders over a checkered shirt, mostly blue. On his feet were black rubber boots up over his calves.

"Ayeh, thought I might see you again," he said as he beckoned her into a room not unlike the one in the gas station Donna had just left. There was a wood stove, an old overstuffed chair, a television set, and a big round wooden table on which were scattered newspapers of the day. She spotted *The New York*

Times and *The Wall Street Journal* and a *Barron's*. Did everyone down here play the market?

"Made the table myself," Bitgood said as he saw her looking. "It was half a big wooden spool the utility company kept its heavy wire on. Two big wheels connected by a thick wooden axle. Just threw it away, they did. So I sawed the axel in half and got myself two good tables. Big enough to hold things. The other's in the barn."

"You must do a lot of reading?"

"Do some. More than I used to. Used to have dairy cows and hay. Brung in the hay myself with some hired help. Too old now. Got rid of the cows and hired some boys to bring in the hay. Good boys. Got to watch 'em though. Get two crops a good summer. Keeps me going. More I read though, madder I get."

Donna couldn't help but smile. Cyrus Bitgood noticed.

"You'll smile the other side of your face when you have to pay off the big debt this country's runnin' up. No way to run things, I say." Did he crack a little bit of a smile? "Sorry I can't offer you much. I'm drinkin' hot water. I guess you wouldn't like some?"

"A cold glass would be good, thanks."

"Right from the well, deepest around here," said Bitgood as he brought her the glass, poured from a pitcher on the kitchen counter. She didn't see a refrigerator. He still hadn't asked her what she wanted.

"Tastes good," said Donna, even though it really wasn't cold. She was growing as laconic as the man sitting across from her in the deep chair, behind the table he made himself. She was in a straight wooden chair with a padded seat. It was more comfortable than she would have guessed. Still she had to sit straight.

"Mr. Bitgood, I wonder if I could ask you some questions about what happened to Mr. Perry?"

"Ask away," he said. "Don't know if I can answer, though."

"You live near that hill Mr. Perry was pedaling up. Do you think Mr. Perry could have fallen off his bike and killed himself?"

"I'm not a doctor. Not a policeman, neither. Just a farmer. It seems to me it would take some squirmin' for a man to fall off a bike backward goin' up a hill. Goin' not too fast and hit the back of his head and kill himself. He had to be leanin' forward to be pedalin' up the hill."

"You didn't see anything that morning?"

"Like I told you, didn't see a thing. Not until that boy, Tommy, came and got me. I was just fixin' to drive down and get my Sunday papers."

"I guess you knew that Perry cycled that way every Sunday?"

"Ayeh. Everybody knew it. Even when he wasn't livin' here last summer he still used to come down with his bike and ride down to Third Beach."

"Was that when he was separated from his wife?"

"Don't know much about that. Just knew he used to drive down in his big station wagon with the bike in the back. And then he'd eat over at Mom's after his ride."

"Alone?"

"Guess so. Once saw him eatin' outside at Mom's with a gal. Didn't think much about it. Sometimes you have to share tables it gets so crowded. Pretty thing, she was. Tall. Blue eyes and dark hair. I like that. The contrast, I guess. My Edna had light hair and dark eyes. Liked that too."

"You eat at Mom's often?"

"Nope. Too expensive. Good place though, I hear. I buy bread there. They bake a good loaf. Used to bake my own. Don't anymore. Too much trouble. Like a lot of things."

Bitgood took a long sip of his hot water, went on.

"Wouldn't make too much of Mister Perry sitting alongside a gal. Even saw Missus Perry with a fella there once. Didn't think anythin' of it."

"Recognize him?"

"Ayeh. Think so. Was a visitor at the Perry house once in a while. Good friend of Mr. Perry."

Bitgood clamped his mouth shut. He wasn't going to say anymore about that. However, nothing ventured, nothing gained.

"Mr. Bitgood, you must have lived here a long time?"

"Since afore the rocks were delivered, like they used to say." He smiled at her and she smiled back. Couldn't help herself.

"You must have known Ron Perry when he was a child?" Donna was beginning to get a picture of the victim. It always helped. "What was he like?"

"Unlike most I don't mind speaking bad about the dead," Bitgood said. "Don't matter much anymore. Ron Perry had a face like a choir boy. But he used to pick on the Levesque boy . . ."

"Frankie you mean?"

"Not n'other. They'd go crabbing together and I once saw Perry toss a big blue claw crab on the Levesque boy when he wasn't looking. Gave him a real fierce bite. Blue claws will do that, you know. Lucky Big Nan didn't kill him. She loves that boy. All she's got left. One of them crabs once bit Perry, I remember. Maybe it's why Ron used to fasten firecrackers under horseshoe crabs, let them try to crawl to the water and they'd blow up."

"Firecrackers?"

"Yep. Only the Perry's could afford that trick. Don't know if horseshoe crabs have any feelin's. Don't care. Still, not a nice thing to do to a fellow creature."

Donna studied the old man. She could have listened to him all day. She shook herself back into cop mode.

"Mr. Bitgood," said Donna. "Why do you think anyone would want to kill Mr. Perry?"

"Sex or money," he said without a pause. "Power mebbe. Sex and money gets you power, or you get power to have sex and money. Same thing."

"Any thoughts about who might want sex or money enough to kill Mr. Perry for them?"

"Haven't had sex or money in so long I haven't given it much thought," said Cyrus Bitgood. Small smile again. Maybe he thought she hadn't seen those stock reports from Merrill Lynch on the table. Maybe he didn't care. Had an act too good to fool with.

"I guess I'm off to see Mrs. Perry then," said Donna as she rose and headed toward the door. She noticed that Cyrus Bitgood rose as well. You could wear rubber boots and still have manners. Suspenders, too. "What's the easiest way to get there?"

"Turn right out of the driveway, left on Bayview Road and follow it to the Perry house. Lookin' for sex and money there? Might find it."

Was there a crooked smile on the face of Cyrus Bitgood as he closed the door? Donna wasn't sure. She was sure that he had had his share of sex in his time. Maybe even now. Especially since he wasn't wasting any energy on cows or hay. She sure liked the old guy.

CHAPTER NINETEEN

Dampened by the drizzle, the Perry house looked smaller, darkly sinister. Donna smiled to herself. Maybe everything looked sinister in the rain. Smaller, too. Maybe the rain shrunk everything. Like some of the wash she had to do when she got home if Al hadn't done it. Then again, maybe she was doing what Borg talked about. Projecting. It was bad enough to project your own emotions into other people. Now, was she doing it to buildings? Maybe she was just plain thinking too much. Still, that was her job, wasn't it?

No sun glistened off the windows of the Perry house, shadows hovered around the door, rushes alongside the approaching road and in the wetlands near the stone building were drooping, bowing to the rain. The dogwoods on either side of the door were sad, not in bloom. This time it was a housekeeper who answered the door, a Latina, short and trim with a high, squeaky voice and a quick smile. Like Frankie Levesque, she was wearing black and white, a short sleeve blouse and a short skirt that swung back and forth as the maid led Donna to the great room where Louise Perry was sitting at a desk facing the big window that looked out on the Bay. Funny how the room didn't look as big as on her first visit. Louise Perry rose to greet Donna.

"I'm sorry to be bothering you again," said Donna, not sorry at all. "I was in the neighborhood and I appreciate your seeing me."

"I'm just writing some notes," said Louise Perry. "Come, let's sit over here. I like to look out on the water when it's raining. However, I have to admit that sometimes when I look out while I'm trying to do anything I end up just watching the gulls."

Donna thought of Borg. He liked the rain too, especially falling on the sea. Maybe all these smart people do, she thought to herself. She joined Louise Perry in a grouping of two chairs and a couch. This was a different Louise Perry than the one she had seen just days before. In control now. Her hazel eyes looked directly at Donna, her hands were folded one over the other. She wore a crisp pink blouse and blue slacks and espadrilles. Around her neck was a strand of pearls. The real thing, Donna thought to herself.

"Now then, would you like some coffee or tea or anything?" she asked, saw a shake of the head and continued. "No? Well then, I'm glad you're here because I have something I want to talk to you about."

"That's what I'm here for," said Donna, recognizing a change in tone.

"I think the Mafia killed my husband," said Mrs. Perry. "I think someone drove up behind him and hit him in the head with a baseball bat or something. This was no accident. I think anyone with any sense could see that."

"The Mafia doesn't usually kill what they call civilians," said Donna. "It's bad business. And killing a newspaper publisher would be very bad business."

"I'm not sure I agree with your theories," said Mrs. Perry. "I'm looking at facts. Ron died from a wound on the back of his head. If he fell from the bike he would have fallen forward and hit his forehead . . ."

Impatient, Donna broke in. "He was on his way up the hill so he couldn't have been going very fast, not fast enough to propel him over the handle bars. He could have fallen backwards . . ."

Louise Perry leaned forward. Donna was sure she wasn't used to being interrupted. She'd better just let the woman talk.

"He was killed by those goombahs up on The Hill." Mrs. Perry glared at Donna, spoke between clenched teeth, still made even "goombahs" sound patrician. Or at least respectable. Donna still hadn't asked a question. While she wouldn't be cowed she'd try to avoid confrontation.

"Mrs. Perry, we're considering every possibility," said Donna quietly. "That's why I'm here. Colonel Rockingham is determined to pursue every lead. I must tell you that our forensic experts say it is possible for someone to have fallen backwards off that bike and injure his head in just the way your husband did."

"Anything is possible, I suppose." Mrs. Perry sniffed. "I don't agree."

Now there was more going on than was being said. Both knew that Mrs. Perry, among others, had called Colonel Rockingham to ensure that the investigation was pursued aggressively. That very morning her boss had told her that one of the United State Senators from Rhode Island, the Republican, had called him the previous evening, asking about the case. Senator Cranston was always polite; always a gentleman, but his questions and the call to Rockingham's home were an indication of his interest. He was also a cousin of Ron Perry's.

"Rest assured, Mrs. Perry, that I will also do everything in my power to pursue the investigation aggressively," said Donna. She took a breath, allowing herself a moment to cool off, to clear her mind, and set her objectives. "Now, I'd like to ask you a few questions."

Louise Perry didn't say anything, just nodded. Her lips squeezed thinner than before, her jaw line almost etched in taut skin. Great bone structure, Donna had to admit. And Louise Perry liked asking questions more than answering them.

"First of all, Mrs. Perry, I wonder if you can think of anyone other than the Mafia who might want to harm your husband? Any reason that anyone might have to want him dead? Anyone who might gain a lot?"

Was there a moment's hesitation, a very slight squeeze, a narrowing of the eyes? Maybe not.

"I suppose there were those who hated *The Bulletin*. No one specific. No one we took seriously. And no one would gain enough to kill him."

"How about something more personal? Bill Hasner and he were close friends since college, I've heard," said Donna. "Will he take over the company?"

"I hear what you're implying and it's outrageous," said Louise Perry. "Bill Hasner and Ron were best friends, you're right about that. And that's all you're right about."

Donna wasn't used to taking rebukes, didn't like it. Especially didn't like being talked down to, felt that now. Gritted her teeth, took a breath and went on.

"Your husband's driver lives in Little Bay." Not a question.

"Yes, and it's a help. He was on call, so to speak. A sweet boy." Except he is over forty, Donna almost answered. She had to remind herself of what she had come for. Patience, Donna, patience.

"Mrs. Perry, I hate to ask you about this, but I must."

"Lieutenant, if you hated to ask me you wouldn't, would you?" Louise Perry looked down her nose even while seated.

"Yes, I'm afraid I would because it's my job. Isn't it true that you and your husband were separated for a while?"

"We were. I don't see that's any of your business or has anything to do with your investigation."

"We try to look into all sides of the situation. I'm sure you want us be as thorough as we can." Donna took a breath. Time to act like a cop. "Did you know if your husband was seeing anyone while you were apart?"

"Just plain snooping is what I would call this. Especially when it's obvious who did it. I don't intend to say anything about the personal life of Ron and myself. I trust I'm not a suspect, so I don't think I need to. If necessary I'll have our lawyer present the next time we talk if you pursue that line of questions."

"I'm sorry you feel that way even though I understand. Certainly, you have a right to a lawyer anytime you wish. What all this means, though, is that we may receive information second and third hand."

"I'll have to take that chance. Moreover, I'm sure you realize that we have ways of protecting ourselves. We are not without resources." Then she seemed to think better of what she had just said. "Every citizen has rights, after all. Now I have to get back to completing arrangements for Ron's funeral if you don't mind. When will his body be released, by the way?"

"The autopsy should be complete by now, so no later than tomorrow, perhaps today."

"Thank you." Louise Perry stood up. She smiled the thin smile, the Yankee smile. The talk was over.

"Thank you. I can find my own way out."

"That would be kind of you," said Louise Perry. Through teeth still clenched. How did she do that? Was it something she learned where she learned posture? Maybe.

Donna saw no one on her way out the door and into the drizzle. It felt cooler than before. Maybe that was just the memory of Louise Perry.

CHAPTER TWENTY

Lieutenant Donna Pacheco needed a bathroom and food. The light rain was getting to her and she hated the way Louise Perry had brushed her off. Society bitch. Maybe Donna was just hungry. Not good. She was proud of her trim figure. Still, she needed lunch. She remembered a roadside place she had seen on her way through Little Bay. Cy Bitgood had mentioned it. Then she saw the sign, red and white, through the mist on the left-hand side.

Mom's was mostly a counter with a few tables in front of it. The rain had started again and played on the corrugated roof. The sides of Mom's were protected by plastic sheets, but not too well. The picnic tables had been edged into the center of the space. A couple occupied one of the three tables with their three children. About the same age as two of her own kids, Sarah, Al Junior, and Mary. Al Junior was becoming a bit of a problem in junior high, a sweet smiling wise guy like his dad. Thought he was smarter than he was. Like his dad? Maybe.

Donna put her coat at one of the tables, on one of the white plastic chairs, and then realized she'd have to go up to the counter to get her lunch. The counter formed an island and circled to the inside of the building where a small shelf held bread and other baked goods for sale. She ordered a chicken pot pie, which seemed the specialty of Mom's, and a Sprite and went around the island counter and inside to the bathroom. When she came out the pie and soda were ready. She sat at her table, checking to make sure the seat wasn't wet.

"Mind if I join you?"

Constable Fred Glasgow loomed over her. The sharp edges of his starched uniform peered out from under a raincoat. His peaked cap encased in plastic made it look more military than ever. He must have emerged from inside or behind the building. He sat down. "When you called this morning to say you'd be doing some work down here I was hoping we'd bump into each other."

"I see you got the chicken pie," Glasgow added. He put his coffee on the table, softly. "Good choice. Well, how'd you make out?"

"I'm collecting an awful lot of information, good and bad. I guess it will begin to make sense after a while. Right now it's muddy."

Donna trusted this big, beefy cop. Maybe it was his eyes. They were blue, but not the steely blue that scared people. Nor the piercing blue of Patsy Doyle. Glasgow's eyes were a little misty, like the day, and that made the deeper blue softer, almost like a baby's. His whole face encouraged trust, a good face for a cop to have. Broad and ruddy and fleshy. And that big body would be hard to push around. Donna wouldn't admit it, but she relied on what a guy like Borg would call her woman's intuition. It had served her well.

"There's something I just learned that might help though I'm afraid it may just confuse things . . ." Glasgow grimaced apologetically, leaned his head to his left, looked like a little kid.

"Not any more than they are." Donna gave him a smile. "Shoot."

"When my second deputy came back to work this morning and we were talking about the Perry case, he said he had a call from Perry a few weeks ago about someone he thought might be following him."

"Name a name?"

"Afraid not. After they talked it out Perry told him to forget it, it was probably just his imagination. He had a lot on his mind. Told Elisha, that's the deputy, not to mention it to me. So Elisha didn't. He went off to check on a report about drugs in the junior high school."

"That seems funny, I mean not saying anything to you."

"That's small towns for you," said Glasgow. "Elisha works the Perry parties, directing cars, sometimes even parking them. Pays good, tips even better. He'd listen to Perry."

"I'd better talk to Elisha."

"Can if you like. Wastin' your time, though. Elisha isn't the sharpest knife in the drawer. Honestly, he'd probably tell me more than he would you. Anyway, I don't know how anyone would follow Perry around this town without being spotted. You can see how open the area is. Besides, I think this is going to end up as an accident."

"Louise Perry didn't say anything about that to me," said Donna. "You think this is an accident?"

"Didn't say I thought it was an accident," said Glasgow very slowly. Sipped his coffee from a white mug with his name on the side. The advantage of being a regular customer. "Just that it would end up being one. What'd you think of Mrs. Perry?"

"Tough and cold," said Donna through clenched teeth.

Glasgow laughed. He had brought paper towels to the picnic table to serve as napkins. Donna had forgotten hers. She wished he hadn't mentioned a drug problem in Little Bay's junior high. Al Junior was in junior high in Arctic. She drove it out of her mind.

"Did you know that Ron Perry had an affair while he was separated from his wife?" Donna spoke between mouthfuls. Her pie was delicious. Lots of chicken, some peas and carrots, terrific crust, flaky and light, crust she could never make in a million years. Neither could Al though he surely thought he could.

"Lot of men do."

"And that Mrs. Perry thinks the mob killed her husband?"

"It would be hard not to know. She's been tellin' that to everybody who'll listen. And, Mrs. Perry being Mrs. Perry, a lot of people will listen. I'm sure you know that by now."

"You're right. You know, when I was learning this job someone once told me that every case was like an onion. You peeled away the layers of skin one at a time. After a while you came to the solution."

"Yeah, I've heard that," Glasgow said as he took a swig of his coffee. "I think it was started by someone who never cooked. When I peel an onion all I get at the end of it is skin and a smell."

Donna laughed. "That's what I might have here?"

"Just a stink? Maybe."

"Would you trust Nan and Frankie and Cy and Mrs. Perry and what they told me today? You know them better than I do."

"Like most people, I'd trust most of what they told me and everything they didn't."

"Thanks, I think. That was a good chicken pie."

"All the food here is good," said Glasgow, emptying his mug. "So's the coffee. You know, there was a writer, a fella name of Jack Kerouac, who once wrote that you should never eat at a place called Mom's, never play poker with a guy named Doc, and never get involved with any woman with more troubles than you have. Well, this place is owned and run by a chef who got tired of New York. He used the name as a joke because of what Jack Kerouac wrote. Says he spent time with Kerouac in New York and the guy might have known something about writin' but not a damn thing about food."

Donna laughed. She didn't read much herself, had never developed the knack, never cared much. She still liked people who did. Especially when they shared some of the book stuff with her.

"For what it's worth," said Glasgow, "I think you're doin' a good job on this, talkin' to the right folks, not getting scared off by people like Louise Perry. Actually, I like her, think she's a good person and a good neighbor. Square shooter." He paused. "I wasn't sure what you'd do when this started. If you need any help, you know where I am."

"Thanks." She felt a lot better leaving Mom's than when she arrived. Nothing like a hot chicken pot pie and a big beefy supportive cop on a miserable rainy day. To say nothing of a truck with a steering wheel on the right side, the confirmation of another woman in Perry's life and word of someone possibly trailing the dead man.

CHAPTER 21

Matt Borg was in a black mood. Otherwise it never would have happened. He would have had more sense. The advertising results were awful, circulation was sputtering, and the old *Valley Times* building needed a new roof. He was mad at himself and with his staff and with the world. Anger combined with disappointment produced a potent emotional stew.

He had stayed late this Tuesday, going over reports, catching up on the dog work that kept a small business alive. It was the opposite side of the coin from the emotional rush of getting out a newspaper every day. The time he had put in with Donna Pacheco had drained his attention from the details of his operation and sooner or later attention had to be paid—or he and the *Times* would pay the price.

It was after nine when he locked the back door and turned to walk to his car. Drizzle had formed small puddles. The light over the door was out. Damn the lazy goddamn maintenance man. The least he could do is change the light bulbs. He did little else. Borg's trusty Caprice Classic rested as far away from the Valley Times' building as you could get. Alongside it loomed a van.

Everybody in the neighborhood used the *Valley Times*'s parking lot. It was big enough so Borg didn't care so long as they didn't start repairing their vehicles on *Times*'s property and spilling oil all over the macadam. Borg didn't even believe in reserved parking spaces. Get to work first and get the best spot. Reporters arrived earliest and parked closest to the back door. They needed to take off fast on stories. So it worked out. Borg tried to set an example by parking as far away from the building as he could but it didn't work. He was the only one ever at the end of the lot.

The parking lot stretched to the next street. Across the street was a body shop business that had gone belly up years ago. A few car cadavers and used bits and pieces were evidence of what was rumored to have been the leading chop shop in the state. At night it looked like a war zone.

Looking down to dodge the puddles and cursing his fate, Borg didn't see the two hulks standing in the darkness until he bumped into the two guys waiting for him. They didn't budge even though Matt Borg carried 200 pounds on his six four frame.

"Don't get nervous," said the first one. A slab over six feet high. Dark green windbreaker. His partner had less of a neck and was shorter. Looked like the old heavyweight, Two Ton Tony Galento. Borg had seen him in Classic Fights on TV. Joe Louis years ago had put him away with a straight right. Green windbreaker with a patch on the front left-hand side. A golf club patch. The gentrification of the goons. Chewing gum. The faces looked almost familiar. Stock figures. Stereotypes. "Just take it easy, no one gets hurt."

"Why should I be nervous?" Borg shot back. "It's my damn lot. What in hell do you want?"

"We just want to talk to you," said the first one, the one who didn't have a golf club patch. Maybe he couldn't get in the club. Probably on the waiting list.

"About what?" said Borg, taking a deep breath. The soft rain was soaking through his jacket. It didn't improve his mood, bad enough to begin with. Common sense was not in play. "I have an office, you know."

"Don't be a wise ass," said the second. They were both close to him. Borg's anger still boiled. He was in the center of Arctic except it was after dark and no one was around. Except for him and the two guys who wanted to talk. Buildings beyond the old chop shop were dark.

He felt a tightness in his shoulders, an emptiness in his stomach, fear as well as anger. He fought to control both and to think about what he could do if worse came to worse. Take a deep breath. Recover. Be ready to run like hell. Bad knees and all, he had a pretty good chance of outrunning these guys to the Chinese restaurant he knew was open blocks away.

"We wanted this to be private," said the first.

"We don't think it's a good idea to be asking around about Angela Rosso," said the second.

"Does Raymond know about this?" No need to mention the Don's last name. Borg watched the two goons look at each other. Surprised. These guys weren't the first team. Probably not even connected. Local muscle. Or what passed for it. Probably not even packing guns. The windbreakers showed no bulges. They still might rough him up, though. Still, the equation had changed.

The two slabs looked at each other.

"That's none of your business," said the short man, his tone more respectful. "We just want you to know that Angela is a nice woman. What's over is over. Leave her alone."

"What's with Angela anyway?" Borg asked, stumbling. He had to focus to even remember she was Perry's girlfriend.

"Don't you hear good? That ain't your business," said the short man, the one who hadn't made the golf club. Maybe the rejection had soured him.

"Listen, I don't want to hurt Angela," said Borg.

"Maybe you ain't listening," said the tall guy, the club member, leaning in close. His breath drifted up to Borg with its memory of a garlic-laced meal. "Maybe we gotta explain better."

The tall one one moved closer yet. Borg waited. Both men leaned toward him. He could knee one of them but could he hurt him badly enough? Or just make him mad. Then they might really hurt him.

He thought about shouting for help. Fat chance. Who would help? Locals complained that the town cops were never around when you needed them and the locals were right. He surprised himself by thinking about an editorial he might write. Focus, you fool. These guys were dumb and not first class muscle. Would he let them push him around?

Goddamnit, he had grown up in Brooklyn, served in the Army's Military Police. Anger and black mood fused together, exploded, overwhelming any common sense. Maybe if advertising had been better and the back door bulb had been changed he wouldn't have done what he did.

"Jesus Christ!" The bigger of the two men screamed as Borg brought his right heel down as hard as he could on his left sneaker. Borg's work shoes, the ones he wore around the newspaper, were the shoes cops use, with hard soles and harder heels. The heel crunched the fat man's foot. Just what he deserved for wearing sneakers, thought Borg.

Borg kept the shoe on the fat guy's sneaker and swung his right shoe as hard as he could into the big guy's shin and then brought the right knee up and into his groin. He managed a glancing blow. A squealing grunt told him it had done damage.

Then he took off. Maybe these guys had more muscle but Borg was willing to bet he could outrun them. Years on basketball courts came in handy.

"You bastard," he heard behind him. He took off across the street and into the chop shop, dodged a couple of rusting exhaust pipes between buildings, almost tripped over a screaming cat. Could he hear footsteps behind him? He looked back. Just darkness. Out of an alley and onto Main Street. The lights of the Chinese Restaurant only a few blocks away now. Not a soul on the street. Finally, he burst through the door. Patrons at the four tables along the wall looked up, then went back to their fried rice. Just another hungry customer.

"Did you call order in?" asked the girl behind the counter, Chinese, pretty, skinny, big eyes considering him. White shirt, black skirt. What else? The linoleum was brown and white and cracking and the walls were a fading brown and held dim light fixtures. One sad, red paper Japanese lantern hung over the cash register. It all looked like heaven to Borg, even the cracked and soiled lampshade.

"No. I'll have spring rolls and an order of pork fried rice," said Borg. It sounded like a chant, a word at a time, between deep breaths.

"It will just be minute," said the girl, unfazed. She showed no surprise at him bursting through the door or even breathing hard. Borg couldn't imagine what the young woman must have experienced as she stood vigil every night behind her cash register and under the Chinese lantern that cast a rosy red light over her face.

Borg looked out the window. Nobody. Then a car pulled up. A police car. Borg knew the cop who came in.

"Hey Brownie, could you do me a favor?" Patrolman Carl Brown was at Cathay Garden to pick up an order for the boys back at the station. He might even pay for it. Borg didn't count on that. Didn't care.

"Not fix a ticket." Brown laughed. "You have to see the chief for that."

Borg smiled with Brown, went on, "Could you run me back to the paper?"

"Matt, it's only a couple of blocks," said Brown. "I'm on duty."

"I thought I saw some guys around the back of my building and a light was out. Maybe we could take a look."

"All right, all right," he said. Borg was grateful for the case of whiskey he gave the cops every Christmas. He and Brownie accepted their bags of food from the girl returning from the kitchen. Borg paid for his.

The light at the back of The Times was still out. No one around though. Borg took his spring rolls and fried rice and settled into the comfort of his Caprice Classic as Brown circled the lot. Borg locked the doors, put both hands on the steering wheel and rested his head on it for a moment. Took a deep breath. Then followed the police car out of the lot.

Who were these guys? Small time mugs, that was obvious. The Don didn't send them. They wouldn't frighten him away and Pastorini knew that. Borg was grateful for intelligence wherever he found it, especially among people who carried guns. The Don would know that this kind of warning would just point everyone toward Angela. If this was a dumb move, maybe other dumb moves would follow. And stupidity in a bad guy is a dangerous thing. He headed home keeping an eye in his mirror for signs of being followed. No one.

The stairs up to Borg's condo reminded him of how tired he felt. What were the lines from the old Burl Ives song: "the hills don't get any higher but the valleys get deeper and deeper." Later, sitting on the couch and sipping a white wine, he gazed out the big window that looked out over the Bay and watched two gulls squabble over a fish. He'd better call Donna.

"Maybe someone is smart enough to do this, to put Angela Rosso on the hot spot," said Donna when Borg told her about the goons who threatened him and what they said.

"Hey, I'm the one who almost got beat up," Borg said. "How about a little sympathy?"

"You got away, didn't you?" She answered. "Rosso is the one this is about."

"Or her husband."

"And her husband," she said after telling him about her visit to Little Bay. And then, "Did you let the cops know about the two hoods?"

"Nope. Didn't think it would do much good."

"We'll talk about that. The two mugs can't be much if you handled them . . ."

"Hey, wait a minute . . ."

"Anyway, lock your doors at least. I'll ask the East Fenwick police to swing by your place once in a while tonight."

"Not necessary. Thanks anyway. Meanwhile I'm trying to remember who I mentioned Angela to and I can't think of anyone. The only time I heard the name was from Jimmy Gleason." Wait. There was somebody. "Hold on. I did ask our sports editor this morning if he knew anyone by that name and he said no, said he'd ask around. I guess he did. I'll try to get him tonight or talk to him tomorrow."

"Is that the short, fat guy who gives me the serious look up and down when I'm at your paper?" She snorted. Borg could sense she wanted off the call.

"That's him. Pete Agnelli. He likes to pretend he's connected. I don't think so. Still, he gets around and sometimes he picks up things on the street that help."

"I'll stop by tomorrow morning. I'd like to see where those two guys stood you up. And talk to Pete."

"He'd like that. Make it after 11:00 when we put the paper to bed, would you?"

"Keep him around."

"I won't have any trouble keeping him around if he knows you'd like to talk to him."

"Good. Listen, I've got to get back to my family. We're playing a serious game of Monopoly."

"Good luck."

"I'll need it," said Donna. "Big Al has Boardwalk and Park Place and a ton of cash."

She paused before going on, "Well, at least we know Louise Perry and Hasner had a motive. They wanted the paper sold. Gleason wanted revenge. Maybe Angela's husband did too. And who were these guys tonight? I'd like to know. See you tomorrow after 10."

"I said 11," Borg answered. She had hung up.

CHAPTER 22

Pete Agnelli cleaned his right ear with his car key. Before he sat, he dug both hands deep into his pants pockets and used them to hitch up his old blue trousers, shiny at the knees and backside. He had scratched himself at the same time. He overlapped the chair. He studied the car key and wiped it clean. Satisfied, he focused on Matt Borg behind his desk.

"What's up, Skipper?" he asked as he began to clean his fingernails with a paper clip. He put out three good sports pages, writing much of it himself, and picked up a lot of information, some of it accurate, at local bars. Most days, he was worth the bother.

"Sheets out?" Borg leaned back in his chair, put a foot up on the bottom desk drawer he kept partly open and empty for that purpose. Pete's presence encouraged informality.

"Being shot. Easy morning. Late Sox game to lead and the Clinton high school baseball team won an afternoon game in the state tournament. Ambrose Lamb is a helluva pitcher."

"Worth another feature on the kid?" Borg waited until Pete nodded, then went on. "I wanted to talk to you about Angela Rosso. I asked you to see what you could pick up about her."

"Sure. I talked to the Parrot yesterday at lunch. I was going to tell you about it after I got the pages out." John 'Parrot' Parrotelli owned a local restaurant, The Come On Inn. Parrot always repeated what you said before adding anything of his own.

"Tell me now."

"Well, Parrot said first of all that I should be careful about Angela. Her husband Ralph is a hard guy. Really hard. He's jealous and she's hot. Not a great combo, Skipper. Parrot said there were stories about her playing around. Parrot said he wouldn't want to be the guy she was playing with if Rosso ever found out."

"Rosso connected?"

"Do bears do it in the woods? You better believe it. He's a loose cannon. Works the construction companies and their unions. Tough guy. Angela was a model for a while, underwear I think. Get it? Was a Christadelphian, whatever the hell that is, before she married Rosso. Anyway, Parrot said that if I was smart, you too, you'd stop asking questions about her. That's all he would say."

Parrot's Come On Inn was a local lunch place that provided good sandwiches and even better soup. Parrot sat in to the back of the bar and dining area and took bets or got you tickets for anything, whether it was a heavyweight championship fight or a Broadway show. Once he had provided Borg with two seats to a Sinatra concert that had been sold out weeks in advance. Borg remembered that the Civic Center had been circled by every limousine in the state, including those borrowed from funeral parlors. A well-placed bomb could have wiped out organized crime on the East Coast. Borg loved seeing all the wise guys in their dark suits, white on white shirts and blonde girlfriends.

"Maybe you better lay off," said Borg.

"Whatever you say, Skipper," said Pete. "Parrot did want to talk about the cops and that porn, by the way."

"And?"

"He said those two guys were making a mistake."

"You mean in breaking the law and hiding behind their uniforms, simple stuff like that?"

"Come on, Skipper. What I meant is that porn around here is wise guy business. Big business, distribution and sales and stuff. I hear Ralph Rosso, Angela's husband, has a piece of one of the strip clubs. The wise guys don't mind amateurs but the Parrot says they don't like people going into business for themselves."

"I thought the old Don didn't like porn?"

"He doesn't," Pete said, shook his head just a bit. "His kid does. Likes it a lot I hear." Now Pete worked the nails on his right hand, carefully noting what he found.

"Think the mob might have used Carl the Cowboy to tip us off?" Borg watched Pete with a mix of amusement, fascination and disgust. How could the man go on cleaning up endlessly? Like a cat. A fat cat.

"Sounds like it." Fingernails cleaned, Pete folded the paper clip into something resembling its original form and clipped it to his shirt pocket. "From what I hear, the business is all connected, from the adult video stores that turn over good cash, to the strip and dance joints to whatever else you want. Drugs play a part. Almost all the topless dancers are into drugs. Have to be to keep moving it all night. You know that, Skipper."

"I didn't, but I do now. Anyway, individual entrepreneurs aren't welcome, I guess?"

"You got it."

"You better tell Aimee all of this so the news side can maybe work it into their stories."

"Just so long as it doesn't come from me."

"Aimee will take care of that."

"Did you see any of that stuff the cops made, Skipper?"

"Not yet."

"Wow, you should take a look. The broad is really hot . . ."

"Time to get back to work, Pete. By the way, stick around. I think Lieutenant Pacheco wants to talk to you."

"She can talk to me anytime," he said and waddled toward the door of the office, stopped, and looked back at Borg. "Why'd she marry that husband of hers, anyway?"

"Maybe she loves him," said Borg.

Pete gave him a puzzled look as he left.

Borg turned to writing an editorial about the Arctic school system which, influenced by a lot of guys like Pete Agnelli, was cutting its arts and music courses and keeping its sports programs. Every bar in Arctic supported the high school cheerleaders and sponsored its own softball team. Nobody sponsored the high school orchestra. His editorial wasn't going to change that. Still, if even one or two parents paused to think about their schools it would be worth it. Besides, he could vent his spleen, always a satisfying process.

Borg put the finishing touches on the opinion piece—and felt a lot better, he had to admit—when Donna Pacheco walked into the office. This time she actually paused for a moment to knock as he rose from his chair.

"Anybody beat you up this morning?" she asked.

"Nice to hear that the law enforcement officers of this great state are concerned about my well-being," said Borg.

"Didn't they used to horse whip editors?"

"Only in the good old days everyone talks about, I guess."

"Let's take a walk so you can show me where you were attacked. You didn't notify the Arctic police. How come?"

"If it appeared on the police blotter we'd have to report it in our paper."

"Don't like stuff about yourself in the paper?"

Borg didn't answer. Donna cackled a laugh, didn't bother to sit down, turned toward the door. As she did, her blue blazer opened a bit and showed a revolver on a belt against the pink shirt. "Let's go look at where those guys trapped you."

"First you might like to talk to Pete Agnelli about Angela Rosso."

"God, I hope he's not cleaning his ears."

Word gets around.

"I'll call him."

Pete was at the door, a big smile mooning his face. Any pretty girl would attract Pete and somehow in spite of being a classic case of "Mister Five by Five" he had a charm that Borg had seen work on some very unlikely objects of his affection.

"I heard you wanted to talk to me," Pete said. "Anything I can do to help?"

"I hope so," said Donna, giving him a shameless smile. Borg leaned back to watch her twist Pete around her finger. Any finger would do. Even a pinky. Pete Agnelli told her everything he had heard about Angela Rosso.

"You don't know how I could get in touch with Angela, do you?" she asked Pete, wetting her lips. Did she actually flutter her eyelashes? Pete was sunk before he left drydock.

"I can find out for you."

Borg looked at him. Not a big cat at all, he thought. A lap dog, really. He raised his eyebrows, shook his head. No response from Pete. Didn't he remember the Parrot had warned him not to talk about Angela Rosso? Obviously something had clouded his mind, a something with big dark eyes and long lashes.

"Maybe we better go outside and I'll retrace my adventure for you," Borg said to Donna. Before Agnelli promised to take on the mob. And get them all killed.

CHAPTER 23

"It really seems stupid now," said Borg as he and Donna emerged from the back door of *The Arctic Valley Times*. Borg looked up at the light fixture over the door. He had flicked the switch before stepping out. The bulb hadn't been changed. He pulled a folded piece of paper from his shirt pocket and made a note. A bright sun had dried the puddles in the parking lot.

"Lots of things seem dumb in the daytime," said Donna as she followed his steps of the night before. He felt like a fool. She knew. She said: "Let's go through it so we can see how really dumb you were."

Borg led her past pick-up trucks, aging cars and one motorcycle, most of them owned by *The Times* staff, some by readers and advertisers bringing in everything from wedding announcements to softball results. Patrons of the diner next door to *The Times* used the lot as well.

"My car was about here and their van was next to it," said Borg, pointing. "It was gone when I got back."

"Didn't notice the license plate I guess?" Donna looked at him and Borg shook his head, felt stupid all the more. The Lieutenant walked around, eyes on the ground. Borg told her how he had escaped.

"Both thugs wearing sneakers?" Donna shook her head in disbelief.

Across the street, even the sunshine failed to warm the chop shop. It still looked menacing, unwholesome, rotting away in the middle of this small town, the opposite of all those pretty picture New England postcards. Arctic, a mill town like most in New England, decayed after its looms went south. Borg pointed.

"There's the alley I ran into, between the main building and the long shed." Borg pointed.

"Tell me about the two guys." Donna stopped her circling.

"One was over six feet, the other maybe five eight. No necks. Windbreakers, dark trousers, dark shoes. One of the windbreakers had a Quonset Country Club patch."

"Any facial marks?"

"The big one had a square face, big nose, strong jaw. The other was round-faced, little piggy nose, soft lips."

"Muscle from anywhere," said Donna and bent over, picked up something.

"Cigarette butt," she said. "One of these guys smokes Salem. Can you imagine? What's a mob guy doing wearing sneakers and smoking menthol cigarettes?"

"Next, we'll find an English Oval," said Borg.

"What's an English Oval?" Donna looked up at him, shook her head.

"A cigarette . . ."

"No wonder you got away." She cackled. "Mix 'em up with smart talk. I'm not going to bother the lab guys with this. Not worth it. I'll pass the word on the two guys. They sound local. By the way, just because you've got this paper doesn't mean you're above the law. If you're assaulted you'd better report it."

"I wasn't really assaulted then."

"All right, wise guy." Donna started to walk back toward *The Times* building. She stopped, looked up at him. "Do you really think the mob is into this? That's the noise Louise Perry is making. Loud. Didn't Pastorini say he wasn't? You still sure his word is good?"

"I've always found it so. He didn't quite say none of the mob was involved. I've gone back over what he said and it was that he wasn't involved and that he—meaning the mob—had no business with Ron Perry. He didn't say all of his people were clean. Couldn't really, if you think about it. And he did point toward a personal motive."

"He was talking like a lawyer. Or you are."

"Well, he's had plenty of experience with them. So have I. I imagine you'll talk to this Angela Rosso and her husband. Ralph is his name, I think. This doesn't seem like a crime of passion to me, though."

"You've had all this experience with crimes of passion?"

"Touché," he said. "I'm not even sure I've had that much experience with passion. If this was murder it had to be pre-meditated, planned well, and executed with a certain amount of precision. Doesn't sound like a Ralph Rosso."

"Don't underestimate passion," Donna said to him with a slight smile on her lips.

"Or lust," he said.

Almost on cue, Pete Agnelli came panting across the parking lot, trailing his shirt tails, a scrap of paper in his hand. Red of face.

"Got Angela's telephone number," he said, leaning over to place his hands on knees, struggling to catch his breath. Borg had long since given up trying to get his sports editor to take off weight. "She works as a hair dresser at Scissors up on Federal Hill."

"Thanks," said Donna. She took a small notebook from her big handbag as Pete recited the number. "You're a big help. I've got to be going now." She gave Pete a smile, payment for the phone number. She turned to Borg.

"Take care of yourself," she said and brushed the back of his hand, squeezed. He was startled and touched.

Pete practically wagged his tail as she took off for her Datsun.

"This isn't going to get you into trouble, is it?" Borg asked as he watched Pete's face return to its normal shade, his breathing ease as he inhaled big one last time.

"Nah," Agnelli said. "I looked up Rosso in the phone book. There was only one Ralph. I called the house and the message said Angie, that's what she calls herself I guess, could be reached at Scissors."

"A regular Sherlock Holmes."

"Listen, do you think I've got a chance with this lady cop?"

"Stranger things have happened," said Borg. "I've got to tell you she's married, has three kids and a husband who works at the prison. Watch yourself, Pete." If he did, it would be a first time. Borg let out a sigh.

"You haven't got anything going with her, have you, Skipper? You're not getting any of that?"

"Not a bit," said Borg. "Why would you think that?"

Pete shook his head. He hadn't heard a word Borg had said.

"So you don't mind if I give it a shot?" asked the sports editor.

"I do mind but there isn't much I can do." Did Borg actually feel a little bit jealous? "Don't get hurt."

"I can take care of myself," said Pete Agnelli. "I've always had good luck with long shots."

Borg knew otherwise. He had paid off some of Pete's gambling debts. He could still feel Donna's touch.

CHAPTER 24

D onna Pacheco felt ashamed of herself. Just a little. She knew she had a smile that guys like Pete Agnelli were suckers for. And long ago she had made a conscious decision that she would use the smile and anything else she could in pushing her career. Well, almost anything. A woman was at a disadvantage no matter what. Especially in law enforcement. Good looks evened things up a bit, even though a pretty woman was seldom taken seriously. Bit by bit, case by case, people who counted were taking Donna Pacheco seriously.

Still, she remembered the police chief in Arctic where she had begun her career in law enforcement.

"Any case a girl cop solves that a man doesn't she should be ashamed of herself." The other cops in his office laughed. Donna didn't. Walked out of the office. Got citations for three cases she solved. Was plucked by the State Police to head investigations. Never talked to the old chief except when she had to.

Driving up to Providence she called State Police Headquarters and got the address of Scissors and how to get there.

Next she flipped on the CD player and listened to Edith Piaf. Borg had put her on to the singer. "Give her a chance," he had said and he was right. Plus, the Frenchwoman was tiny, peppy, and had a big voice. Even her husband, Al, was warming up to Piaf. Her kids? Rock, period. Loud. Oh well, as Al would say.

She turned her thoughts to the woman she was on her way to see. What did Donna know? That Angela Rosso had an affair with Ron Perry. That her husband was a wise guy. Were they connected to the death of Ron Perry? Time to find out.

Scissors was on Abbott Avenue, one of two main streets of Federal Hill, the Italian district of Providence. All the street names were white bread. Donna had no trouble finding a parking space not far from the sign, which was under a huge pair of neon scissors. No mistaking the place. Under the scissors, almost as an afterthought, was a red sign, BEAUTY SALON. Probably a barber shop to begin with.

"Angela Rosso here?" Donna asked the receptionist at the front desk. Behind the girl chewing gum was a half wall with an opening to walk through. Behind the wall were seven or eight chairs in a row and then another half wall with a few chairs behind that. Mirrors tried hard to make the place look wider. Most of the chairs were filled. On the walls the posters with hair styles seemed almost up to date. Almost.

Donna flashed her badge to make sure she was taken seriously. The receptionist, a thin kid with red hair and freckles and a jaw strengthened by years of Wrigley's, didn't exactly shudder in fear. Donna gave the kid a look and her card.

"I'll see if she's here," the kid said, still chewing. The laughter and chatter in the place quieted as Freckles showed the card to a woman dressing hair near the back of the shop. The hairdresser was tall. Looked to be five nine or so. Thin with long legs and full bust. Not a very pretty face by Donna's standards.

A strong nose framed by a full head of dark hair. Big, dark eyes, almost as black as the hair. Weakish chin. Puffy, full lips men might find sexy. A short blue skirt and red shirt gave her a gypsy look. Maybe just a little bit cheap? A woman's view, Donna admitted to herself.

"Something I can do for you?" asked Angela. "I'm with a client right now."

"This will take a few minutes," said Donna.

"She's about to go under the drier. Give me a minute and I'll be with you." Donna watched Angela move the woman to another chair, place the drier on her head and return almost within the minute she had promised.

"Is there an office or do you want to step outside?"

"Let's go outside," said Angela. She called to the back of the shop to remind someone to watch her client. Or at least, her hair.

Outside the spring morning still held the faintest reminder of winter in its breeze. Stores were open and in front of a few restaurants the sidewalks were being swept. Across the street was Luigi's, known for its cheap, good spaghetti and its cheaper, lousy, wine. Down the street was the small office of the company that provided vending machines for this state and beyond. It also served as headquarters for the mob.

The two women walked away from the front of the shop, Angela leading, until they were by a small window still advertising winter vacations with pictures of models in bikinis. The posters were curling at their corners.

Donna didn't remember what she expected. A working hairdresser wasn't it. Angela Rosso seemed sure of herself, contained, intelligent. Not chewing gum. Not the floozy who might have blackmailed Ron Perry for his money. Well, Donna would see about that.

"Busy day?" Donna asked. She had noticed a sheen of sweat on the woman's forehead and above her upper lip. No air conditioning in the shop this spring.

"Average," said Angela. Waited.

"You know why I'm here," Donna said.

"Tell me," said Angela.

"All right, if you want to play it that way. You saw my card. That told you I'm Lieutenant Donna Pacheco of the State Police. I'm investigating the death of Ron Perry. I hear you were involved with him."

"Who'd you hear that from?"

"Enough people to lead me to believe it's true. Now listen, we can do this easy or we can do this hard. You want to go downtown and talk or do you want to stay out here in the sunshine? Personally, I'd like to do it easy." Donna took a step back from Angela so she wouldn't have to look straight up. Stopped herself from rolling forward from heel to toe to gain an inch.

"All right." Angela took a deep breath. "Why don't you tell me what you want."

"Let's begin by you answering a few questions. You know anyone who would want to hurt Mr. Perry?"

"Did someone hurt him?"

"You tell me."

"I don't have a clue." She stopped, realized what she had said. Smiled. Donna liked her for that. "I thought it was an accident. Didn't he fall and hit his head? Anyway, I haven't seen Ron Perry in months. I've talked to him on the phone maybe twice in that time." Angela Rosso didn't look cowed. She stood with legs apart, chest and chin out. A man in a white butcher's apron walked by and gawked. Angela's red shirt had two top buttons undone.

"You talked about what?"

"None of your business." The trigger response. Afterward a sigh. A second thought? Then: "I'll tell you because you'll probably find out anyway. The first call was about some personal problems I was facing and some choices I was making."

"So you still stayed in touch with him?"

"I did," she said, after a pause. "I could still talk to him about anything."

"He was married and so are you."

"So? So there's a law against talking?" Angela paused, took a breath. "All right. Yeah, Ron was married when we met. He was living apart from his wife. Yes, I was married. I'm separated now."

"Because of Ron Perry?" Donna could see Angela's jaw tighten, her eyes moisten, her hands turn to fists.

"Yes, but not in the way you think. He showed me I could be more than I was, that I was settling for too little in my life."

"By marrying him?"

"No, not by marrying him." Another sigh. "No chance. He had a family and he wasn't going to give that up. He was old-fashioned in that way. He encouraged me to go back to design work and I have. That's what I wanted to talk to him about when I called him last week."

"Think Perry would have married you if he got a divorce?"

Angela sighed again. Deeper. Took a breath. "I'm not a fool, Lieutenant. No Perry is going to marry an Alves . . ."

"An Alves?"

"My maiden name. I'm Portuguese like you. A Perry wouldn't marry a Rosso either, so it didn't make that much difference."

"That's all?"

"That's all."

"So you're going into design work?" An obviously smart woman like Angela Rosso knew she never had any chance of marrying Ron Perry. Must have realized he gave her a smart brush-off, and was as kind as he could be.

"Surprised?" Angela bcame more assertive. "Most people are. Listen, I completed a year at the Rhode Island School of Design before I married Ralph and took up hair dressing."

"Your husband happy with what you're doing?"

"Ralph doesn't understand that we're growing in different directions. I know that sounds like something out of a magazine. It's still true. How about your husband, Lieutenant?"

Donna paused. Angela Rosso had touched a chord. Dennis cooked, did housework, drove the kids to school more often than not. How did he really feel while his wife starred at her job, got the publicity? He always said he loved it, that he had a job and she had a career. She knew, however, that her career was providing her with new worlds to experience and explore. Were they growing apart? She pushed the question out of her mind.

"This isn't about me. How did Ralph feel about you and Ron Perry?"

"To be honest, I'm trying to convince him that Ron had nothing to do with me going back to RISD—or our separation."

"Hard to believe there were no hard feelings."

"I said I'm trying. I'm not saying I've succeeded. Listen, if Ralph wanted to go after Ron he would have done it with his fists. That's his way. Not while Ron was riding his bike. If you knew Ralph you'd laugh to think he'd sneak up behind Ron and hit him on the back of the head."

The pride showed in her voice. Maybe Ralph didn't know much about design but Angela obviously wasn't willing to run him down, even now. Donna admired that about her.

"I have to be getting back in there. I've got a customer under the dryer."

"Wait a minute." Donna didn't want this getting too personal, too much woman to woman stuff. "Listen, I told you we can go downtown if you like. I don't want to do that. So you'd better just stand still for whatever questions I've got." She gave Angela Rosso a cop stare.

"All right, all right, I'm sorry."

"Good. Now, where were you last Sunday morning?"

"You've got to be kidding?" laughed Angela. "You think I could have killed Ron Perry? I would have parked my slippers under his bed anytime. The sex was great and so was he. He opened up whole new worlds for me, worlds I never even knew about. And, by the way, I was in church with my mother, as a favor to her. The whole church saw me, all the Christadelphians in the state. Probably wanted to pin an A on my shirt, first for marrying a Catholic and then for leaving him. What else?"

"What's a Christadelphian?"

"A religion. Like a Seventh-Day Adventist or a Mormon or whatever. Anyway, I was in church."

"How did you know Ron Perry had a wound in the back of the head?" That information had not been made public. Yet somehow everyone seemed to know about where the wound was. Nan had mentioned it as well. Talk radio? Maybe. So much for tripping up suspects.

"It's all over The Hill," Angela said, referring to the Italian neighborhood. "Go figure. And here's a tip: Ask Bill Hasner about the company and about Louise Perry."

"Why would I do that?"

"Because you're a cop and that's what cops do." She laughed again. Donna could see her appeal. A big, good-hearted woman with a great body. Like a lot of women these days, struggling through a new world, a pioneer in a way. Like Donna herself.

She wouldn't judge Angela. Still, that's what cops do all the time.

"Isn't Angela an Italian name by the way?"

"Yeah, my mother's Italian but my dad's Portuguese. My mother must be the only Italian Christadelphian in the world. She converted, and you know how they are."

"I guess. Anyway, you won't be going anywhere, will you?"

"Not really. I'm just waiting for my prince to come along. Another one, that is. If you find one, send him in for a haircut. On the house."

CHAPTER 25

Matt Borg spent too much of his time at meetings. There were meetings in town with local businessmen and advertisers, meetings with other newspapermen to compare notes on industry developments, meetings with staff, meetings that connected him with politicians to keep him plugged into their vision of the future—though they seldom had one—and last and sometimes least, meetings that had little reason at all. His favorites.

Wednesday night was when the DC Club met in the back room of the Arts Club. Once a month. Always on the first Wednesday. The DC Club had been formed more than 100 years ago, in the wake of the Civil War. First, only Supreme and Superior Court Justices and a few others were invited to join. Republicans all. Then, when Democrats were appointed to the Courts, the membership expanded to include lawyers, businessmen, and even an occasional journalist. Now it stood at 20.

For a long time members gathered in a room on the second floor of an old barn owned by a member. Very reverse snobbish.

A woodstove provided the heat, and oil lamps the light. The barn finally burned down, and members were forced into a back room of the Arts Club, which in its genteel shabbiness provided an appropriate home for the DC. The assigned space contained a table almost as long as the room itself. Stucco walls featured silhouettes of past Arts Club members, all of them quite dead and unidentified.

The format of the monthly Dis Cussion Club meetings was simple. A speaker, often a guest, provided the topic and then he and his talk were attacked unmercifully, ridiculed, and diced. Occasionally a speaker was invited to join the Club. Sometimes they accepted. Occasionally the speaker was a Club member in which case the hazing was intemperate, especially because dinner was always late and too much time had been spent at the cocktail hour.

"Is the treasurer honest and/or sober enough to report to this gathering?" asked President Randall Ransom after he had called the meeting to whatever order it could achieve.

"Neither, sir," the treasurer, Dayton Thomas, an eminent attorney, replied, amidst murmurings of feigned discontent. "I am pleased to say that the Club is solvent."

"Hear, hear," bellowed Ralph Bettinger, a retired public relations executive sitting at the end of the oak table. "Move that the report be received, approved,and enshrined and the treasurer be embalmed and impeached, if he is not already."

"So be it," said the president. Randall Ransom wasn't going to ask for discussion. He might get it. Or a vote. That might lead to a discussion. Besides, he knew the treasury contained only $178.53. The Club's expenses were the dinners, which the attending members paid for, and the stationery for invitations, which cost $84 a year and which the secretary usually paid for himself. BYOB was the rule and the room was free. At least DC had never paid for it.

Matt Borg had settled about halfway down the table, carefully avoiding a covey of Brown graduates. He knew from grim experience they would talk endlessly about their college days, and even the gossip, such as it was, contained serious particles of dust. Next to him, instead, sat Dayton Thomas, who endlessly relived his trips to exotic places. At least he was pleasant and of a sweet nature. If in his tales he reduced those exotic places to rather dull neighborhoods. Then again who ever claimed that Timbuktu was anything more than a trading center built of mud huts.

Borg liked the bonhomie, the feeling of comradeship, the irreverence of the group. And also, for the most part, the intelligence, even when soaked in wine. Better than the endless talk of golf and business that mired most of his meetings.

Tonight's speaker was a treat. For Borg anyway. Anthony A. "Toby" Fragnoli, the charismatic, colorful, and allegedly crooked mayor of Providence, was on hand and in full flower. Most of his talk was about a new ice skating rink he was having built in downtown Providence. And about how wonderful Toby Fragnoli was. So wonderful that to express his appreciation the mayor was naming the skating rink after himself. The fun would be in the questions. And the answers.

"How do you explain or justify all the corruption in your City Hall?" asked Roger Wellstone, a retired surgeon. Everyone who read *The Bulletin* knew Fragnoli was being investigated.

"I don't," said Fragnoli and laughed. "You men are too intelligent to believe everything you read in the paper."

Moans and chuckles. Fragnoli paused. He is so good, thought Borg. I'll miss him when they finally catch him. If they catch him.

"You know," the Mayor continued. "If one day I walked across Narragansett Bay without getting wet, *The Bulletin*'s headline the next day would be, 'Fragnoli Can't Swim.'"

He waited for the laughs, which always came. Borg, who had heard the line a dozen times, still chuckled.

"What do you think about the death of Ron Perry? Was it murder and did you do it?" Randall Ransom, president of the club and a revered artist, dared ask anything. Especially after a few martinis. And with a smile.

"No I didn't and I presume you didn't either—in spite of Mr. Perry's taste in art as reflected in his paper." More laughs. The Mayor paused. "I don't know any more than you do, gentlemen. The investigation is being conducted by Donna Pacheco, whose reputation you all know. She's top flight and a woman, of course. I don't see any females among your membership, by the way." He looked up and down the table as some DC members shifted in their seats.

There were few questions after that. Fragnoli, faster on his feet than any DC Club member, posted another notch in his belt. Few in the room would love him for it. Too smart for his own good. Like me? Borg wondered. Toby Fragnoli could also be mean, almost cruel. Not like me, Borg hoped.

The evening dwindled to a conclusion, not much beyond 9:30. On his way out the big green door of the Arts Club, Borg felt a tug at his elbow. It was the Mayor himself, smiling that mischievous smile, a Cheshire cat in a political tree.

"Come have a drink with me," he said to Borg, who really wanted most of all to get home. But he enjoyed Fragnoli and he imagined one drink wouldn't hurt—even though he knew from experience that Toby was able to consume and expand an evening endlessly. Still, he agreed to meet the Mayor in a favorite hangout, The Menagerie on Witherspoon Street. You never knew what you could learn. Or what would provide another column.

Once upon a time Witherspoon Street had been the heart of the Portuguese community, where fishermen and laborers lived close to the Providence River, which emptied into Narragansett Bay. Gentrification had set in and the Portuguese had moved to the suburbs and now college students and some professors and professional people lived there. On the street itself were antique shops, art galleries, and places like The Menagerie, which pretended to be a French bistro. Toby had a favorite table near the back, across the narrow room from the old and hissing espresso machine. His driver, a city cop, sat outside in the limo.

"Drinks are on me," said the Mayor. Borg knew he would be running a tab that had as much chance of being paid as a South American loan.

Toby Fragnoli put his elbows on the table and leaned forward. His blue blazer was still lightly pressed, his red striped tie flowed neatly down and over the buttons of his light blue shirt, his hairpiece remained the best one Borg had ever seen. Fragnoli was always ready for the TV cameras. A broad smile of white teeth contained just enough gaps to make it interesting as it lit up his moon face. Was he just looking for company, an audience, or did he have something to say? Borg bet on the latter.

After one funny tale about his negotiations with the laborer's union in which the Mayor emerged as triumphant as he usually did in his stories, Toby sipped his Campari and soda and looked down for a moment.

"I hear you're interested in the Perry business," said Fragnoli after a while. Borg noticed he didn't say death or murder. "Business."

"Well, it's an interesting story even for a simple, country editor like me," said Borg. Two could play this game. Fragnoli gave a half-smile.

"What do you think happened?" Fragnoli asked. Which meant that he had something to say.

"I'm really not sure. He was an interesting guy. The family thinks it was murder. You know that from the paper." When people said "the paper," they meant Perry's newspaper, the only statewide daily, *The Bulletin*.

"Not the whole family," said Fragnoli. "Just the wife."

Oops, thought Borg. There's something. "The others don't?" he asked.

"You might want to check it out," said the Mayor. "Or tell that slick-looking police lieutenant you run with to look into it. You might also ask who wants to sell the paper."

"I don't run with Donna Pacheco and you know it, Toby. Couldn't keep up with her for one thing. Not with these bad knees." Why would Toby suggest that? "What do you hear?"

"I hear there's real disagreement in the family, that a number of the cousins aren't satisfied with their dividends and want to cash in, to sell. Some think newspapers are dying. You should talk to someone. Might get a story or even a clue."

"You seem to know a lot about the paper," said Borg.

Toby laughed out loud. Like most politicians, and journalists and almost everyone else, he loved people to believe he had inside information. "Maybe," he said finally. "Maybe."

"You know Bill Hasner pretty well, do you Toby?"

"Why would you ask that?" The laugh had died on the Mayor's face. His left hand went to the back of his neck. Adjusting his hairpiece? It looked perfect to Borg.

"Don't you have a boat down in East Fenwick harbor?" Borg smiled as he asked the question. Softening the blow? Maybe.

156

"Just a piece of it. A small piece. Why?" No smile from Toby.

No use playing cat and mouse with the Mayor. Toby was better at it. "I heard that Bill Hasner has been out on it once or twice," said Borg. "With a friend. A good-looking blonde."

"I give rides to a lot of people. Cocktail cruises mostly. I'm not much for fishing. Mr. Hasner would be someone I'd like to spend a few hours with. After all, *The Bulletin* is a big employer in the city, almost the biggest. It's a good idea to know how businessmen feel, what they want."

"And influence them a little?"

"Matt, you know the Temple of Truth is unassailable," said the Mayor, referring to *The Bulletin* with a smirk. "Besides, as I understand it, Mister Hasner is on the business side and you know those people have no influence on the news department. Hardly even talk to them."

Borg wouldn't be put off that easily. "Remember who Hasner had with him, the woman?"

"Can't say I remember." The Mayor struggled to seriously consider the question. "Seemed nice enough."

"Sure you don't know her? Not someone called Lulu or something like it?"

"Doesn't strike a chord. Sorry." He paused. Borg could see the gears working, watched him put it together. Finally, "Talk to Peeps, did you?"

"Can't say as I remember," said Borg.

The Mayor chuckled. He liked to parry, to thrust and withdraw. Sometimes you could learn something from him. Sometimes you could be sorely misled. The trick was to know the difference. Not easy.

"Toby, you know Louise Perry thinks the Mafia did it." Borg resisted being a wise guy and calling her LuLu.

Toby smiled. "Do you really think the mob would kill a newspaper publisher? Come on. You know Mister Pastorini."

"How about your friend, Hasner?" Borg might as well see what else Toby would say. "Sounds like he'd have a lot to gain."

"No way." Toby hadn't lost his smile. Now he shrugged as well. "Those kind of people aren't murderers. They can kill you other ways. Financially. Your reputation. Why would they murder anyone?"

"Same reason anyone else does, I guess, money or love." Borg watched a pretty waitress begin to clear a nearby table, pick up a tip, frown, rub the table vigorously with a wet cloth.

"So if it was murder, why then?" Borg went on, took a sip of his drink. It began to taste sour. "A personal thing? An affair of the heart? Revenge? How about you, Toby?"

"I'm a politician, Matt. The only violence we resort to is verbal violence. Politicians never even fight in the wars they start, you know that." He smiled. "They don't even let their sons fight. If they did, there would be no wars."

They did once, Borg thought, but that was hundreds, maybe thousands, of years ago. And there were wars anyway. The evening was still mellow. Borg had switched to Amontillado and Fragnoli was sipping his second Campari and soda. Borg couldn't remove his reporter's cap or lose his curiosity. Especially about Toby Fragnoli.

"Toby, why do you think this small state is so corrupt?"

It said a lot about the Mayor that he didn't jump back or open his eyes wide or act surprised in any other way. His smile just widened.

"Is this off the record?"

"Sure, unless you say otherwise. My pen's in my pocket."

"OK. First of all, it takes a little bit of grease, a little corruption to run anything. A city. A country. Anything. The squeaky clean places are run by dictators and you know what? They end up being most corrupt of all.

"You know something else? I'm not sure when corruption began in this state. Maybe it goes all the way back to when our founding families made their fortunes on slaves or using little kids in their cotton mills. Remember the Senator who ran this country from his estate down on the water, the guy they called the Boss of The United States? Aldrich, wasn't it? Married a Rockefeller, I think. He did it for the benefit of the railroads and the people who owned them. And most of the people you know call those the good old days.

"Now everyone plays the game. It's grassroots corruption. The average citizen wants a state or city job he turns to someone he knows. You want a contract you find a friend. Even if you want a vanity license plate you talk to someone—your state legislator, your councilman. You expect a favor. Even if you want a liquor license you talk to someone you know. And in their hearts people don't want that to change.

"Why is that? I'm not sure. Maybe because at least a favor is personal, it's not a lot of red tape and paperwork. Maybe it's because people here are convinced it's the way things work. They know it better than people in big states because government in big states is a distance away from the average citizen. Here, everyone sees exactly what's going on, how things get done.

"I'll give you two examples, Matt. How did you raise the money when you wanted to buy your paper?"

"From friends and relatives and the bank," Borg said, and knew where this was going. "And yes, I played tennis with the president of the bank."

"And when you were thinking of buying a monthly here in the city who did you call about getting legal advertising from this city?"

"You know damn well who," said Borg, and laughed. "You."

"And I said yes, right? At least you don't pretend to be holier than everyone else like those hypocrites at The Temple of Truth," said the Mayor. "You know that they look for favors in the same way you did, for their new production plant and its construction, for parking, for help with their property taxes. And you know the boys from the Hill are involved in trucks—which is how *The Bulletin* is delivered."

"You're saying what?" Borg remembered that Gleason described how the mob had helped *The Bulletin* in its circulation battle with Gleason's paper.

"Not a thing. Just thinking out loud."

Matt Borg knew that Toby was simplifying, that asking for a favor was not strictly illegal—though it might be—and that what Fragnoli was being charged with was racketeering. And the mob and the Perrys? Tired, he let it pass.

"Toby, do you think that they'll finally nail you for something? Honestly."

"Listen, I'll deny anything you repeat. And yes, they'll probably get me for something. *The Bulletin* is running such a strong campaign for it, using its news columns, headlines, columnists, editorials, that sooner or later my indictment will seem the only thing to do. So will they get me? Sure. It will be circumstantial and will be overturned eventually. But they'll get me."

"And so that's why you're selling your house and your boat and all the rest?"

"Whoa," said the Mayor. "That's just a change in lifestyle. Don't expect me to be too honest." He laughed again. So did Borg. Toby widened his eyes, raised his hands in a supplicating gesture, finally said, "I wanted to simplify my life, that's all."

"Toby, just to go back to the Perry thing, do you know anything about the affair he had?"

Toby hesitated. Borg knew the mayor couldn't resist sharing anything he knew, especially when it was juicy. And didn't hurt him. Then again, maybe this is what he wanted to talk about all along to help point suspicion away from his friend, Bill Hasner. With the Mayor, it was hard to know.

"Sure I knew. I'll tell you something not everyone knows," said Fragnoli, his smile wide enough so that every gap between his teeth was visible. He loved gossip as much as he loved politics. "Do you know how Ralph Rosso met Angela? You know who she is. She was doing some part-time modeling and somebody was trying to get her to do porn flicks. Ralph saw her picture and that was that. Ralph is into the porn racket as well as construction."

"Did she make any porn?"

"Not that I know of. Ralph fell in love and so we'll never know how good Angela might have been."

"How did she meet Perry?"

"You won't believe this . . ."

"Try me."

"They met at a parade. Angela was a Mrs. Federal Hill or something. Perched on the back of a red convertible, I remember. Great legs and knew it. Short skirt. Mr. Publisher was at the reception afterwards. Separated from his wife at the time, if that mattered. Bingo."

There was some more small talk and then Borg had to be going. Borg knew the Mayor didn't expect him to swallow his whole message. Then what? The hint about *The Bulletin* family wanting to sell? Or was it Angela and her husband? It sounded as though Ralph Rosso was being hung out to dry. Borg was thinking about that as he walked to his car parked down Witherspoon Street. The Mayor's limousine had been in front of The Menagerie—blocking a fire hydrant. No ticket. Of course.

CHAPTER 26

While Borg chatted with Buddy Fragnoli at The Menagerie, Donna Pacheco, her husband, Al, and their three children shared dinner at home in Arctic. It was not pleasant. Donna had been late, held up at work and then, always the punisher instead of nice guy Al, she scolded Al Junior for his behavior at school. Sarah smiled at her brother's discomfort while she ate her vanilla ice cream. Her high school grades and behavior were impeccable. Mary, a youngest child, held her peace.

"Well, at least you made the football team," Al said.

"The JV," said Junior. He stopped scowling.

Then the phone rang.

"Always during dinner," said Al. "Always during dinner."

"At least we got to finish," said Donna. "The chicken cacciatore was delicious, Albert."

"They don't make it right in restaurants anymore," he said. "Don't soak the chicken in the sauce overnight."

His wife had already taken three steps to the living room.

"Lieutenant Pacheco," she said.

"You told me you were looking for two muscle guys," the Arctic chief of police said. No small talk for him. He didn't like her. She didn't like him.

"Right," said Donna.

"A short fat guy and his buddy, a big guy with a buzz cut."

"Right." Her family and dessert waited at her table. More vanilla ice cream.

"They're in the Franco-American Club on Main Street, having a few beers. Want me to pick 'em up?"

"Please."

"Charge?"

"Make it vague. Questioning . . ."

"That Borg isn't pressing charges, hah?

"No."

"Pain in the ass."

"Sometimes. I'll be down in a half hour. You can hold them that long?"

"No problem. They're not bad guys. Just dumb." He hung up.

Donna went back to the table, spooned her ice cream. Al and the kids waited.

"Gotta go, dontcha?" Albert had finished his ice cream, smiled a sad smile. The kids just looked at her.

"Just in town here. Be back in an hour or less."

"Uh huh. Well, at least we're not in bed yet. I'll check out the homework and maybe we'll watch some TV."

Guilt trailed Donna to her car. It took her less than ten minutes to get to the police station. The chief practically greeted her at the door. He grabbed his briefcase from the top of the receiving officer's high desk.

"They're in Six," he said, indicating the cell number. "Sergeant Medeiros will release them about ten minutes after you leave unless you tell him something else."

"Thanks," said Donna. Chief Carriere left without a word.

"Names are Big Al Sorrentino and Tubby Costa." Sergeant Roger Medeiros smiled down from his desk. He was a cousin or something, married to a Pacheco. He'd watch her back. She knew that and so did the chief. Sergeant Medeiros followed her down the hall, through the door to the line of cells.

The tall guy was standing, the short, fat one sat on the bottom bunk bed. Donna took it in through the bars. Cement walls. Stripped toilet in the corner. Stink.

"The Lieutenant here has a few questions," Sergeant Medeiros said. "Pay attention." He left the hall door open as he went back to his desk.

"What's this all about?" It was the big guy, but now he wasn't playing tough.

"A few questions, you answer them and you can go back to the Club, OK?"

"We're not looking for no trouble," said the fat guy on the cot.

"Why'd you want to talk to Matt Borg last night?"

The two guys looked at each other. Both still wore their windbreakers, plastic of some kind, over T-shirts. Jeans. Sneakers. The big guy shook his head.

"Just giving some advice," he said finally.

"Nobody got hurt, right?" The fat guy looked down at the floor, cement like the walls.

"Right," said Donna. "I just want some information. Nobody knows where it comes from. Nobody says a word. Just give me a nod and you're out of here."

Both men looked at her.

Donna returned the look and went on. "I know you were doing a favor, right? Can't blame you for that. A favor for a friend. No harm done. A favor for Ralph Rosso, right?"

They hesitated, then both looked down at the floor. You had to watch carefully for the nods to see them. Donna was watching.

"Right," said Donna. "Don't be offering any more advice, you hear. Or you won't be getting off so easy."

She knew it wouldn't do any good. Without Borg, no charges would be filed. She gave Medeiros a smile and a wave and a "thank you" and headed out the door and home to her family and maybe just a little bit more vanilla ice cream. And, oh yes, Ralph Rosso deserved a visit. More than ever.

CHAPTER 27

Citizens for a Free Press (CFP), like most organizations of its kind, was formed to protect publishers, their newspapers and, most important, their profits. *The Bulletin* was its founder, its primary funder, and its driving force. That's because CFP was organized to make sure that a vengeful state legislator didn't have his way and pass a bill taxing all newspaper advertising.

The legislator had been exposed in *The Bulletin* for questionable dealings by his law firm, which did a lot of business with the state. The state senator swore he had gained all the business fair and square, above board. Other law firms, privately of course, knew very well how his small outfit got all the work selling new bonds the state issued. *The Bulletin* had made the senator look bad though it had proved nothing. Because there was nothing. At least nothing illegal. The legislator drew up a bill that would tax every inch of advertising in all of the state's newspapers. His target was *The Bulletin*, of course, but singling that paper out would have been too blatant and illegal as well.

The bill, even as it stood, would never pass and wouldn't stand up in a court of law if it did. *The Bulletin* wasn't going to take that chance so it enlisted the five other daily newspapers in the state to join in this battle for freedom of the press.

"I think we agree on the need for strong editorials against this bill," Bill Hasner told the five others who were gathered in an upstairs and private room of the Benevolent Club this Thursday morning. Coffee stood on the sideboard, as well as Danish and muffins. The oblong table the newspaper executives sat at was of the same rosewood as the wainscoting around the room. It was plumy, thought Borg, a place where men of ample proportions had probably plotted against anarchists and union organizers and the drive to have United States Senators elected by popular vote instead of by state legislators.

The Benevolent Club was the most prestigious of the state's several clubs, a three story red brick mass on College Hill. It was one of the few clubs its age, over 100, that was built as a club. Its kitchen was on the top floor and food was lowered by dumbwaiter. There was a courtyard at its center with a fountain whose vertical stream of water kept a ping pong ball constantly dancing. Often that was the only sound during the summer as members quietly obeyed the old adage that soup should be seen and not heard. Or slurped. As should children, women, and waiters.

Bill Hasner provided the room. He was the member of the Benevolent Club. It would have been more convenient for the meeting to be held in a conference room or his office at *The Bulletin*. But that might have revealed the sponsor too obviously. As though it mattered. So here they were at the Benevolent Club.

"Do you think we should write letters to the Governor?" asked Tuck Gilchrest, whose family owned the daily newspaper in Oldtown. Like most who inherited wealth he had convinced himself that he deserved it.

"Probably talking to your own local legislators would do the most good and you probably see them around town anyway," answered Hasner, who had assumed leadership of the meeting, most of all by taking the seat at the head of the table. It was his Club, after all. "I do have some copies of editorials and some editorials I'll pass out. Not that any of you need them, I know. However, you might get some ideas."

Borg knew that most of the men—there were only white men at the table—couldn't write an editorial if their careers depended on it. Once upon a time newspapers were run by newsmen, former reporters who had become editors. Now they were headed by advertising executives or men from the business side, accountants who could turn a profit. And most newspapers were owned by chains, parts of a large corporation whose essential reality was the bottom line.

There was some friendly lying during the last few minutes it took the meeting to break up. It was the typical banter of a thousand locker rooms after a day of golf or the annual meeting of a company whose executive committee decides everything. The meeting began to break up.

"Have you got a minute?" Borg knew that his staff made fun of him because that was always the way he gathered them, whether briefly or for an hour or more. Hasner nodded acceptance and, after shaking hands with his guests, came back and sat at the table, now littered with coffee cups and rapidly aging Danish.

"Now, what's up and how have you been?" said Hasner. "Sorry, we haven't been able to get together."

Years before, briefly, they had been colleagues at *The Bulletin*, working together on several projects, even sharing a social evening or two. Ron Perry and Hasner had come aboard but Perry was not yet publisher. When Borg left to buy his own paper the relationship ended. Hasner never afterward accepted an invitation to lunch. His eye was on the big prize. Now he had it.

"You running the company?" asked Borg.

"Pretty much," said Hasner. He sat tall in a chair. He was about six feet and made the most of it, chest puffed out, taking long strides when he walked. The receding hairline made him seem taller. There were cold blue eyes. The domed head was almost always shiny. He could be a Prussian cavalry officer. Except that his lips were fleshy and soft and squeezed into his lower face above a weak chin.

"For good?" said Borg.

"Who knows? The family may bring in someone from the outside."

Fat chance, thought Borg.

"Bill, I heard some things last night that raised several questions. I thought you might be able to help me answer them."

"What kind of questions?"

"That *The Bulletin* might be up for sale."

"I hope you don't mind me asking how this is any of your business—unless you want to make an offer. This is a little bit outside the scope of your circulation and well beyond your financial capabilities, as I understand them, isn't it?" He smirked.

"You have me there," said Borg, not being baited. He pasted on a smile. "If *The Bulletin* were sold it would be important to the whole state so it would interest me and our readers at *The Times*. I'm also very interested in the death of Ron Perry."

"How would Ron's death have anything to do with any possible sale of *The Bulletin*?"

"I've heard Ron was against the sale and a lot of the family would like to cash in and this would be a good time to do it."

"Listen, can we talk straight here as old friends, off the record?" Suddenly they were old friends again. Well, Borg guessed he could use any friend he could get. Or reclaim.

"Why not?" he finally answered.

"Let me begin by saying that I don't think any of what I'm going to tell you has anything to do with Ron's death. I think it was an accident, pure and simple."

"I got the idea from some stories in your own paper that you agreed with Louise, Mrs. Perry, that it might be murder," said Borg.

"I will support Louise as much as possible and I certainly wouldn't want to publicly disagree with her. Privately, I wonder if she's a little overboard on this."

"Does she want to sell the paper?" asked Borg.

"She's not sure," Hasner paused, clasped his hands on the table in front of him on top of a legal pad without a scribble on it. "Besides, Louise may not have much to say. The majority of the voting stock, the stock in the trust, now reverts to the Perry family, a committee of the cousins. They have always given that voting power to the publisher of the paper."

"So you could end up making the decision?" said Borg. "If they make you publisher."

Hasner smiled, a thin smile. He picked up the freshly sharpened pencil on the pad, rolled it in thick fingers. "I could become publisher, I suppose. No decision I made would stand up, however, unless the family agreed with my decision."

"And what would your decision be, Bill?"

"I'm not sure yet. The fact is, there's a lot of money out there that wants this newspaper. We're practically a statewide monopoly—with all due apologies and deference, Matt—and a lot of the family would like to see the money. They've been getting very poor dividends for a long time."

"Why is that?"

"Ron built this new plant and filled it with expensive equipment, for one thing. It cost a ton of money and has strained our resources. We're going to have to cut back in a number of areas. You know we're staff-heavy. Ron was even going to give up his private car and driver . . ."

"You mean Frankie Levesque would be fired?"

"It was as an important gesture to the staff and our stockholders. Results have not been all they should be lately. Most of the family have all their wealth tied up in The Bulletin Company. They have a right to a fair return."

"Was Frankie told? Do you know?"

"I think Ron was going to tell him privately last Saturday, down in Little Bay."

"Did he?"

"I don't know."

"You've had trouble with the presses too, haven't you?"

"We'll straighten that out. We're on the trail of the cause already."

"Sabotage?"

"Maybe. That doesn't mean the plant and presses were a good idea."

"So there are a lot of reasons to sell, from a business point of view?"

"And from a personal one as well. People talk about newspapers as a trust, however, they're businesses first of all. You don't find any great newspapers that don't have a lot of money. And owners have a right to get a return on their money. Reporters and other editorial types squawk about that. You don't see them hesitating when another newspaper or TV station offers them a lot more money to leave. Off they go. They're only generous with other peoples' money."

"I don't want to get into a discussion about responsibility and the press," said Borg. "And I sure am not going to defend reporters. Still, what I think you're saying is that Ron may have been the major roadblock, maybe the only roadblock, to a sale of *The Bulletin*."

"I didn't say that at all," said Hasner. "I'm just trying to give you some background. I repeat I don't think Ron's death was anything but an accident."

"The dynamics have changed, haven't they?" said Borg. "And changed radically."

"Of course. Let me add one more thing, Matt, and this is for your own good. The Internet is coming in and it's going to hit all of us very hard, especially in classified advertising. It's starting already."

"I just find it hard to believe that people will give up their papers."

"Some won't but they're dying off. Get smart."

"You mean, sell out, like you want to do?"

"Don't be a dinosaur."

"Too late for me, Bill, but I guess not for you. And you sure will come out way ahead." Borg figured he didn't have anything to lose. The conversation was over anyway. Maybe he could puncture the pomposity.

"Perhaps. We have yet to see." Hasner's smile was as thin as his pouty lips would allow.

"By the way, Bill, have you ever been on the Mayor's boat? For a cocktail cruise or something? A nice romantic cruise? I hear it's a beauty. The one down in East Fenwick Bay."

"Not that I recall." Hasner rose from his chair, his face turning red and the color rising up his forehead. "If you're trying to sneak in an insinuation about me and the death of Ron Perry, forget it. I owe everything I have to him. He was my best friend. You're still too much of a two-bit reporter, Matt. Now, I've got things to do. If I read a word of accusation or innuendo in your paper we'll sue you out of business."

Losing his temper, was he? At last.

"Let me remind you too, my friend, that we've never really competed with your little paper as hard as we might . . ."

"You might face anti-monopoly charges if you did, my friend."

"And they'd take so long to prove it wouldn't do you any good at all. We could lower prices on our zoned pages." Hasner now talking between thin lips and teeth tightly clenched. "I'm sure you wouldn't like to see that. Might even put you out of business."

"Good to talk to you, Bill," said Borg as he left the room. He had been threatened with competition that could destroy his paper. Put the thirty-five men and women who worked for him on the street. What the hell was he doing playing detective?

On the other hand, his mother's Irish side in him was up. He wasn't sure he was able to back off. It just wasn't in him. His paper might go down anyway. But hell, it would go down fighting. And Hasner might not have the last word. *The Bulletin* would be sold, no question about that. And Bill Hasner's future was as uncertain as his own.

Borg's paper and its survival filled his thoughts as he took the stairs down to the back door of the Benevolent Club and out to the parking lot. He had no trouble finding his lone Chevy Caprice Classic among the Mercedes and BMWs. There was only one Bentley. Probably cost a quarter of a million. Enough to keep him in business for a while. Maybe he'd steal it. Instead he got into his Chevy.

CHAPTER 28

Jimmy Gleason loved the presses. He loved the smell of them, the inky mist that filled a pressroom and seeped through old newspaper buildings and lingered in closets and desks and the floors. He loved the throb of them when they were humming, the pulse of a newspaper, its very heart. He loved the racing of the cylinders as they turned out page after page. Sheet after sheet as some called them.

Now, though, he hated the people who owned them. Which is why he had contrived to hurt these particular presses in small yet destructive ways. You always hurt the ones you love, he smiled to himself. Some Irishman must have said that. Had to be. Someone as mixed up as himself. Let Perry blame the Mafia or the Germans; it was a Gleason behind the press malfunctions.

Pausing on the metal walk he looked down on the great units that could pour out a million copies in a few hours. Gleason leaned over the low guard rail and admired the machinery, breathed in the ink fumes, thinned by environmental rules but still present in any working pressroom.

Gleason loved to be up here on the walk. He felt at home. Even though none of this was his, never would be. Still, he felt a fit, a part of a great engine that printed a newspaper. Nowhere else, really, gave him this same feeling of comfort as a pressroom.

Gleason wouldn't do anything now. It would be too obvious. Anyone might walk by below and see him up here. Best to be careful. Ron Perry was dead. Maybe Gleason ought to give up the vendetta. A good Italian word. Only the Irish and the Sicilians really knew how to keep a grudge. Now maybe the debt was repaid.

As far back as Gleason's memory could reach, there were presses. He could remember when the old letter presses— were they Harris or Goss?—had knobs that the pressmen painted different colors to signify something or other. Or maybe the colors, orange and red and yellow, were just to pretty up the machines. They turned though, Gleason remembered, they sure turned.

Those colored knobs were a part of him, the knobs and the power of the presses. They were the heart of any newspaper, no matter what anyone said. Reporters claimed it was news that gave newspapers their name but free newspapers all over the country contained no news at all and were still successful. Just so long as the ads were printed clean and readable. And the ads wouldn't exist without the presses. In the old days you hardly needed to sell ads. There was a Main Street in a newspaper town and the merchants brought their ads in. They had to. There was no place else to go. They brought their ads in and they brought them to be printed on the presses. Even the constitution guaranteed a free press. Not a free newsroom. Not a free circulation department. A free press. Because if you owned the press, you had the freedom.

You poured information and ideas and dreams and even bullshit into the presses and the presses performed their magic and out came pages that gave importance to everything on them. People still believed what they read in spite of everything.

Jimmy Gleason's heart had been broken when the family had to sell its newspaper and the presses that went with it. For peanuts, as he recalled. Forced out of business by *The Bulletin* with its wealth and power. The power to buy all the good comic strips for itself exclusively and the best syndicated columnists.

Jimmy Gleason had his share of fun before everything came apart. Always around the presses. It was somehow appropriate that he even lost his virginity while the presses hummed their encouragement. Not that he needed much. It was during the last year of *The Tribune*, the day of the Christmas party. Jimmy had volunteered to stick around while a lot of the senior people went home early or took the day off altogether. He was down in a small circulation department office off the pressroom, fielding calls from readers who were disappointed because they hadn't received their paper yet. Sadly, there weren't many calls.

Maria had brought a drink down for him. In a plastic cup, a Dixie Cup he remembered. She had one herself. Not the first obviously. Jimmy had lusted after Marie Rostelli. Who hadn't? Before that there had only been girls in Jimmy's life. Maria was older. Maybe even thirty. Not a teenager, not a cheerleader. Tall, almost as tall as him in her heels and full bodied. Dark hair pulled back straight, very pale skin, dark eyes, full lips. She had a freckle on her lower lip. She had laughed about that when they stood in line in the lunchroom. She worked in the business department and looked sad more often than not. The half-hearted rumor was that she was in an unhappy marriage. That might have been wishful thinking on the part of the men at *The Tribune*.

"All alone down here?" she asked Jimmy as he stood up after opening the door. She was swaying just a little bit. "A young guy like you should be upstairs enjoying the party."

"I'll get up there pretty soon," he said. "I just want to make sure about the last calls."

"Serious, serious," said Maria. "You're too young to be so serious. There will be plenty of time for that later. Trust me."

Maria was wearing what she wore most often, a light cream sweater, brown skirt and darker brown shoes. The joke around the office was that the cream sweater was evidence she didn't fool around: No fingerprints on it. There were no clean hands in an old building filled with the ink fumes.

"What are you so serious about, Jimmy?" she asked him as she gave him the drink. Gleason was leaning back against a roll-top desk. It belonged to an assistant circulation manager who had locked it. Gleason had been working on the only other desk in the room, an old oaken relic with a dial phone and his blank papers on it. Maria was up against him now, smiling that sad smile of hers.

"What are you so sad about, Jimmy?" she said.

"Nothing, now that you're here," he said and felt like kicking himself. Clever? Maybe for high school. And he was sad. He knew the family company was collapsing around them. That wasn't on his mind right now. Instead, he couldn't help the effect Maria was having on his seventeen-year-old body. She had to be aware of it and maybe that's why she smiled a little smile.

"You know, I've had a few drinks so I can tell you that I've admired you, how serious you are, how hard you work when you're here, how you don't take advantage of who you are, how you've never made any wise remarks to me," she said, looking up at him as he squirmed back deeper into a desk that wasn't giving him any more room. "I also like the way you look. Aren't the holidays time for a little bit of celebration?"

"Maria, you're going to get ink on your sweater if you don't look out," he said as one of his hands gripped the Dixie cup and the other reached toward her and stopped.

"Not if you reach under it," Marie said. He did. Jimmy had fondled high school girls. Marie was a full breasted woman, filling his hand as he caressed her. She moaned softly. Then her dress was up and Jimmy was trying to pull aside her white lace panties. Maria brushed his hand aside and pulled them down. He was in her almost before he knew it. But he was seventeen and it was over before it should have been.

"Stay," she murmered. He could feel her move and it seemed as though she was massaging, coddling him.

"Be patient," she said, and kissed him more deeply now. Both of them came up breathless. "Just be still. Let me do the rest." She shrugged her breasts out of the bra.

Soon, they were moving together again, Maria whispering and moaning in his ear, then quiet cries of satisfaction. Jimmy felt as though he might pass out as he reached a climax.

The moment was enshrined in his memory. Everything about it. The titillation he felt, the fear that someone would come through the door and catch them. The surprise when he was aroused for a second time. The magic somehow combined with the presses in an experience somehow never duplicated.

"That was nice, Jimmy," Maria said finally, still holding him, both now leaning against the desk. He hoped she meant it. "Merry Christmas."

It was the merriest, most memorable Christmas Jimmy Gleason ever had. Soon the company would be in receivership. He would see Maria again but what happened during the Christmas party never happened again. She was friendly yet distant. He guessed his heart was broken, yet there was so much else happening that he noticed it less than he might have otherwise. And he was seventeen. Maria was soon gone with the rest of *The Tribune* staff. He never knew what brought on the holiday celebration. Still, he remembered it vividly always.

Jimmy Gleason smiled at the memory. Sex for him had never been the same. Nor had life—as that afternoon with the presses running when he and the world were young, even though the presses were old. Relationships had been fleeting, his life fragmented, chapters in a book without meaning and continuity.

Now there were decisions to make. He knew what happened to Ron Perry wasn't an accident. And he knew who the killer was. Had almost seen the crime itself. And the killer had seen him. Maybe if he told what he knew about the murder it would calm things down and help his union secretary. Pat Doyle was a square shooter and Gleason knew and appreciated that Doyle had gone out of his way to get him this job and keep him in it. Even Pat's brother, Michael, wasn't as bad as some foremen he worked for. Maybe it was time to return the favors to the Doyles. He knew they didn't like him much now that they suspected him of damaging the presses, saw the way they watched him. They probably were sorry they ever let him in here.

Jimmy Gleason was considering that and remembering Maria and how surprised he had been to find that she used Chanel perfume and how he had liked it ever after.

Standing here looking down on the presses, James Francis Gleason II was thinking he hadn't amounted to much since that holiday party. He had still been seventeen when the company had gone belly up and he had been left with nothing. His father took care of his wife and daughters. Little Jimmy, as he was called, had to fare for himself and not in a prep school anymore. So he got a job as a pressman at a Massachusetts newspaper, helped by the old *Tribune* press foreman and union president, an Irishman named Clancy. By the time he made his way back to *The Bulletin,* few remembered Gleason and those few in the pressroom kept quiet about it. As usual the news department knew little about what was happening in the rest of its own building.

That didn't solve the problem of whether to share what he knew with Pat or Mike Doyle. Jimmy Gleason never had to make that decision. While he was thinking about what he knew and admiring the presses and remembering Maria, someone had quietly joined him on the catwalk.

That someone wore old sneakers. There was no need. The roar of the presses covered any sounds. The heavy steel wrench was carried loosely so if anyone saw it they could think it was about to be used on a piece of machinery. That wasn't its purpose now. As Gleason leaned over the presses he was struck on the back of the head and tumbled into the presses he loved so much. They swallowed him. It was not an easy way for James Francis Gleason II to die, crushed by the huge cylinders, squeezed no thicker than the sheets of a newspaper. Even the murderer shivered as Gleason's body disappeared and his screams were consumed by the roar. The murderer dropped a pen on the catwalk and trotted to the catwalk and down.

CHAPTER 29

"**I**'m looking for a favor."

It was Pat Doyle calling at 6:45 a.m. Matt Borg had finished breakfast of Quaker Natural Cereal and blueberries and was sitting on his couch looking out on Narragansett Bay where it flowed into East Fenwick Bay. Then the telephone rang. Borg resented the disturbance. This was a time in the morning when he sipped his coffee and watched the early morning boats go out, led by the first quahoggers, those strange rowboats with the box cabins on them sitting aft just in front of powerful outboard motors.

First time he saw a quahogger go by Borg remembered that the ironclad *Monitor,* had been described as a cheesebox on a raft, a turret set on a deck that hardly emerged from the water. Outhouses on dories, that what these small boats looked like. Even though they had small heaters in the cabins he wouldn't want to be out there on the Bay on a freezing morning, dropping those long rakes down through the water and into the bottom of the Bay to dredge out the clams called quahogs.

This time in the morning was special for him, a time when he could watch the sun come up, think about the day ahead, maybe even meditate. Even before he read the morning newspapers. Before he listened to NPR. He needed this private time in a day. Even though it often turned melancholy, into memories of Jane and him together. Sometimes, now, he wondered how Donna was doing. His private time was seldom interrupted. It was now.

"Sorry to be calling this early. I knew you'd be up." It was Pat Doyle.

"It better be damn important if you're up and calling me now," answered Borg. He knew the union secretary was a night owl.

"It is," said Doyle. "Damn important. I don't suppose you've heard—Jimmy Gleason is dead. Died late last night."

"How, for God's sake?"

"In the new presses."

"How in hell did that happen?"

"That's what I'd like to know. The Providence Police seem satisfied that it was an accident, that Jimmy fell into the presses."

"You don't think so?"

"You're kidding? Jimmy had been around the presses too long for that. The cops say he must have been up on a catwalk over the biggest units when he slipped and fell into them. Or maybe threw himself."

"Painful way to kill yourself." Borg watched a lone sailboat join the quahoggers on their way out, the sailboat running before the wind, elegant and classic, the clamboats chugging out into the Bay, leaving a trail of noise.

"Damn right," said Doyle. "The only way they knew it happened was the blood coming out with the papers. That and the scream one of our guys thought he heard. Listen, Jimmy would never have fallen from that catwalk."

"What was he doing up there anyway?"

"Who the hell knows? Grabbing a smoke maybe. My brother told me Gleason used to go up on the catwalk once in a while just to watch the presses. He was a strange one. A pain in the ass, but a good pressman. God, it seemed like he could feel if anything was wrong with a press and find it and fix it in no time. Kept to himself, mostly. No friends. Maybe it was because of all the crap his family had been through. Reliable and straight. Never called in sick. Not the kind of guy to fall from a catwalk."

"That wasn't what you were saying a day ago, Pat."

"I know that. Jimmy went strange when these new presses came in. He was still one of ours. And I'm asking for help."

"What do you want from me, Pat? He didn't fall into my press." Borg snickered, finished his coffee. His few minutes of quiet were shot.

"Your press isn't big enough to fall into," Doyle shot back. "If someone did fall in they'd probably break the damn thing." Doyle paused. Back to business. "I know you have some pull with that police lieutenant and the Colonel, too, and the word is you helped with a couple of investigations. I'd like you to look into this. As a personal favor. We won't forget it if you do."

"Who's the 'we' here and why are you so suspicious? It must be more than you've said, Pat."

"It is. Remember you asked me about Gleason and his history in connection with the Perry death? I think he knew something. I think he was going to tell me about it."

"What makes you think that?" The sailboat had disappeared around the bend of the point across the Bay. The clam boats kept coming, noisy little buggers.

"He mentioned that he wanted to have a beer after work pretty soon. It's the first time he ever suggested anything like that. I think he had something to say."

"Not much to go on. Have you told the cops?"

"The Providence Police? Don't make me laugh. They haven't solved a murder in twenty years. And they've never been on a union's side since the big mill strikes. We're looking after our own here. The pressmen want to make sure someone pays some damn attention. And, in spite of all our disagreements, we trust you."

"I'm flattered, Pat." Borg took it with a grain of salt, took a sip of coffee as well. "I guess I'm curious myself. I'll talk to Lieutenant Pacheco and then I'll nose around. But it has to be after I get the paper out and take care of my own business."

"We know that. It's all we ask. And don't worry about your paper getting out on time. We'll make sure of that. We won't forget this."

"Any idea where I should start?"

"How about some of those who could walk through the production plant without arousing any suspicion?"

"Like unionized pressmen?

"Forget them. Like executives. Don't know if the Providence cops will tell you but a ball point pen was found on the catwalk."

"And?"

"It was one of the personalized pens that Bill Hasner had made for his desk. He gives them away. Talk to my brother Michael. He's the foreman on Gleason's shift. Any help you need, let me or Michael know. Especially if you run into trouble."

"How about a little help with the next contract so I can stay in business?"

"I said any help and I meant it." He hung up.

Borg knew it wasn't an empty promise. This was a labor state and unions played a big part in everything, including getting people elected. Not as much as in the past but they still got the voters out. And politicians never forget those who get the voters out. Besides that, the pressmen were a tough lot. Not as tough as Teamsters. No one was as tough as Teamsters.

Borg washed his coffee cup and slipped on a jacket from the closet. He felt sorry about Jimmy Gleason's death, even though he hardly knew him. Like Gleason, like Doyle, at forty-seven Borg thought of himself one of the old style newspapermen, fewer all the time. Maybe that was because he often felt a lot older. In any case, he didn't appreciate a murderer thinning the ranks.

CHAPTER 30

Aimee couldn't wait to get at him. The Managing Editor pounced as soon as Matt Borg opened the second-floor door of *The Times* and walked into the newsroom.

"The Attorney General is going to bring charges in that Clinton porn case," she said with a satisfied smile as she followed him into his office. "Against the cops and maybe against the woman."

"You know for sure?"

"Attila the Nun told me herself," said Solante, referring to Hilda St. Jean, the attorney general who had once been a Sister of Mercy and now showed none, having given up the veil in favor of verdicts. "Called this morning. Told me to give you her regards. She sounded as though she was looking forward to a fight."

"Hilda always sounds that way. Some priests must have picked on her when she was a nun. Her heart's in the right place even though it mostly gets lost behind her temper. What else did she say?"

"You can guess. The same old stuff about public morality going down the tubes and how the police are our last line of defense. That stuff."

"She didn't mention that it's an election year, did she?" Borg barked a laugh. Good old Hilda. Transparent as glass.

"Must have slipped her mind." Aimee joined him in a laugh. "Anyway, it's great stuff. Can we run a still from the movie itself, do you think?" Aimee followed him into his office, wagging her head, shaking the papers in her hand. He finally turned toward her.

"Will you let me catch my breath?" He tossed his briefcase on the desk, motioned with his hand for her to calm down. Sat down himself. "Now calm down. Let me see the still picture from the porn movie. As long as you can't recognize anyone in it or what they're doing I suppose it's OK. Don't forget we're a family newspaper."

"Don't you forget my family reads our paper. In other words, no dice?"

Borg shook his head. He knew every reader would gobble up the paper to see such a picture. And would then complain to high heaven and beyond about the paper printing such disgraceful stuff.

"Aimee, have you seen this film?" Borg looked at the grainy picture she handed him. It showed two men and a woman in the Clinton quarry. No faces and no bare parts that would offend anyone. Still.

"I felt it was my duty as your managing editor to see what everyone is talking about," she said.

"And what did you think, if I may ask?"

"I sure as hell have never had as much fun as the men or that woman do in the film. Maybe I'm not as agile either."

"Enough, enough."

"So how about it?"

"Amy, I just don't think we can run it. Any other local stuff you'd like to go over?"

"That's what I thought. Anyway, the Indians are inviting the townspeople to a public meeting next week to tell them about the casino they'll build if they get an OK to go ahead. And we've got a report from the state that the Arctic River is the cleanest it's been in years. And a couple of profiles of candidates for the school committee in Arctic."

"Good stuff. Everybody will read about the porn flick and the casino and the candidates' families will read the profiles. Make sure they're exactly the same length."

"God, that's so dopey. Do we really have to do that?"

"When you're running for office every word counts and so candidates count every word. Believe me. Make sure the damn things are the same length. By the way, it might be a good idea to get one of our young reporters in a canoe with a photographer on the Arctic River to get a good look at the river."

"Do you think we have to pay for life preservers?"

"Depends on which reporter you send." Borg laughed. "Make sure the photographer has his own camera and not one of ours. In case he goes overboard."

"The heart of a publisher is a cold, cold thing. You going to write anything? Everybody is eating up your stuff about the Perry death. It sounds like you're on the inside, like a super sleuth. They can't get enough of it."

"Probably not. I'll see. Let you know in ten minutes or so. I'm going to try to get out of here before noon. I may not get back today so catch me while you can. Anything else?"

"Felix was up and wanted to see you," she said.

"Next time you're downstairs tell him to come up anytime," said Borg. "By the way, if you haven't got it yet, ask the AP for something on the death of a pressman last night at *The Bulletin*."

"After the publisher's death? You sure you don't want to write something?"

"OK, I'll try. I'm just not sure they're connected."

"Maybe you should try to connect them," said Aimee as she cocked an eyebrow, rose from her chair and then dashed out the door.

He turned to skimming *The New York Times*, *Wall Street Journal*, and *Bulletin*. He had barely finished when press foreman Felix Unger knocked on the door, nodded and came in.

"I hope we haven't got a problem with the press," Borg said. "Tell me we haven't."

"We haven't," said Unger with a quiet smile. Unger was yet another demonstration that people constantly surprised you. In his late thirties, he had started in the five-man pressroom eighteen years before as an apprentice, a quiet kid who just did his job and listened. Now he was foreman, his dark hair was sprinkled with white and he had Borg's absolute trust. Unger not only ran the presses, he also managed all the purchasing for *The Times* and was a master at getting newsprint for the best price possible. Because paper and people were the two big expenses in a newspaper, Unger was a key supervisor.

"Then what's up?"

"Do you know that I live over in Little Bay?"

"No, I didn't know that. I'm not sure it makes me happy. That's a long drive in the morning if there's a snowstorm."

"I haven't missed a day yet, have I?' said Unger. "And I won't."

"That's good enough for me. Where you live isn't what brought you up here is it?'

"In a way it is. I hear you may be looking into the death of Jimmy Gleason. You know that he lived over in Little Bay?"

"The place must be getting crowded."

Felix didn't smile. He was a serious man. The kind of guy you want around your presses.

"He has a big old place, something left over from the time his family had dough," Felix said. "It was a summer place, I guess, going down hill now."

"Know anything else about him?" In spite of the fact they worked together every day, Borg had a formal relationship with Felix. Didn't know much about him while respecting him as much as anyone he knew. His blue work shirt was always buttoned, with just the white triangle of a T-shirt showing. His blue work trousers always had a crease. His heavy, black shoes were cleaner than most.

"Sometimes I hear things around town. It might be a good idea for you to talk to Cyrus Bitgood." Felix still stood. Not at attention, but surely at parade rest.

"Why's that?"

"He used to do some odd jobs for the Perrys and Gleason and he were fishing buddies."

"Thanks for the tip. He talked to Lieutenant Pacheco, didn't he?"

"Yup. Talk to him, OK?"

"OK. You wouldn't happen to know where I can find Bitgood this afternoon, would you?"

"At Marr's General Store by the potbellied stove. It's on Main Street. He had a fall on Monday. Hurt his hip. You might want to ask about it."

"Thanks again. Pat Doyle talk to you, did he?"

Felix Unger just smiled as he left the office. The editor's first call after Unger closed the door was to the Attorney General, Attila the Nun. He looked forward to it.

"Hilda, how are you? Is it true you're hot on the trail of our little porn ring?"

"Absolutely. You should be delighted I'm going to clean up your Valley."

"And take some heat off the investigations into the Perry and Gleason deaths?"

"I'm not sure I'd qualify those as investigations," Hilda said. "We're looking into them and that's about it."

"No pressure? No important people calling?"

"There's always pressure in this job, you know that. And I regard every citizen in our state as important."

"Especially in an election year."

"Goodbye, Matt." She hung up. Borg didn't mind. It seemed to happen to him a lot.

Next he called Donna Pacheco.

"Early for you to be in the office," he said. "Must have been a late night with the Gleason death."

"The early bird gets the worm," she said and cackled. "Obviously, you've heard about Jimmy Gleason. What's going on?"

"Are you up for lunch today? To compare notes?"

"I can't get down there, Matt."

"How about the Arts Club in Providence? I can stop on my way to Little Bay."

"Haven't been there since the Crowe murder. On your way to Little Bay?"

"Tell you about it. Twelve noon?"

"If they let me in."

"They will." Borg, hoping the small and private space under the old stairway hadn't already been reserved. It would give them some privacy. He called.

It was available.

CHAPTER 31

"**P**eaches are what make my summer," Dayton Thomas said to Borg as the editor entered the Arts Club from the cooling spring day outside. Thomas sat in the small library and waiting room off the entrance hall. White-haired and with a blue-and-white bow tie, Thomas looked every inch the attorney who had won two notable cases before the Supreme Court. Yet when he worked was anyone's guess. He seemed always to be sitting in the Club, reading the day's newspapers, which he never bought himself. Borg always had the same response.

"I like blueberries myself," he said.

"Good," said Thomas. "Not as good as the first peaches of spring on breakfast cereal. Anything new on Perry's death?"

"Just what you read in the paper," answered Borg. Satisfied that one of spring's rituals had been observed, Thomas went back to reading *The Bulletin* the Club provided. Was it a matter of honor by the lifelong Democrat not to buy the Republican newspaper himself? Or just thrift? Borg asked himself the questions not for the first time as he made his way past the fireplace in the Green Room and to the cubby. Probably a little bit of both, he decided once more.

Donna Pacheco was already seated.

"Paper out?" she asked as he squeezed into the short bench on one side of the small table. Pacheco had taken the bench under the slanting roof that was the bottom of a now unused stairway to the second floor. She wore a white shirt under a blue jacket.

"Put to bed, as we used to say. Every last sheet."

"I like those expressions. Anything good in it?"

"Attila the Nun is going after that little porn ring down in the Valley and we have a long-shot chance at getting an Indian casino."

"You guys love to run scandals and sex, don't you?" she asked with a half-smile. "You really think that stuff sells newspapers?"

"And murder. You don't?"

"I just worry that my kids might be learning a lot of stuff they don't need—and learning it too early."

"They're learning a lot more from TV and from other kids than they'll ever see in any newspaper."

"I guess. Anyway . . . I hear you're looking into Jimmy Gleason's death for the pressmen."

"And for myself. You do get the news pretty fast. I only agreed to sniff around this morning."

"Remember I'm a trained detective." She cackled. "Maybe I can help you with your sniffing. Maybe we can help each other. Let's not forget, Matt, that I'm the one in charge of the investigation. Did Pat Doyle say anything that might be useful?"

"He didn't but someone else, our production foreman, Felix Unger, did this morning. Told me Gleason lived out in Little Bay. Told me to talk to Cyrus Bitgood some more."

"Do you think there's some connection here? Aside from the fact that both deaths were accidents. So far that is."

"Both accidents, both Gleason and Perry lived in Little Bay, at least some of the time, both worked at *The Bulletin*."

"You believe in coincidence, Matt?" Donna buried her face in the menu, a typed page clipped to cardboard.

"Not much," he said. "There's also that Perry's driver lives in Little Bay and Bill Hasner spent a lot of time there. Do you know if the Mafia has an annex down there?"

"How about your Indians?"

"We're clean. That's another tribe over there."

The waitress peeked into the cubby. Donna looked up at Borg. "I remember you once told me that everything here tastes like the pot roast and the pot roast tastes like cardboard." She turned to the waitress: "Pot roast."

"Me too," said Borg. "Don't forget the johnnycakes. Extra butter." The waitress nodded, said not a word. Like most students from the local art school she focused more on the visual than the verbal. Finally volunteered a question: "Drink?"

"Pinot grigio." Borg had started drinking the wine because he liked the way it sounded. On the other hand, anything in Italian sounded better than in any other language. Lots of vowels. And soft consonants. Rolled off your tongue. Like the wines.

"Water," said Donna. No soft consonants for her. Then she weakened. "Slice of lemon."

"The pressmen are convinced the Gleason death is murder," said Borg. "At least Pat Doyle is convinced. Doesn't believe a pressman could be careless enough to slip and fall into a press and it's possibly the worst way in the world to commit suicide."

"What do you think?"

"Makes sense."

"So if Perry was murdered it looks like Gleason knew something and was murdered to shut him up."

"Looks like it. And it boils down to the motive for killing Perry."

"Always the reason, it's always the reason," said Donna as she labored at her pot roast. "Talk to me about this. Not the pot roast. The motives."

"Here's how I see it." Borg watched Donna saw at her meat, tried his and then turned to the johnnycakes and green beans. "If Perry was killed, the problem is not too few but too many motives. Greed to begin with. Perry stood in the way of a sale that could have made a lot of people a lot of money, including his wife and best friend. If the motive is sex, he had an affair with a mob wife."

"And maybe there was someone shadowing Perry," Donna had given up on the pot roast. "A wild card. I thought it might be Gleason, but he's gone."

"It still could have been Gleason following Perry. Maybe he wasn't the only one. I don't think the mob is involved, however."

"It could be a mob guy," said Donna.

"Maybe," said Borg. "But then the Gleason death doesn't seem to fit. Would the mob guys be in the press room of the paper? No. It all comes back to *The Bulletin*."

"The Perry family will all get very, very rich, no question," said Donna. "And both Louise Perry and Bill Hasner were alone for a time on Sunday morning. Mrs. Perry didn't seem unhappy enough in her marriage to want to kill her husband but who knows?"

Borg interrupted her. "Think she was on the boat with Hasner?"

"Yes," said Donna and looked up. Then she went back to the pot roast.

"Hasner and her together?"

"Maybe. I'm not sure it means anything. She seems pretty straight. What do you think?"

"I don't like the guy much so I have to be careful about passing judgment," said Borg. "I agree with you about her. Hasner gains the most, though. He'll become chief executive and manage the sale if there is one. He says he loved Ron. Now that's he's dead, everyone loved him. Or so they say. I guess you noticed that Hasner drives a vintage Jaguar with the wheel on the right."

"Easy to reach out and hit someone on the side of the road, even while driving," said Donna. "Sure I noticed. And Frankie Levesque has a right side drive truck, as well. He seems to have loved Ron Perry too . . ."

"That love might have turned sour," said Borg. "Hasner told me Perry fired Levesque."

"I can't see Frankie being smart enough to plan the murder of Perry, can you?" Donna shrugged. "He seemed pretty slow. Anyway, I'm talking to Hasner this afternoon and then I'm after Pat Doyle and some of the other pressmen. It would help if you talked to Anne Black this afternoon? The Colonel asked me if you had."

"I'll try. I've called her a couple of times and haven't got an answer so I'm just going to drop by. Her house is up the street."

"Great," said Donna. "Now listen, maybe we better get a little better organized or we'll be stepping all over each other."

"Just remember, Donna, that I'm after a story as well as a possible murderer . . ."

"Fair enough, but we can help each other or get in each other's way here. I know you've helped me a lot, Matt, but I'm in charge of this investigation, so can we organize a little bit maybe?"

"Fair enough, Donna. The last thing I want to do is screw you up, you know that. So, tough as it is for me to say, what do you suggest, Lieutenant?" He smiled at her.

"You'll see Anne Black, right? Then what?"

"I'm driving down to Little Bay afterwards to see Cyrus Bitgood. The press foreman at our paper, who lives in Little Bay, told me Cy might have something to say about Gleason. The pressmen want to find the killer of Jimmy Gleason as much as we do. Maybe more. How about you?"

"I'm going to see Bill Hasner here in Providence again and talk to a pressman myself while I'm at *The Bulletin*'s production center. Maybe one of the Doyle brothers."

"Good luck." Borg paused and smiled his twisty smile at Donna. "You don't mind if I fill my car with gas down in Little Bay, do you, and maybe say hello to Big Nan?"

She smiled back at him. "Don't give me a hard time, will you?" She cackled. "Listen, I don't even care if you talk to her son as well."

"Thanks, Lieutenant, Ma'am."

"I'd like you to stop off here in Providence on your way back to Arctic so we can compare notes," said Donna.

"I'm not going into that Providence police station if I can help it."

"How about I buy you dinner," said Donna. "I'll make sure it's on the state."

"Let's put it on hold," said Borg. "I'm sure you want to get home to your family and I may be too bloody tired."

"Call me around eight," she said. "Like after dinner. At home." She gave him her number.

He signed the check but they didn't reach the door before Adele, the receptionist, stopped him.

"Call for you," she said, handing him a phone.

"This is Anne Perry Black, Mr. Borg. I hope you remember me."

"Of course." How could he forget the widow of the man who was the richest baby in the world when he was born. Or so it was said. And she must have known he had called her twice in two days. Ah well, the rich are different from us.

"I wonder if you could possibly stop by to see me since you're up here anyway?"

"I was planning to, as a matter of fact, even without benefit of an invitation. By the way, how did you know I was here?"

"Dayton Thomas," she said with a chuckle. "Lovely man though he's obsessed with peaches. He says the very best come from China, of all places. Dayton is my attorney and we were just talking on the telephone. It's a small state. See you in a few minutes?"

"Of course." He told Donna and they left together, walking up the steep hill to the Club parking lot. His knees ached as he pushed up the hill as best he could.

"Hear anything about a pen on a catwalk, Donna?" He had to puff it out.

"OK, so you got me. Yeah, and with Hasner's name on it. Providence cops asked me to keep it to myself. Sorry. How'd you know about it?"

"Pressmen, who else? I just forgot . . . ."

"I hope you don't make it a habit. Not if we're trying to help each other out."

Donna said nothing, gave a face, practically flew, her arms churning, high heels clickety-clacking along, to her Datsun. He knew, like all cops, she hated sharing information and wished she could just tell him what to do and where to get off. Borg turned away, in the opposite direction toward the Black mansion. He was whistling.

CHAPTER 32

"**M**rs. Black is in the War Room," the butler told Matt Borg as he led him toward the back of the hall. He kept a straight face. Under the beautifully curving stairway, almost hidden, was a door. "You can walk down or take the elevator in the back if you like."

He chose to walk as he had just walked the several blocks from the Arts Club down Bounty Street to the Black house. Actually it was the second Black house, across a narrow street from the original, now a museum, that John Adams had called the finest mansion in this country. This second Black house was a three-story wood frame in yellow with white trim. Borg had noted the license plate with the number "One" on the ancient, brilliantly shined Rolls in the driveway in front of the four-car garage, once a stable.

The War Room was almost the entire basement. Borg remembered that from a previous visit when Mrs. Black had helped him plan a trip to Italy, introducing him to Frascati and suggesting he visit the small town after which the wine was named. Ron Perry, a cousin of some kind, had made the introduction. Borg's trip produced a very profitable magazine for *The Bulletin*.

"Come in, Mr. Borg," said Mrs. Black, wearing a plain dress the same color as her name. Around her neck dangled a cord from which hung reading glasses. She was standing alongside one of a number of large tables upon which were arrayed miniature soldiers, cannon and horses all taking part in battles. Villages sprawled across the tables and even small streams that actually flowed water.

"This is the battle of Quatre Blas," she said. "You remember it was just before Waterloo. Marshal Ney hesitated and that allowed Wellington to bring up his troops even as Napoleon was winning the victory of Ligny."

"I've always been surprised you don't have Waterloo," he said.

"Too large. Actually even this battle is a little oversized. For my purpose, the best battles are those of the Cavaliers against the Roundheads during the English Civil War. Most of those were small, but the uniforms weren't much fun. I love the Napoleonic uniforms. The Old Guard and the cavalry, light and heavy, the cuirassiers with their breastplates and wonderful plumes, the chasseurs with their capes, all of them almost as colorful as the Austro-Hungarian cavalry. Now they were magnificent. Not a very good army but beautiful."

"I remember the first time I saw all this and I said something about toy soldiers and you almost hit me."

"I would have too," said Mrs. Black. "You weren't within reach. I trust you've learned these are all military miniatures."

"Indeed I have. You haven't agreed to talk to me to discuss Napoleon's strategy at Waterloo, though. Or are we?"

"You are still direct. Well, in a way, perhaps I do wish to discuss strategy." Mrs. Black picked up a member of the Old Guard in her right hand and looked at it. She was a tall woman, built like a Wagnerian soprano. Handsome, with wise blue eyes that occasionally twinkled.

"Do you believe in free will?" she asked Borg.

"I guess to some degree. However, I think we're all limited. I couldn't be a jockey, for instance, or a gymnast or a diver. Just too tall."

"Nor could I," said Mrs. Black. "Nor could this Guardsman. They had to be tall as well. Do you know, Mr. Borg, that it is said the French were a tall race before Napoleon?"

"So I've heard. I probably couldn't be a Guardsman anyway. I don't take orders well."

"I've heard that about you."

"I wasn't thinking of enlisting in any event."

"Napoleon probably could have used you at Waterloo. All he had was his poor old Ney. The great marshals of earlier days were elsewhere. Napoleon could have used some of those who could act on their own, could anticipate rather than react. Grant didn't have his great success in the East until he had his team with him, Sherman and Sheridan and the like. "

"OK, now that you've taken away my Marshal's baton, may I ask you a question or two, Mrs. Black?"

"You may. And I wanted to talk to you as well."

"Then let the battle begin, Mrs. Black?" He laughed. So did she.

"You haven't changed. As irreverent as ever. I guess that's a good thing in your profession. What I wanted to talk to you about is *The Bulletin* and Ron Perry's death. I suppose you know that he's a cousin."

"I know."

"Actually I'm a pretty distant cousin. Now I've become a family sage. When you get older people think you get wiser. I'm not sure about that. Anyway, the family knew about our little Italian collaboration and they asked me to talk to you."

Matt Borg waited. Mrs. Black put the Guardsman back in place. Little did he know that soon he and his compatriots would face the British guns at Waterloo and die. Almost to the last brave man.

"Mr. Borg, I think you're an honest man, if a difficult one. I hope you think I'm honest as well."

"I do."

"That will make what I have to say easier. None of the family had anything to do with the death of Ron Perry or of that poor Gleason man. Certainly some of us believe it would be best to sell *The Bulletin*. Some of us believed, as well, that it was inevitable in any case. The time for independent operations like *The Bulletin* is past and Ron would have recognized that sooner rather than later. You will recognize it, as well, Mr. Borg, and you too will sell your newspaper. Don't smile. I know you're a romantic. You would have been a cavalryman. Bill Hasner would have been a quartermaster, in the commissary. Like our own Nathanael Greene in the Revolutionary War. You remember what Greene accomplished in the South. This is a time for quartermasters.

"What I'm saying is that the plot was set. Just as surely as it is on this table. Just as inevitably. No one was going to kill anyone to push it along. No one was desperate for money. Please don't stir up matters that are best left alone. I hope you believe what I've told you."

"I do, Mrs. Black, and I hope you know that I am sympathetic. I trust you understand it does not surprise me that you would defend your family. It would surprise me if you didn't."

"And disappoint you?"

"Probably. I suppose I can tell you that it is conceivable the sale of the paper is related to the murder, but perhaps not directly."

"Now you are being subtle, Mister Borg. I'm not certain it becomes you. What are you saying, precisely"

"As delicately as I can I'm suggesting there might have been a romantic triangle that motivated the murder to gain the money to be made by the paper's sale."

"Not very delicate at all, Mr. Borg." She picked up another soldier, this time a cavalryman. Her knuckles went white as she gripped it hard. Mrs. Black showed no emotion but her face had turned a pale pink. Just as quickly, the color faded.

"I am no longer young, Mister Borg. Still, I am not unaware of the part passion plays in our lives. Was I aware that Ronald and Louise had troubles? Yes, I was aware of that. My belief is that they had solved those problems, or at least learned to tolerate them. If you are suggesting a love triangle of some sort that deserves public display as a part of this investigation I would strongly recommend you do not follow that train of thought."

"Mrs. Perry and Mister Hasner stand to gain an awful lot and I have already been threatened today, Mrs. Black . . ."

"Excuse me, Mister Borg. You are mistaken. Mister Hasner has not a major share in The Bulletin Company. If the company is sold and he expedites the sale he will be rewarded, but perhaps not nearly as much as he would have gained if Ronald, his best friend, had lived. By the way, for your information, I believe that Mister Hasner understands better than Ron did the threat of the Internet and associated technology to newspapers.

"As for Louise Perry, she has no shares in the company. All of what Ronald owned is in trust for his two daughters. Louise will not go hungry, needless to say. She too might have gained more if her husband had lived. Louise is one of the best people I have ever met. She has put up with a lot. I would trust her with my life.

"Moreover, I do not know what you mean about being threatened. I assure you that did not enter my mind. I hope that no member of my family threatened you either."

There was a pause. Mrs. Black caught her breath. It had been a long and emotional explanation. Borg regarded her with sympathy. It had to be hard to talk about family, to say what she had just said. She was a private person. So he wouldn't repeat what Hasner had said to him. Not yet, anyway. If his paper and his employees' jobs were on the line he just might. And Mrs. Black might just be capable of a lot more than she would let on.

"Thank you for what you have told me," he said, finally.

She hesitated, picked up a mounted cavalryman. "I respect your judgment—and your discretion." She put the soldier back. Borg noticed she placed it backward on the table. And out of place. Mrs. Black was seriously distracted. "We have used the word, 'trust', a lot today. I hope it retains the same meaning for you as it does for me."

"Thank you," said Borg. "I believe it does. I hope Ney does better this time around."

"He won't," said Mrs. Black. "Not a thousand times around. It's not in him."

CHAPTER 33

"**S**ssst."

It was the sound of spit hitting a hot wooden stove in the front room of Marr's General Store in Little Bay. Five elderly men were sitting around the stove, enjoying what might be the last fire of the late spring.

"Afternoon, Cy," Borg said as he stood across from Bitgood and, like the rest, faced the stove. All the men wore checked shirts. Probably L. L. Bean. Jeans. Boots. Not a clean shave in the group.

Pssst. Someone else spit, hit the stove and interrupted Borg's reverie.

"Ayeh," said Bitgood.

"Hear you had a fall," said Borg. "Hope you're feeling better."

"Fall's less trouble than my heart," said Bitgood. "Heart keeps me from walkin' much."

"Sorry to hear that."

"Yep, can't walk into the wind, the doc says. Still, did a mile out to the cemetery and back this mornin'."

Borg chewed on this for a while as a couple of other psssts interrupted the quiet of Marr's General Store.

"I can see how you walked out there with the wind at your back but how'd you walk back without facing the wind?" asked Borg.

"Backwards," said Cy Bitgood and his cronies shared a chuckle at the expense of the newcomer. Borg wondered if they had been waiting all day for him and his question. Probably.

"Cy, I wonder if we could go outside and talk for a while?" He asked after the one joke of the day at Marr's had settled down.

"Awful cold out there," said Bitgood.

"We can sit in my car. It's plenty big."

"Question is whether it's plenty warm."

"That too," said Borg.

Bitgood got to his feet—slowly, Borg noticed. With some cracking of knees, they made their way through the cold and into the Caprice Classic. It still retained some heat and Borg put it on full blast as Bitgood squirmed into the comfort of the passenger seat.

The drive down to Little Bay had been a smooth one but Borg found it difficult to focus on the matter at hand. His paper dominated his thinking. Strong women were also on his mind. Lots of them involved in the deaths of Ron Perry and Jimmy Gleason. Louise Perry for one, and Anne Black and, of course, Donna Pacheco. Angela Rosso? Probably.

He focused on the present. "Why'd you take that walk this morning, anyway?" Borg asked Bitgood, to get it rolling.

"Like a walk for exercise," Bitgood said. "And had to check on the cemetery. No telling what that Joshua Arnold or the Constable were up to out there."

Bitgood was the caretaker of the cemetery and Arnold was the volunteer fire chief of Little Bay. Their feud was legend.

Bitgood insisted on burning leaves in the fall and Arnold insisted it broke the law. The result was that the lone Little Bay fire engine went screaming out to the cemetery regularly in the autumn to quench the fires and charge the cemetery for the service. Bitgood refused to pay. There was even the tale, which seemed to be supported in fact, that Bitgood burned leaves on Halloween every year so the kids in town could see the fire engine roar through town. Joshua Arnold was not amused.

"Everything all right at the cemetery?" asked Borg.

"So far," said Bitgood.

"Cy, I hear that Jimmy Gleason lived out here and you know he just died. His friends have asked me to look into it. Can you tell me anything about him?"

"Guess Felix Unger told you about Jimmy. Nice boy, Unger." Bitgood paused, looked out the windshield. He was sitting ramrod straight, a bony old man with a profile of sharp edges, like Dick Tracy. He fiddled with the door, trying to open the window.

"Got to spit," he said and Borg opened the electric window from the driver's side and noticed that Cy Bitgood checked the wind before he let fly.

"Jimmy Gleason kept to himself pretty much," said Bitgood. "Lived in one of those old summer cottages near the beach. Been in his family forever. Worked nights, I guess, so you'd see him shoppin' and such around town during the day. And fishin'."

"Did he live anywhere near the Perry place?"

"Not too far. Matter of fact, he fished down on a beach you could see right across a little creek and into the Perry place. Wasn't much of a fisherman, though."

"How'd you know that?"

"Well, the shed on the east side of the cemetery is right close to that beach and I'd see him out there. Couldn't cast worth a bad penny. Never saw him pull much in. Even when the blues were runnin' so hard you had to beat 'em off."

"That part of the beach near the Perry place, you say?"

"Not near but within sight." Bitgood had closed the window by himself, a chaw of tobacco still in his left cheek. "You might say."

"Watching the Perrys, was he?"

"I'd say so. Not bad watchin' either. Have to admit I did a bit myself. That Mrs. Perry used to play tennis in a little skirt and tight shirt. Long legs she has. Nice to watch her chase the ball."

"Playing with her husband?"

"Mostly with her daughters and that Hasner fella. Friend of the family, I guess."

"That beach was where Perry was going on Sunday, wasn't it?'

"Guess so. It was close to his house. Couldn't get there direct, though. You have to go all the way around to the little bridge over the creek. Perry used to go to the beach once in a while to sit in his car and read his paper. Biked there most every Sunday."

"So Gleason and he were at the beach at the same time."

"Didn't say that. Matter of fact, they never were, now that I think about it. Gleason always had somethin' else to do when Perry was there. Made sure he was never on the beach with Perry."

So there was a Little Bay connection—or telling separation—between Gleason and Perry. And both were dead. So what did it mean, if anything? Maybe Bill Hasner's tennis was more important than Gleason's fishing. Even though Gleason may have been watching the Perrys.

"Cyrus, do you think someone killed Ron Perry?"

"Why ask me?"

"Because I think you're a smart man and you watch a lot of what goes on at the beach from your perch at the cemetery. I also hear you used to do some odd jobs for Perry." Borg didn't add that he was sure old Bitgood heard a lot more at his spot by the stove at Marr's. Bitgood chewed for a while before he went on.

"The odd jobs were a long time ago." Bitgood paused, swallowed hard. "I'm goin' to tell you somethin' and I'll tell you why. It's because you hired that boy, Roy Ketchum, as your maintenance man. The boy's not all there, I know, but you hired him even though Felix didn't want you to. Felix told me that himself. I had a son. Nobody remembers that now. Buddy was a good boy, black hair, blue eyes. What you call autistic. Died young." Bitgood's expression didn't change, but Borg watched his Adam's apple rise and fall with another swallow.

"I guess the more you know about any family, the more you realize they've been touched by many of the same things, cancer and mental sickness being a couple of them." Borg looked away from the old man, allowed him to recover.

Finally Bitgood went on. "Guess you could say that. Anyway, I think Gleason was out to get Ron Perry sooner or later. And I think someone who knew Perry real well killed him. Knew where he went on Sunday mornings especially."

"Anything else?" That really hadn't told him anything he didn't know.

"You might fill up at Nan's on your way home. She knows more about Little Bay than I do. More than anybody, I reckon. Might ask about Frankie's father." He opened the car door. Nothing more was forthcoming.

"Thanks, Cy. I appreciate it," he said to the old man. "I hope you have good memories of your son."

"Only good memories," said Cy Bitgood as he got out of the car slowly, knees cracking all the while. Cy Bitgood and his cronies were one of the reasons he loved his job. Nan was Borg's next stop.

CHAPTER 34

At Nan's you could pay for your gas by credit card at the pump. Borg was surprised. The place looked so decrepit he imagined cash as the only exchange. He filled his tank, the pump read out a "Thank You" with its receipt, and Borg went inside to say hello to Big Nan Levesque.

"I remember you from when you worked at *The Bulletin*." Nan sat in her armchair in front of yet another woodstove. At least she wasn't spitting, thought Borg. Not yet anyway. She was wearing brown corduroys and a checkered red-and-black shirt over what looked like a red sweatshirt. On her feet were brown boots. Unlaced. The town was an L. L. Bean advertisement.

"Talking to Cyrus about the Perry death," said Borg. "So I thought I'd stop in and say hello."

"Nice of you," said Nan. "Don't get many customers when it's cold and this sure feels like winter this afternoon. Boys down at Mars spittin' away?"

"Spitting away," said Borg. "They've got pretty good aim. Seem to always hit the stove."

"They been at it long enough. I guess practice makes perfect, even if it's just spittin'. Look at all those baseball players. Spittin' and scratchin'. Must be experts by now."

"A couple of Jimmy Gleason's friends have asked me to look into what happened to Jimmy. Pressmen your son probably knows. Nothing official about it, of course. I wonder if you could tell me what you know about his life."

"Kept to himself mostly. Paid his bills. Went to pieces after the family paper went out of business. Let his teeth go. Too bad. He was a nice lookin' kid. Always said hello."

"You must know a bit more than that."

"I guess I do and I guess it don't do no harm to talk about it now. It sure won't hurt Jimmy. Not any more than the poor fella was hurt in his own life. A lot like the rest of us."

"How's that?"

"You know his family was ruined by Perrys. Drove their paper right into the ground. Just like with the mills. They all went broke or went south. The owners came out on top, as usual. Only the workers suffered. You know the song? The rich get richer and the poor get children. Old Eddie Cantor song. Remember him? Probably not. Anyway, the rich sure do get richer around here."

"I guess some people say the big strike of '29 and the unions helped kill the mills." Sorry as soon as he said it, Borg knew he had let Jimmy Gleason out of the conversation. Big Nan would surely go on about the mills. She did.

"The strikes were just an excuse to move the mills south where labor was cheaper. Got rid of the old buildings and old machines and old workers. None of the owners gave a damn. They never do. Bottom line. That's all that counts. I know because my husband was killed by those people. I still remember him taking me to the mill. He was as proud as though the mill was his. Wasn't though. He found that out."

"How's that?"

"He was a foreman at the biggest mill in Fall River. Owned by the Perrys. They never even offered him a job down south when they moved. Even though he went to work right through the strike. So the workers hated him and then his bosses left him high and dry. Murder is what it was."

"Same Perrys as own the newspaper?"

"Cousins or something. Same breed."

Nan's lips were tight. Her hands were gripping the arms of her chair, clenched like claws.

"Nothing's changed. It's what they still do. The bottom line. It's all they give a damn about. Loyalty to workers? Forget it. If *The Bulletin* has to cut expenses, you know damn well who'd suffer. Not all those people in the executive offices. Oh, no. It would be all the poor bozos down the line. Like my Frankie. Just like always."

"I guess your son would be safe though, wouldn't he?" Borg fished, wanted to hear what Nan's answer would be. Had Perry fired Frankie? Hasner had said as much.

"Who knows? He isn't in a union. Who knows what will happen now that Mr. Perry is dead. After all that my boy did for that man. They'll kill him just like they did his father and grandfather."

"His grandfather?"

"They took the mill business from our old country store and took it to the cheap outlets in the city. Grandpa Sheldon never got over it."

"Doesn't sound as though you're grieving for Ron Perry?"

"Good riddance," said Nan. "Good riddance to all of them."

"What did Frank do exactly, besides drive the car for Perry?" Borg would let Big Nan talk. She sat alone most of the time. Probably grateful for an audience. Seemed that way.

"Anything he was asked to do. Drove Perry to dates with that Italian bitch." She pronounced it "Eye-tal-ian." "Defended him to the pressmen. Frankie would have died for Mr. Perry. He worshipped him."

"And Ron Perry took pretty good care of Frankie, I guess."

"I suppose. Until push came to shove."

"You think Frankie might be laid off? I heard something about that from Bill Hasner." Borg gave Nan time. Watched her make a decision.

"Not that I know," said Nan. She looked him in the eye, rolled her powerful shoulders, daring him to contradict her. He couldn't. There was no way to establish that Perry had laid off Frankie now that Perry was dead. Borg knew that. So did Nan. They paused, letting the standoff sit for a minute.

"By the way, Nan, how did your husband die?" Borg tried to sound apologetic. He didn't do that very well. "You don't mention him much."

"Worked in the mills just like I said. Just after it went under he went fishin' one morning. By himself. Drowned."

"I'm sorry. Must have been tough?" To Borg on this cool and damp day New England seemed littered with broken lives and empty mills.

"Tough enough." Big Nan paused, grimaced. "He knew I had the union insurance long as it wasn't suicide. It was all that was left. Young Frankie was old enough to go to work. We managed."

Borg shook his head in sympathy, looked down at his hands decided to sit in the straight chair that stood against the wall. Dusty. Borg didn't dare brush the dust it off. Not much more to say, really. Sorry he sat as soon as he did.

"Just as well," Nan added finally, looking down at her hands now clasped in front of her. "Broke his heart, the mills dyin' and all. A victim he was, one more victim."

Her voice trailed off. Borg waited before the next question. "Did Frankie know Jimmy Gleason well?"

"Knew him enough to see when he came in for gas. Young Frankie used to go fishin' down on the same beach as Jimmy but nobody knew Jimmy real well."

Nobody knew anybody real well in this small town. Or would admit it. Even though they all seemed to be watching each other.

"Young Frankie's not around right now, I don't suppose."

"He's runnin' an errand. You leave him alone, you hear? You can see he's just a simple boy, means no one any harm."

"Mrs. Levesque, listen, I don't want to make anyone uncomfortable here. I would like to see Frankie again."

"All right, all right. Why don't you go up and talk to Louise Perry if you're lookin' for someone to talk to? She's the one's probably gains the most by Mr. Perry's death. Not afraid of her, are you? Most people are."

"Mrs. Levesque, there are times I'm afraid of my own shadow, but I think you have a good idea. I will go and talk to Mrs. Perry. She's home, isn't she?" He wasn't about to let Nan know that Louise Perry wouldn't get as rich as Big Nan thought she would. Still, he took it for granted Big Nan would know whether she was home. He was right.

"Yup. Had the funeral and burial. Small and private. I hear she wasn't too beat up."

Borg didn't ask her how she knew. Instead he opened the door—it was still sticking—and made his way to his car.

It was getting colder as the day wore on.

CHAPTER 35

The stones of Isle de l'Espoire looked as cold as Borg felt when he drove up to the front door. A chill wind off the Bay roiled the net of the clay court off to the side of the big house. He had once played on that court, when he was a senior editor of *The Bulletin*, and had been invited for a weekend with his late wife before he left *The Bulletin* to buy his own newspaper. Louise Perry was in tennis gear, a white sweater over a white shirt top and short skirt. Her manners were still perfect.

"Matt, it's good to see you," she said. "Come in out of the cold. As you can see I thought I might hit the ball a bit this afternoon, but it's too damn cold. Especially with that wind. The children have gone upstairs to read. Or so they say."

She led him into the great room where a small fire huddled in the center of the huge fireplace. They sat in a couch facing the fireplace, on either side of which were windows looking out on the Bay. There was what looked like a coffee pot on the table in front of them.

"Would you like some hot cocoa? I'm having some."

Borg nodded yes, Louise Perry poured, then looked at him and waited. She had the remarkable ability to look down her nose at you even while she was actually looking up.

"Louise, first of all, I'm awfully sorry about Ron's death. We were never very close, competitors almost, but I always had a feeling that in a different world we might have been closer friends."

"I think Ron had the same feeling. I don't want to gild the lily, but I think he liked you. In his own way. Did everything in his own way, of course. You didn't come here to tell me you liked Ron, did you?" She smiled a very cold smile.

"No, I didn't. Some of Jimmy Gleason's friends—you know he died in an accident—have asked me to look into his death and I was surprised to find out he lived down here, that he and Ron occasionally shared a beach. Or almost anyway. So I've been talking to Cy Bitgood and Nan Levesque this afternoon and thought I might stop by here even though I know how you must be feeling."

"And you're surprised to see me in whites?" Louise Perry said. "I've never been one for pretense, Matt. If you knew me better you'd know that. Ron and I had what I would call a good marriage. Perhaps for the last few years it was more one of convenience than anything else. We lived different lives after a while. And we had hurt each other in ways it was difficult to overcome. Why am I telling you this?" Her smile had turned sad. Louise Perry was one of those women with the high cheekbones whose smile is enhanced by the crinkles that flare from their hazel eyes. "Maybe it's because you seem to really listen. Part of your job, I guess."

"I guess. I do appreciate any help you can provide."

"To catch a killer?" she said. "I hope you can do that, Matt. I'm not sure the police will. Still, I promise you I won't let this whole thing go away if I can help it."

"Do you still think someone killed Ron?"

"Absolutely. I think it was the Mafia and I don't think the murder will ever be solved."

"How can you be so sure?"

"They hated Ron because of the stories that were run in *The Bulletin* about them and there were personal reasons as well."

"I think I know what you're referring to."

"I suppose it doesn't matter now," said Louise Perry. "That was the final straw between Ron and me, however. A little hairdresser, for God's sake, an Italian one at that. I thought he had better taste than that."

"Actually, she's Portuguese."

"Same thing." She sniffed. Borg let it pass. Sipped his cocoa from a white mug. Delicious.

"There are some who think that Ron's death might have cleared the way for *The Bulletin* to be sold, that he would never have allowed it if he were alive."

Louise Perry sat up straight in her armchair so abruptly that she spilled a small spot of cocoa on her white sweater. The stain didn't spread. Instead it remained, sharply edged, almost like a bullet wound below her left breast.

"Who have you been talking to?" Louise pointed a beautifully manicured finger at him. "Certainly, there were some members of the family, cousins and such, who wanted a lot more than the dividends they were getting. I can't imagine any of them killing Ron. You know them, Matt. Can you imagine it?"

"I guess not, but some might. I've learned long since, Louise, that some awfully respectable people do some awfully bad things. Some might even suspect you, Louise."

"You've been talking to that awful Levesque woman, haven't you? She lives in her own world of mill owners and mill workers, the bad guys and the good guys. We're the bad guys and everything is always our fault. You know that her husband came back from the Vietnam War and killed himself. She says it was because there were no jobs at the mills or at the paper. Everyone with any sense knows it was something left over from that awful war. And her father turned to drink when the mills moved. Contrary to what she says, he was offered a job. Her father wouldn't move down south.

"You know, Matt, when I first came here from Boston, we tried to be friends. We even had a picnic at the Fourth of July for the townspeople on our lawn here. Hotdogs and hamburgers and those things. And you know what happened? They used the bathrooms and stole all my cosmetics. Can you imagine? Not even the jewelry. But cosmetics! That's how they think. Us against them. Workers against owners. It's left over from the nineteenth century, for God's sake. Maybe the whole state is."

"Maybe, Louise, and I've run into the same thing. But none of them stood to benefit from Ron's death."

"And I did? Perhaps I did. Then again, perhaps I benefited more by his life. Do you think any woman in her right mind would want to be a widow in this state, even a rich widow? At forty-four?"

He gave her a look. Who was she kidding. With her money and looks she'd be a catch. She didn't seem to notice and went on.

"I'm looking forward to a life of raising my two girls and probably dodging fortune hunters. And let me tell you, Ron Perry had his faults but he was a good father and tried his best to be a good husband. I honestly believe he was learning how."

"I guess that's the best that can be said of any man and I know how you're feeling, Louise. Don't underestimate yourself, however, and don't go fishing for compliments in my pond. You know you're a very attractive woman and a lot of money doesn't make you any less attractive." He wondered if she knew the details of her husband's will. He wouldn't put it past the shrewd Yankees involved to keep her in the dark. "Anyway, let's go on. Can you think of anyone else who might have wanted to kill Ron?"

"God, you're as blunt as ever." She took a breath. It ended in a sigh of exasperation. "To answer your questions as best I can, Ron had competitors like you, Matt. Frankly, they were not really a problem, too small to cause any real trouble. His struggle was against the economy and the future of the news-paper business. Those were his real enemies."

"Did you know the connection between Ron and Jimmy Gleason?" He emptied his mug. Funny how cocoa filled you up. A lot better than coffee or tea.

"That funny little man who died in the pressroom?" She shook her head. "Awful. Ron never took him seriously. Skulking around for years, working at *The Bulletin*. Probably even imagined Ron didn't know. He was a threat only to himself, as it turned out."

"Did you know he used to go fishing on First Beach and could see this house pretty well from there? Used to watch you play tennis."

"Hope he didn't expect to learn anything about tennis from me. Especially a backhand."

"I'm sure your backhand wasn't on his mind." Borg smiled at her and she returned a laugh, a small laugh but a laugh nonetheless.

"I guess I should be flattered," she said. "Thanks, Matt, I guess."

He let it go, looked out the window at the Bay. Situated on the tip of a peninsula, the Perry summer house had a water view from three sides. Finally he shook himself free from the weariness and torpor the fire and cocoa invited. This wasn't a social call in spite of how smoothly Louise Perry tried to make it one.

"Bill Hasner would seem to come out of this pretty well."

"You can't think Bill would hurt Ron. They were best friends ever since college."

"And what did you think of Bill? You played tennis with him, didn't you?

"That was it. If you're trying to imply something else, you're dead wrong. I never much liked Bill Hasner, if you want the truth. Thought he took advantage of Ron's friendship. Bill's no killer, though. An operator, maybe, and an opportunist, but no killer."

"He got around, I hear." Borg hesitated and then figured what the hell. "Used to go out on Mayor Fragnoli's boat, I hear."

Louise Perry's eyes flashed open and her jaw dropped. In a flash they shut closed, then opened to look as normal as ever. If you weren't watching closely you might have missed the whole thing. Borg was watching closely.

"Actually." Louise squeezed it out from between clenched teeth, repeated it again, "Actually, I went out on the Mayor's boat myself once. The Mayor had asked Ron and Bill and me. Ron couldn't make it, so Bill and I went. We talked about the paper, if you must know."

Cute. Ron couldn't deny any of it and the Mayor wouldn't either. Too clever to remember any details of the cruise as well. Knowing what was good for him, Peeps would have forgotten too. Now, Louise Perry was in no mood to continue the conversation. She rose and so did Borg and she led him to the door.

"Matt, I hope you're not going to stir up a lot of muck," she said to him as he stepped onto the cold granite from the steps. "I wouldn't have thought that of you."

"Try not to, Louise," he said. He didn't add that a lot of people believed that was his business.

CHAPTER 36

Frankie Levesque drove his old mail truck, painted blue, the same pure color as the sky, a color to break your heart. Frankie pulled up behind Borg's Caprice before he had a chance to drive away from Isle de l'Espoire. Borg got out of his car and went back to the truck. Frankie was getting out with two brown bags in his arms.

"Delivering the mail, Frankie?" said Borg. "Remember me? I used to see you around *The Tribune*. Matt Borg's the name."

Frankie Levesque looked puzzled for a moment. Then he smiled as recognition dawned. He put the bags back on the driver's seat of the truck and shook hands. He was almost as tall as Borg, comfortably over six feet, and at least twenty-five pounds heavier. A strong man with the smile of a child.

"No, Frankie's not delivering mail, Mr. Borg," he said, taking the question seriously, thoughtfully. "Just run some errands for Mrs. Perry. She was short of things so she called Frankie. I picked up her list. Heard you was at the General Store."

"I asked because of the mail truck," said Borg. "I was just kidding."

"Oh," said Frankie and, after a pause, he laughed. "My Mom bought this truck for me for when I deliver the paper. I drive and put the paper in the tubes just like a mailman."

"Real handy with the wheel on the same side as the curb," said Borg. "How have you been, Frankie? Know what you're going to do with Mr. Perry gone?"

"I been good, Mr. Borg, try to listen to my Mom. We'll figure out something for me to do."

"Maybe Mr. Hasner will need a driver, Frankie."

"No, no. Mr. Hasner doesn't like Frankie much."

"That's too bad, Frankie. I'm sure you'll be all right."

"I hope so, Mr. Borg. But it's bad since the mills went away."

That was fifty years ago, Borg wanted to say. Before you were born, Frankie. But he didn't say it. It might just confuse the issue. And confusion would not help Frankie Levesque. Besides that, he wasn't the only one who lived with the memory of the mills haunting him. Not in this state. Better to go on.

"Frankie, did you know Jimmy Gleason?"

Levesque thought for a minute. Looked down at his shoes, heavy black shoes that went with his black slacks. Over his white shirt he had on an open yellow parka. He smiled at Borg.

"Mr. Gleason fished down on First Beach." There was a pause. "Never caught no fish."

"That must have been a disappointment for him."

"Didn't seem so. Didn't seem he thought he'd catch any fish."

"Did you catch any fish down at First Beach, Frankie?"

"I did. You have to be patient. Frankie's a good fisherman, Mr. Borg."

"Did you talk much to Mr. Gleason?"

"Some. Not much. Mr. Gleason would move away if I got too close. Like he was afraid I'd take some of his fish. I wouldn't take his fish. You know that, Mr. Borg." Then he smiled. "Mr. Gleason didn't have none."

"So you and Mr. Gleason just stood and fished?"

"Yes," said Levesque. "And he would look over at Mr. Perry's house."

"Did you look too, Frankie?"

"Frankie would, Mr. Borg. Frankie liked to see Mrs. Perry play tennis. She's pretty."

"Very pretty, Frankie."

"She played with Mr. Hasner."

"Did they play a lot?"

"Yes. They liked it a lot, too."

"They did?"

Frankie giggled and put his hand to his mouth. "They had fun. They would laugh. They liked playing."

"I guess so. You must miss Mr. Perry."

"Frankie never had an accident with Mr. Perry's car. Frankie liked to drive and he kept it clean. Never a mark on the car."

"You'll miss driving it for Mr. Perry?"

"Frankie likes to drive. Mr. Perry is gone now."

"Did Mr. Perry ever say anything to you, Frankie, about you not driving for him anymore?"

Frankie Levesque looked puzzled. His mouth dropped, then hardened. Borg could see him putting words together before he spoke them.

"My Momma says not to talk about that stuff. I keep his car as clean as I can. I never had an accident."

That was going nowhere without Mama Bear being present to give approval. Borg changed direction back to Gleason.

"So you saw Jim Gleason around a lot, Frankie?"

Frankie perked up, glad to get away from Ron Perry.

"Frankie never drove Mr. Gleason. Mr. Gleason always drove himself. Mr. Gleason always walked by himself, too. He was alone a lot."

"That must have been sad."

"My Momma says sometimes it's good to be alone. Sometimes people are mean and bad. It's better to be away from them. I always do what Momma says."

Borg was about to ask who Mrs. Levesque found to be mean and bad when the door to the big house opened and Louise Perry was there.

"Frankie, do you think you would like to bring those groceries in, now?" she asked, smiling a thin smile.

"It was my fault," said Borg. "Don't blame Frankie. I was just asking him a few questions."

"Oh, I wasn't blaming Frankie," said Louise Perry. "Not at all. I do want the groceries though. Goodbye now, Matt."

"Goodbye, Louise."

CHAPTER 37

"So Louise Perry and Bill Hasner liked tennis so much they laughed and probably hugged during their games," said Donna when Borg called her to review his afternoon. She cackled. "Wonder what they did in the shower?"

"Anyway, it sure doesn't sound like she disliked Hasner as much as she said she did," said Borg. "And no one said they hugged."

"Isn't that what you people do after you play?"

"I think we want to be careful about Louise Perry. All we have is insinuation."

"You're right, but we don't have much more about anybody, Donna said. "Anyway, we've had a busy day. Bitgood and Nan and Frankie and Louise Perry. Canvassed Little Bay. Talked to Mrs. Black too."

"She voiced the family line. Fine old stock and all that stuff. They just don't do things like murder."

"Believe her?"

"I like a lot of people I don't believe. You talked to Pat Doyle, right?"

"I like him," said Donna.

"This is beginning to sound like a goddamn popularity contest." Borg laughed a tired laugh. "I didn't like Big Nan very much if that makes you feel better. Listen, I'm hanging up. I've got an early morning."

"Thanks for the information," said Donna and sighed. "Now I've got a meeting with the Colonel to bring him up to date. Talk to you tomorrow."

"Good night," said Borg. No promises about the next day.

Donna had called from her office, one down from the office of the commander of the state police, Colonel James T. 'Rocky' Rockingham. Her office of three years was as bare as a newborn baby. Nothing on the green walls and only a family picture shared the phone on her standard metal desk. Two metal chairs faced the desk. Not a home away from home.

At her home in Arctic earlier, Al had grilled hamburgers, a favorite of the kids, and cooked peas and carrots and mashed potatoes. For dessert he served them brownies. Donna, a worrier, liked her burgers well-done to burn out any microbes. She was convinced all meat needed scorching. The kids followed suit. On the other hand, Al knew in his cook's heart that beef should be medium rare. Donna was tired of the argument.

"You think the government would let them sell bad beef?" Sarah had asked her father.

"Where you been?" he shouted back at his daughter. Both looked at Donna to referee. She got up and retired to the bathroom. When she got back the argument, if there was one, it had gone away and dessert had been served. The brownies were delicious, hot from the oven, melting in your mouth. She had to drag herself away after a cup of coffee to return to State Police Headquarters, a fifteen minute drive.

Donna counted the twenty steps she took to her boss's office. More than twice the size of her own, it shared the same approach to interior design. A family picture and phone on the desk. One difference was that between two big windows behind the Colonel there hung a certificate from the FBI. No one in the state police had ever asked him what it stood for. Donna took one of the uncomfortable chairs the Colonel waved her into.

He was as always. White shirt as crisp as morning, white hair in a brush cut so short his scalp shone through, eyes the same color as the pewter cream and sugar set an aunt had given Donna as a wedding present. As lifeless. That wasn't fair. But cold. He sat straight in his chair, elbows on the arm rests, hands clasped before him. No papers, no distractions.

During a shootout at a restaurant when the Colonel was a rookie state cop years before, he had shot dead three men attempting a robbery. He had used only three bullets from the clip in his standard Army Colt .45. He had never explained what he was doing at the restaurant. "Stake out" was all he said. He was the only person Donna was afraid of. Aside from her mother, of course.

"Well?" he asked.

Donna as briefly as possible told him what had been done, how the suspects lined up: Hasner and Louise Perry, Angela and Ralph Rosso, less likely the mob, someone who knew the press room of *The Bulletin*.

"Murder then?" The Colonel didn't move.

"I think so."

"Need help?"

"Not so far."

"May I make a suggestion?" It wasn't a suggestion or a question. Both knew it. The Colonel issued orders.

"Yes, sir."

"Let's wind this up one way or the other. Soon. Talk to Jerry Zampato. Talk to the Doyle boys again."

She had just questioned Pat Doyle. And why Jerry Zampato? But she got the message. Leave the Perrys alone. Don't stir up any mud from the state's pond of wealthy and powerful.

"Yes, sir."

"You carry a heavy load with the family and your job," said the Colonel as he rose to indicate the meeting was over.

"I can handle it," said Donna.

"I know that," said the Colonel. "Or you wouldn't have the job." And he swung his chair around to look out his window at the woods behind the headquarters of the state police. He had seen a fox slink past the day before with a squirrel in its mouth. Vixen taking food home for her kids. Thought of Pacheco. Smart as a fox that one. You didn't need to draw a map for her.

CHAPTER 38

"There's a lot of pent up emotion there," said Alex. "As usual in your little, repressed state."

Borg had returned her call from London where she was still auditioning possible pirates. He looked out on the Bay, watched seagulls hover in a brisk breeze and two boats taking advantage of the wind that filled their sails. He put his feet up on the table that sat within the "L" of his couch, settled in for a conversation. The pirates came first.

"I like British actors so much more than Americans," she had said, almost as soon as she picked up the phone. "For one thing, they drink more. Maybe because of that they take themselves less seriously. I think they're influenced by the Welsh and Irish. I guess they're all Brits, aren't they? Anyway they are a funny and charming lot."

"How about your American boy director?"

"He's a royal pain in the ass, as you might expect. Keeps asking these guys about their motivation, for God's sake. Most of them have played Shakespeare and studied at the Royal

Academy and this guy has made a couple of MTV spots and he's asking about motivation. I think he read a book about Stanislavski once."

"A little knowledge is a dangerous thing."

"Thanks for that pearl. Anyway, it's funny to watch these actors put him on. He doesn't suspect a thing of course."

"And you're not telling him?"

"I'm not sure he'd believe me if I did he's so full of himself. How can a guy who's making a movie that's really just about a Disneyland ride take himself so seriously? It's beyond me. The money's good, however, and I don't want to lose sight of that. Anyway, enough about this fool. What's going on with you?"

Matt Borg told her about his paper's continuing struggle to stay alive—Easter advertising had been even weaker than in previous years.

"When do people spend their money if not at Easter?" she asked.

"Halloween is now the second biggest holiday after Christmas."

"What does that say about America?"

"That we like masks better than bonnets? I haven't the slightest idea. One thing is for sure: People don't get dressed up for church anymore and that makes a real difference."

"They do get dressed up for Halloween?"

"Absolutely. And undressed as well. You should see some of the slave girl outfits they're selling at a store right down the street from *The Times*."

"Speaking of which, how's that porn case going?"

"As you'd expect, this being an election year. The attorney general, Attila the Nun, is promising a crusade, which will probably be as effective as most crusades, in that it will probably get her re-elected."

"You love to say that Attila name business, don't you? Well, I like Hilda, even though I only met her once."

"So do I. She's a lousy administrator and too enthusiastic, but she's mostly honest and on the side of the angels, which is what you'd expect from a former nun, I guess."

"How about the death of that publisher? You and that sexy little lieutenant involved in that?"

"I am helping out a little bit mostly because there's been another death, this time a pressman named Jim Gleason. Fell into *The Bulletin*'s new presses. Or they say he fell anyway. The head of the union asked me to nose around a bit. I owe him and he can help make or break *The Times*, so I am."

"Is there a connection between the two deaths?"

"I think so, even though there's no hard evidence to suggest it."

"To do with the newspaper?"

"I'm not sure. One way or another probably."

"And so you're working with that Donna again?"

"Guilty, I guess. Both the Colonel of the State Police and Donna asked me to help out and honestly, Alex, it gets me away from the paper for at least a few hours. And I like puzzles. Maybe that's why I like you."

"Because I'm a puzzle?"

"No," said Borg, and provided a dramatic pause. "Why you love me is a puzzle."

"You old smoothie. Anyway, I hope Donna and you keep a distance."

"Will you cut it out? She's happily married with three kids."

"That never stopped anyone before . . ."

"Maybe not in Hollywood . . ."

"Maybe not anywhere. All right, all right. I'm just kidding. It sounds as though there's already enough hanky panky involved in the death of the publisher, though. Still, you and Donna sure seem to find reason to get together."

"Come on."

"You know, a wise man I know, probably an underpaid writer, once told a dinner party I was at that the most important thing in the world was relationships."

Borg chewed on that for a moment, watched one of the sailboats begin to tack and one of the gulls begin a long, smooth descent to the sea.

"And that means what?" he finally asked Alex.

"It means your case sounds like a tangled web of relationships, some going back generations. That's all."

"And if we untangle the right one we might have a killer . . ."

"And maybe not."

"Thanks a lot. To focus on another relationship that I hope needs no untangling, you still coming in next Friday?"

"At about 9:30. And now I'm a little worried. I may bring some pirates."

"As long as you don't bring that director. I love you and can't wait to see you Friday."

"I love you, too," said Alex from London.

Borg went to the kitchen, poured a glass of Italian wine, one of the big reds from Tuscany, a Barola, and returned to sit for a few minutes and look at the water. He turned the lights out so he could better see the darkness of the Bay. There were lights in the parking lot of the state park across the inlet and the very occasional red and green flickering of boats moving slowly through the dusk that had fallen this early in the spring. His townhouse was at the mouth of the smaller bay that opened onto the larger Narragansett Bay so there was always traffic, fishermen and yachts and, on occasion, those damn noisy cigarette boats. Borg liked the traffic.

His conversation with Alex didn't go away. There had never been any formal declaration between them. Had there been an unspoken understanding of sorts? He hoped so. Yet assuming makes an ass of you and me. Especially in love. And they were apart a lot. They had to be with the weight of his job and hers. And the fact that she lived in Beverly Hills and he on the East Coast. He still found it hard to understand her interest in him when she had so much to choose from in California.

Still, Alex would be here on Friday, and that would be time to talk about all of this. They were adults, after all, though he knew from grim experience that maturity didn't necessarily wash away the most basic of emotions. Sometimes it even increased their pull. The damn truth of it was that he was in love with Alex but couldn't figure out a way for them to take a next step, to be together more, to grow their relationship. And there was Donna. She kept slipping into his thoughts. Impossible. Ten years younger. Married. With three kids. Forget about it.

He took another sip of wine, let it fill his mouth with its strength, and returned to a consideration of the case of the two deaths, one at the top of the newspaper pyramid, the other in the bowels of the pressroom. He agreed with Donna that the deaths were connected and that both were murders. And that someone at or connected to the newspapers had committed them. The murderer had to know his way around the pressroom, enough not to be noticed. And the murderer had to know Ron Perry's routine.

Louise Perry and Bill Hasner, Hasner especially, had to be at the top of the list. Both would benefit from Perry's death, at least a little, no matter what Anne Black said. Both had been watched by Jimmy Gleason and Gleason might well have seen something. If they were lovers that made them even more likely suspects. Borg couldn't discount Ralph, the husband of Angela. Or maybe even Angela herself. There's nothing more dangerous than a woman scorned—except perhaps a husband who's been cheated on. Even with a Mafia don looking over his shoulder, Ralph Rosso could have lost his temper. And Borg couldn't forget the guys who had threatened him in a dark alley of Arctic.

He had told Donna he would see if there were any rumors about *The Bulletin* being for sale. There were. Borg washed the glass and headed for the kitchen again for a quick salad. Then it would be on to his desk to work on some financial projections for his newspaper. He just had to find more revenue or layoffs were a necessity. He hoped he could sleep with this stuff rattling around in his head. Surprising himself, he did.

CHAPTER 39

Matt Borg didn't know whether April was the cruelest month. It sure was the one with the most sneezes. You didn't know what to wear. Put on a sweater and it was warm, leave it off and it was cold. He tried to outsmart Mother Nature, something he knew in his soul was impossible, by keeping sweaters at the office and even a scarf and an umbrella and overshoes.

Mother Nature won, of course. He had imagined that summer was on its way and the hardy cardigan had been taken to the dry cleaners and it was cold this morning. Almost freezing. He had spent Sunday walking a South County Beach and going over the books of *The Arctic Valley Times*. It had been warm and hazy.

This Monday the cold sneaked through the wooden frame of the old tenement in which *The Times* lived and chilled him as he sat down at his desk. He turned on the electric heater full force, shoved it under his desk, and looked up to see Aimee Solante looking at him.

"Wish I had an electric heater," the Managing Editor said.

"You've got a sweater and you're young," he answered. "I'll buy you another sweater for Christmas or your birthday."

"Young isn't an excuse for low wages and endless work and a freezing workplace," she said.

"It is in my book," answered Borg. "Now stop sniveling and tell me what's going on."

"Attila the Nun is arraigning the porno trio this morning in County Courthouse. Charges like public nuisance and something about endangering public morals. She told me she'd try to do it by 9:30 so we could get it in today's paper."

"You should have something anyway, a picture of the trio arriving for arraignment or something like that. Get the photographer back here as soon as he gets any kind of shot. He should know that anyway."

"I don't count on a photographer knowing anything, so I've already told him. Are you going to write anything about the Gleason and Perry deaths? People are eating it up. I think we're beating *The Bulletin* with our stuff. They're really walking on eggshells and you have a lot more behind-the-scenes stuff in your columns. The AP is picking it up with credit to us. I'm surprised *The Bulletin* hasn't complained about that."

"I think they'd just as soon not carry the ball on this one. Yeah, I'll write something. I may want to get out of here early again today."

"To sniff around? Are you turning into a super sleuth or something? And, if you do, can I have your electric heater?"

"Funny. Actually, I want to drive down to check on our Indian paper. What else have we got besides dirty movies for the paper?"

"The profiles of two more school committee candidates in the primary as our public service snooze. And we have a tip that there's something wrong at the sewage disposal plant and it may really stink up the Greenwood area this summer."

"That again? God, I know you live in Greenwood, but sewage plants usually smell just the way airports are noisy. If you live near one you have to expect that. I'm sure you'll look into it, however, no matter what I say."

"Damn right. I've got to get going on this arraignment. Let me know when the column's written."

"Will do. Now get out of here and do some work. It will warm you up."

Aimee left, muttering under her breath, and he turned to face his word processor. Actually, writing about the case helped him in trying to solve it. Put something in simple declarative sentences and clarity emerged. You couldn't write clearly if you weren't thinking clearly. So he tried to do both before he would change hats from editor to publisher, from the editorial side of the operation to the business, advertising, and circulation.

What did he know? What could he write and still obey the primary law of journalistic truth, that it be limited and verifiable? At least that was the old rule. Well, two men were dead, both by way of suspicious accident. The homicide lieutenant of the State Police was looking into the deaths, adding to the questions surrounding the cases. Could he find out if *The Bulletin* might be sold? Usually newspapers didn't print anything about other newspapers. Professional courtesy or fear of giving anyone or anything free publicity? He didn't know but if the only statewide newspaper was going to be sold it was big news regardless of whether the two men had been murdered. One more newspaper with distant, absentee ownership.

No broker would tell Borg anything about a possible sale. At least no reputable broker. There was one person Borg could call. Jerry Malloy was often quoted in *The New York Times* and

The Wall Street Journal as a media expert and broker though, to Borg's knowledge, he had never been responsible for selling anything. He had a rich wife, however, was at all the newspaper conventions, and was the only man Borg knew who wore a driving jacket and shoes until he arrived at his destination and then changed into his business attire. Borg remembered Malloy once going through this act in a Connecticut mill town where a small daily newspaper was for sale. The paper was probably worth less than the shoes and jacket Malloy changed into. The paper finally went out of business without ever changing hands. Malloy was also a great gossip and made it his business to know about everything. Borg liked him. Then again, like Holly Golightly, he appreciated real phonies.

Malloy might also be available at 8:00 in the morning since he worked from his home in Westport, Connecticut. And was an early riser. Or so he said. As it turned out, he was telling the truth.

"Jerry Malloy here," Jerry said, in a robust baritone.

"Matt Borg here, Jerry."

"Nice to hear from you. Finally getting around to selling that paper of yours? I could drive up to talk to you tomorrow."

"Not quite yet, Jerry. I'm looking for some information. Won't credit you unless you want to be. To get to it, have you heard anything about *The Bulletin* being up for sale?"

There was a pause, which was unusual enough when you were talking to Jerry Malloy. Usually he filled any gaps with patter so inconsequential that small talk would be a flattering description.

"What have you heard?" asked Malloy right back at Borg.

"Come on Jerry, we've known each other too long and too well for you to play games with me. You know I won't repeat what you say. Now, what have you heard?"

Another pause. Was Jerry recalling their long friendship? Was Jerry recalling the time at a convention when Borg had found him at a hotel bar with an airline stewardess (An attendant now, though stewardess more accurately described the blonde Jerry was with)? Borg had kept his mouth shut about it and Jerry had expressed his gratitude more than once. Jerry also just loved to share what he knew.

"It can't come from me." A pause to add importance to the information whether it deserved it or not. "A possible sale of *The Bulletin* has been discussed for several months. Very big money."

"For several months? You sure?"

"For several months."

"Know any of the players?"

"The usual suspects. Gannett. Knight-Ridder. In this case, *The New York Times*, but I hear there's an outfit in Oklahoma that wants it most of all."

"How come?"

"Because *The Bulletin* owns some radio and TV stations in the Southwest that would be a perfect fit for the Oklahoma company. I don't know how that happened but they have them. And *The Bulletin* itself could be trimmed down, you and I both know, to be much more profitable."

"I can hear the news staff squealing already."

"I hear that discussions were at a very preliminary stage. Your former boss was the fly in the ointment. Now he's a dead fly, of course."

"Makes sense. So his death would clear the decks or purify the ointment or whatever metaphor you want to use."

"You mix the metaphors, my boy. I'm just a simple broker."

"Know any more about this deal?"

"Just that the money involved is very big and your friend, Bill Hasner, will come out of it very well."

"How so?"

"Word is that if he pulls it off, he'll be rewarded by the buyers for arranging it. A top management job for three to five years, probably publisher. And by the family members who want to sell it with a bonus."

"You don't know where the widow stands in all this, do you?"

"I don't have the foggiest, my boy, not the foggiest. Interesting question, though."

"Who's the broker handling all this, by the way?"

"Your friend, Van Ness Brown. Don't mention my name, I repeat. And he won't tell you anything, you know."

"Yes, I do. Thanks a lot, Jerry. Look forward to seeing you at the next publishers' gathering."

"See you then and keep me in mind if you change your mind about selling. Not many independent dailies left, you know. Prices keep going up."

"I always keep you on my mind, Jerry. Thanks."

So there was plenty of money involved with Ron Perry out of the way. Anne Black was wrong about Bill Hasner not benefitting. She obviously put family before truth. He couldn't blame her for that. Or wouldn't, anyway.

Borg had enough to work something about the possible sale into a column. Near the top. It would raise *Bulletin* hackles, he knew. Well, what the hell, wasn't it journalism's job to afflict the comfortable and comfort the afflicted? That's what they said in journalism school, anyway. Of course, none of the professors at "J-School" ever had to meet a payroll.

Borg was reminded how lucky the professors were in their ivory towers during his first publisher's meeting of the morning.

It came after he had finished his column and sent it off to Aimee.

Bob D'Orio was always optimistic, so optimistic at times you had to remind yourself of reality with a good hard look at the advertising lineage figures. Bob was the marketing and advertising manager, typical in almost every way, a nice guy who drove the composing and business departments nuts. He handed his ads in late, after deadline, and was always trying to give advertisers a price lower than the rate. "Off the rate card," as the business manager said, quite rightly, always adding, "Why do we have a card if Bob doesn't pay any attention?"

"Matt, can we get some stories in the paper about the new car dealership on Route 2?" Bob began. "It will open in a week or so. Could be big bucks."

"Bob, the last time you told me that, we ran three stories about a new indoor tennis bubble and we didn't get a cent in advertising out of it. What makes you think this Korean car company will be any better? Who are they going to sell their cars to anyway?"

"They tell me college kids are their target. We have a lot of community college kids here."

"Bob, those kids are struggling for tuition. They buy old Volkswagon bugs. If these guys are counting on them they won't be around in a year. And, by the way, as new advertisers, make sure you get the money up front."

Bob D'Orio smiled. He was always agreeable, which is what made him such a good salesman. He was also a poor collector of money from advertisers, which made him the bane of the business department. After D'Orio, there was Art Bottlebaum, who was a real estate broker while also serving as circulation manager. As he pointed out to Borg, the jobs really were compatible. He knew about new residents in the area and he was out on the road almost always. Besides which, for what he was paying Bottlebaum, Borg couldn't do any better.

"I've got to get out of here," Bottlebaum said as he sat down. He had a bushy mustache, hair to match, and an edge. He's probably making more money than me, Borg thought to himself. Bottlebaum went on, "We have two carriers who have called in to quit and a driver who quit last night. So I have to take his place and maybe deliver the routes for the carriers, too."

"Then get out of here," Borg said. He was spending his morning ordering people out of his office. They seemed happy to comply.

Rosie O'Neill was next in line. The business manager was, as always, a few minutes late. She had dark hair, was just over five feet tall, pretty, and had a mind as sharp as a razor. She watched his money more closely than he could.

"I have to finish out the month," she said. "So if you don't have much I'd like to get going."

"Everybody is dying to get out of my office this morning," said Borg.

"Just this morning?" O'Neill laughed. "Listen, will you remember to turn off that heater when you leave the office. It costs money, you know."

"I thought maybe I'd let Aimee take it."

"Let her wear a sweater. She's young."

His wasn't the only cruel, cruel heart in the room. "That's what I told her. How does the month look, by the way?"

"Not too bad," said O'Neill. "We did pretty well on the spring circulation drive and the special sale we promoted for garden advertising. I've got to go. Oh, by the way, could you speak to someone about the Perry things you're writing?"

"Sure, what's up and who is it?"

"Roland Alves. He's a cousin of mine."

"Know why he wants to see me?"

"He was seeing one of the Perry girls."

"All right." Borg said it out loud. He felt like rubbing his hands together in surprise and satisfaction. Sometimes good things happened even in newspapers.

"So you'll talk to him?"

"Absolutely."

"I'll send him up."

Borg hadn't given any thought to who the Perry girls dated. Maybe he should have. He'd soon find out.

CHAPTER 40

"Wait a minute, I know you," Borg said as Roland Alves walked into his office. The fisherman was about five nine or so, but looked wiry and strong in a black turtleneck and jeans, an Arctic High School orange football jacket, and short black rubber boots.

"From the fish store," said Alves. "Flounder. Small to medium pieces to fill your frying pan, right?"

"Right," said Borg. "I never knew your name. So you're the guy who was seeing Samantha Perry?"

"I hope I still am."

"Your cousin tells me I should talk to you and, by the way, I trust her judgment maybe more than my own. What's on your mind?"

"I wanted to get some things off my chest. I didn't want to go to the police because I don't know if what I have to say really matters and I don't know anyone on the State Police force. My cousin Rosie says you're a straight shooter and I can trust you."

"Hold on," said Borg, searching his memory. "If you're an Alves, isn't there some connection to the Pachecos?"

"My mother is a Pacheco."

"So you're related to Lieutenant Donna Pacheco?"

"Distant cousins and not on the best of terms. You know how families are."

"Yup," said Borg even though his only sister lived on the other end of the country and didn't like him much. He knew the state though, and the edge was always who you knew. No wonder the Mafia flourished here. First you trusted your family, next you trusted friends, and then there was everyone else. Well, sometimes that was useful. Like now. Good government suffered in the process. Right now Borg put that thought aside.

"If Rosie says you can trust me I guess you can," said Borg. Or you wouldn't be here, he thought to himself.

"I wanted to tell you about Mr. Perry and that family," said Alves. "Mostly because I don't think anyone else will say anything and I think there'll be a cover-up."

"I have to tell you if there's something important to the investigation I may have to tell the police—your cousin, Donna, as a matter of fact."

"That's OK. I need someone else's judgment first, though. To begin with I have to tell you that Ron Perry was a bad guy."

"There are a lot of people who would disagree with you, especially since you're obviously a prejudiced witness. He didn't want you to see Samantha, did he?"

"No, he didn't and that's part of it. He was against it because I'm Portuguese. The guy was a bigot. Against Italians, Jews, Portuguese."

"Maybe he just thought you weren't good enough, that you were a fortune hunter," said Borg.

"Listen, I'm not poor. We have three fishing boats, my brothers and me, the big market down in Bethlehem, the small market near you and we supply about half the restaurants in the state with their fish. I couldn't buy *The Bulletin*, but nobody's going to have to put on a tag day sale for me."

"Maybe Perry just didn't like fishermen," said Borg and smiled. "The smell or something."

"I'll let that pass," said Alves, bristling. Borg couldn't blame him. It was a stupid thing to say. Sometimes his big mouth got no help from his brain. No wonder people were fleeing his office.

"What I wanted to tell you is that the Perrys were not all they seemed. You've got to know he was playing around and people said so was his wife. They were so holier than thou and so was their newspaper. That was all a show. They did pretty much what they wanted to do while they tried to make everybody else toe the line."

"Like Samantha?"

"Especially Samantha. It was driving her crazy. I know she loved me." Roland Alves stopped for a moment, took a breath. "She loved her parents, too. The family is important to her."

"Doesn't sound good for you two. Have you seen her since the death of her father?"

"Just once. Tuesday night we had dinner at the Lakeside. You can get lost in that place. We had a chance to talk. I don't know what's going to happen. I know I still love her."

"I hate to tell you this, my young friend, but true love doesn't conquer all in spite of Walt Disney." God, he could be pompous. "By the way, how did you know that Ron Perry was cheating?"

"Angela's husband works right down the highway from here, at Zampato's. Didn't you know that?"

"No, I didn't as a matter of fact," said Borg. "How about Mrs. Perry?"

"Samantha thinks she was cheating with Bill Hasner. All that tennis and kissy facing. Samantha thought it went beyond that. She had an awful fight with her mother one time, probably about me, and accused her of cheating on her dad. Her mom just cried, said she was surprised Samantha would believe such a thing. Samantha came out of it feeling like hell, kind of agreed with her mother. Things haven't been the same between them since."

Borg was beginning to think that he and Donna should turn this whole investigation over to the fisherman. Maybe he could throw out a net and keep the best suspects and throw back what he didn't want. Borg liked the kid. He sounded like an American success story, a little bit like Borg himself. He hoped fishing was doing better than newspapering. Way back when the country was young it was probably a kid like this one who started the Perry family fortune. Borg remembered that the first Vanderbilt began his climb to fame and fortune from a ferry boat he sailed from Staten Island to Manhattan. Probably did a little fishing, too.

"You obviously knew about Angela Rosso," said Borg.

"Sure. Perry didn't give a damn about where he dropped his line. He wasn't taking that catch home with him, you can count on that. Damn lucky he didn't get killed fishing around there."

"Maybe he did," said Borg. "Jealousy can be a strong motive." He looked at Alves with what he hoped was a piercing and searching gaze. Probably didn't work but what the hell.

"Maybe," Alves answered. "Anyway, there was enough cheating in the Perry house to go around. Just wanted you to know about it."

"I appreciate it," said Borg. "And I like your fish a lot. Freshest flounder anywhere."

"Any fish—if it's fresh—just filet it and throw it on a pan with some butter and you can't beat it," said Alves. With that, the conversation was over and Alves was out of his chair. Not before a final question by Borg.

"Before you leave," he said. "You have to tell me how you and Samantha met. It has nothing to do with this case, but I'm curious."

"Hard to believe, isn't it? She was down by the shore last summer and was taking some out-of-state friends around, showing them places like Bethlehem, which is a cutesy little fishing village if you're not working there. Anyway, they came into our market where I was working a counter. We got to talking about the kinds of fish we had. I guess she was surprised that I had a degree in oceanography from the university. The next thing I knew I was showing her friends and her one of our fishing boats and how it operates. The next week I took her out on one of our working trips and that was how it started."

"So she can handle the smell?" Borg smiled but kicked himself. God, he was an ass. This time Alves took it better.

"I guess so." The fisherman was smiling as he left the office.

Borg called Donna Pacheco as soon as the fisherman disappeared down the stairs. He told her about Ralph Rosso and where he worked. And about his talk with the newspaper broker and Donna's cousin, the fisherman. He waited a minute, let her digest what he had said.

"So you think Mrs. Perry and Hasner were getting it on?" said Donna. "And that the paper is gonna be for sale. Their motivation just jumped a notch. Think the fisherman is straight?"

"I do," said Borg. "But I don't believe Louise would cheat on Ron. "

"You're a romantic . . ."

"Maybe, or maybe I just know people."

"Anyway," said Donna, "I'm on my way to see Zampato now." Her voice turned official, "At the Colonel's suggestion. I should have asked Angela or your two thugs where Ralph Rosso worked. Lousy police work on my part. Maybe that fisherman is a better cop than I am."

Borg laughed. "I thought the same thing about Alves and me," he said. "Don't be too hard on yourself. You've got a lot on your plate."

"I can handle it," she said. It sounded like a credo.

CHAPTER 41

Jerry Zampato could only happen in a state as small as this one. At least that's what Donna thought as she drove down Route 2. Then again, she didn't have much experience anyplace else. Maybe Zampatos happened everywhere. Not as many people would know about it though. On a small stage a guy like Zampato could look big.

Zampato had first come to Donna's attention and everyone else's some years before when Zampato's partner in their construction company stole his wife. Not only was the guy a partner, he was also Zampato's best friend. Or so Jerry thought. Most men might have been ashamed. Not Zampato. The case caused some noise when Jerry tried to beat his partner up on the exit ramp of a parking garage, Zampato went on a national TV show to explain himself. Donna still had a tape of the show. Then he ran for the town council in Arctic. He won. He married a model. Blonde.

Zampato was a six-footer with a smile that could blind you and a mop of black hair. He was cheerful and charming. To

Donna he looked more like the guy who would steal a wife rather than lose one. He made a lot of money using ex-convicts in his construction projects. They were cheap labor and gave his company the stain and advantages of mob connections. Since everyone assumed that all construction companies had mob connections anyway, the fact that Jerry openly carried crooks on his payroll added to his reputation. What his reputation added up to no one quite understood.

Jerry had moved onward and upward after that, being smart enough to buy property along a road that turned busy almost overnight. He built strip malls and his own offices. After he married the blonde model (he made sure he had no partner this time in his business), he built a big house in East Fenwick. He didn't notice when some of the snobbish natives shunned him. Or he pretended not to. He built an even bigger summer house on Block Island, just off the coast. The last time Donna had read anything about him, Jerry was telling newspapers and the TV that the President of the United States was going to visit him on a day trip from Martha's Vineyard. That didn't happen, but Jerry rode the story for a week or so.

You couldn't miss Jerry's business. It was a one-story building with a three-story tower over its front door and a couple of columns to frame the entrance. A big white sign proclaiming ZAMPATO ENTERPRISES in large blue lettering hung over the door. A big parking lot was torn up and a crew of men with a small Cat earth mover were working on it. Donna parked her orange Datsun on the shoulder of the highway.

Donna picked her way between hunks of concrete freshly torn up and watched her high heels sink into the mud and dirt. They were new shoes. Nine West. Her mood was not improved by the gang of huskies who grinned, whistled, and called, "Hello, baby." Maybe later she'd say hello.

There was a blonde—what else?—at the reception desk and furniture that was all black and chrome. The blonde didn't pay much attention until Donna flashed the badge. Even then her glance was cool. Her hips swiveled inside her tight red skirt as she sauntered through the door behind her desk, closing it as she went.

She looked a little bit surprised and disappointed when she led Zampato back into the reception area. She actually sniffed when Zampato greeted Donna with a smile that bounced off the chrome and warmed the black leather chairs.

"Donna, it's great to see you," said Zampato. "I was just thinking I hadn't seen you in a while. Since I moved out of Arctic. Come on into the office and have a cup of coffee or something. Veronica, will you bring us two coffees and some sugar, honey?"

Donna knew that Zampato hadn't given her a thought since the developer moved out of Arctic. She also knew that like all good liars Zampato really believed what he said when he said it. He might even believe it for a while afterward. Not for long. They went down a hall of quiet beige walls and into an office large enough to garage one of Zampato's earth moving machines. Almost as soon as he sank into a too comfortable chair, Veronica Honey was handing him a mug of coffee and offering sugar and cream or milk from a tray.

"Pretty fancy," said Donna.

"Joel Swartzman decorated it for me," said Zampato. He must have noticed the look of incomprehension on Donna's face.

"He did the New England Bank offices in Providence. I really liked them so I had him do these. What do you think?"

"Pretty fancy," said Donna. "A lot better than the trailer you used to work out of in Arctic."

"Hey, what a country, hah?" laughed Zampato. "You work hard, you make a buck, you get new furniture . . ."

"And Veronica Honey brings you coffee." Donna finished the sentence.

"You know, the thing I like about you, Donna, is that nothing much impresses you. At least I think I like it. Maybe I'm not so sure anymore."

"I hope you like it long enough to answer some questions."

"You got it."

"I'm investigating the deaths of Ron Perry and Jimmy Gleason. I hear that Ralph Rosso works for you. He may have something to do with it. How well do you know the guy?"

Zampato laughed. Big teeth and big dark eyes were aglitter. Watch the eyes and the hands. They say a lot. Also watch the feet. Zampato had his legs crossed as he sat facing Donna in a matching chair. The crossed leg was bouncing, almost doing a jig.

"Hey, he works for me and he's a friend," said Zampato. "What, you think because he's Italian he's got to be connected or something? Come on, Donna, I thought you knew better."

"Cut the baloney, Jerry," said Donna. "You know about Rosso's wife and Ron Perry and that Rosso isn't the kind of guy to like that much."

"Who would like that much?" Jerry looked directly at Donna, both recalling when Jerry's wife cheated on him and the time he tried to beat up his best friend because of it. Jerry sure had recovered. Or looked it anyway. You couldn't miss the tailored, button-down blue and white dress shirt he wore, sleeves rolled up to reveal a Rolex on one wrist and a gold chain on the other.

"Listen, Jerry, I'm not trying to nail anybody here. I'm just looking to answer some questions for myself."

"Unless Ralph's a killer, you mean."

"You're right on that. Now tell me about Ralph Rosso."

"Remember the definition of a caffone, a guy who no matter how expensive his suits and his shirts, you can still smell the shit on his shoes. Ralph's a diamond in the rough."

"How rough?"

"Pretty rough."

"What does he do for you, anyway?"

"Runs one of my crews. Makes sure things go right on the job. That the guys do what they're supposed to do. Does some union negotiations, if you know what I mean. He's good at it, very good. Listen, if you want to talk to him, let's go out back. He was out there checking changes made to his crew's schedule. I think he's still here."

They walked briskly down the hall and into a stark room that seemed to stretch the entire width of the building, with doors that opened onto the rear parking lot where pickup trucks and SUVs sat cheek by jowl. Desks were parked inside at random as were a couple of tables. Standing over one was a big, beefy man and a smaller one with glasses and a pullover vest and glasses. He was doing the talking and pointing at blueprints. Nobody at any of the other desks looked up.

"Hey, Ralphie, come over here for a minute, will you," Zampato called. Several men at the desks looked up and then looked down again. Fast. Ralph Rosso came over, bigger up close. He wore a lumberjack shirt of red and black, jeans, tan work boots, and a Red Sox baseball cap, bill out front.

"This is Lieutenant Donna Pacheco of the state cops," Zampato said to Rosso.

"I know who she is," said Rosso. When he reached out Donna reached deep into the handshake so that Rosso couldn't put a squeeze on her. She wouldn't put it past him.

"The Lieutenant has some questions for you," said Zampato.

"Maybe I don't have any answers for her," said Rosso.

"Maybe you better think harder," said Donna.

"Listen, Lieutenant." Rosso's jaw jutted out as he spoke. "I know you been sniffing around. Sniff someplace else. I was in church last Sunday morning and I got witnesses who saw me. I never been in *The Bulletin* in my life and I was at DaVinci's up on the hill the night the guy died in the presses. You want more, you talk to my lawyer, John Cicerine."

He turned and walked away. No one looked up from a desk and the clerk started talking and pointing as soon as Rosso returned to his table. Zampato smiled and patted Donna on the shoulder. She moved a step away.

"Diamond in the rough, what did I tell you," he said to Donna.

"Think that guy doesn't cheat?" Donna said. "Involved in porn and all the rest?"

"Ralph's a good guy and that's different."

"For men, right?" Donna stopped. Stupid. She didn't want to get into an argument about values and the different standards for men and women. Especially one in which neither side would even understand the other. She was just beginning to understand it herself.

So she took a breath, buried her temper, and looked to the end of the room. Two men working at back-to-back desks looked at her with wide eyes. Like kids caught cheating on a test. One of them had on a windbreaker with the Quonset Golf Club windbreaker. She'd let them off this time.

"It's great to see you, but I'm kind of busy," said Zampato, who had watched Donna and the glances exchanged with the two men. He began to click a ball point pen. "We've got to get together some time."

"Who are those guys at the end of the room, Jerry?" Donna asked, just to pull his chain.

"Just some of our crew," said Zampato, as he moved toward the door. "Nobody you would know."

"More diamonds in the rough?"

"You got it."

"One of them got a sore foot?"

"Could be."

"Listen, Jerry," Donna said at last as Zampato clicked the pen faster and faster. "You hear anything you let me know."

"Those two guys at the end of the room made a mistake going after Borg. They know it. Ralph made one sending them. You can go nuts with jealousy. I know that. But Ralph didn't kill Perry or the press guy. He's alibied up. Want some advice? Leave it alone."

"I'll think about it."

"You do that. I got work to do."

Zampato opened the door out of the big work room and almost trotted down the hall, into the reception room, and to the front door. Donna followed slowly enough so he had to hold the door for a while. She wouldn't let it be a bum's rush. Donna believed Zampato. She didn't think Ralph Rosso had killed anybody.

She still simmered enough that when the hunks outside in the parking lot whistled and one of them grabbed his crotch, calling out, "Want some of this baby?" she walked right at the four men by the tractor.

"Want some of this?" she asked, flashing her badge and opening her blazer to show the revolver in its belt holster. What the hell, throw a little fear into the bums, probably parolees, every one. Four grins dissolved. Shoulders dropped. Four heads wagged. Good enough.

"You don't want a disturbing the peace or sexual harassment charge, do you boys?" She probably couldn't make anything stick but they wouldn't know that. They wagged four negatives.

"OK then, behave, and don't make me talk to your parole officers." They nodded and she walked to her car. No whistles. No remarks. Donna was reminded of who she was. She liked it.

CHAPTER 42

Borg tried to focus on the Indian paper as he drove to see Quonset colleagues. *The Quonset Indian News* was almost a pure labor of love. Like most of those it was doomed to heartbreak.

Every week Borg motored down to Greenville, a ride of about 40 minutes, and spent time going over results and plans with Chief Roger Crandall and Evelyn Clear Creek, and whoever else was around.

Matt Borg wondered how many amateur sleuths had to worry about printing and delivering a 32-page tabloid to an Indian reservation every month. He was finding it hard to focus on *The Quonset Indian News*. The murders nagged him. So did his own struggling paper. And his relationship with Alex Cord occupied more of his heart all the time. There was also Donna, the wiseacre cutie pie with face and figure to match. He just plain enjoyed being with her.

He was on the old state highway, the one that had been replaced by a new federally funded road several years before. What had been predicted as a disaster for old Route 2 had turned out to be a blessing. Not only had Zampato relocated along the old road, but so had a number of restaurants and other businesses.

And on old Route 2 there was still Allie's, which was known for producing the best doughnuts in all New England. Every morning there would be a cluster of cars around the simple one-story white shop. Borg thought twice about stopping for doughnuts even though it was almost lunch time. He resisted. Nobody down at the Quonset Reservation needed another doughnut. Then again, the same could be said about almost everyone in this small state with the big waistlines.

So he cruised down the road, past fields where corn would be ripening in the summer, past the turnoff to the state college, past the shops that rented canoes and horses and even lawn mowers. Past the mill where they still ground cornmeal for johnnycakes and the best buttermilk pancake flour in the world. Soon he was driving through Greenville, a collection of motels, restaurants, and bait shops along the old Post Road.

His pastoral mood was shattered when he turned into the dirt road entrance to the Quonset reservation. Shouts and screams and sirens blasted the woods, State Police cars were everywhere, their lights flickering, their doors open.

Before them an entanglement of state police and Quonsets struggled in front of the one-story white frame building that served as the Indian lodge and all purpose store.

"Freedom," roared a huge Quonset. Borg recognized Running Bear, who had played nose tackle for the University of Rhode Island football team.

"Freedom Now," echoed a woman almost as tall but not nearly as hefty as Running Bear. She held a carton of cigarettes over her head. Deer in the Woods was on the Quonset Council and a croupier at the Pequot casino in Connecticut.

Reaching for the cigarettes had to be the shortest state policeman Borg had ever seen. A cousin of the Governor? Must be to have made the grade. As Borg watched, Colonel James T. Rockingham, in full uniform, his .45 strapped to his hip, strode over and took the carton from Deer in the Woods with a smile. He threw it in the nearest state police car. Then he noticed Borg getting out of his Caprice Classic and strolled over, deftly neglecting the struggle between his troopers and the Quonsets.

Slowly, the dust-up settled down, several young Indians throwing cartons at troopers and sitting down in protest. They were carried, arms still folded, to patrol cars.

"Selling cigarettes without paying state tax," said the Colonel. "Governor sent us down to stop it." He leaned up against Borg's car, relaxed while watchful. "Election year. Be over in a couple of minutes. Nobody wants to get hurt."

"Gonna raid the mob next and collect all the cigarettes they hijack and sell around here?" Borg wouldn't forget he was an honorary Quonset and the state police were invading his people's sovereign land.

"Thought you gave up smoking?" said the Colonel. "This'll give you a helluva story. Your Indian editor is over there shooting pictures. Smiling, as a matter of fact."

Evelyn Clear Creek waved to Borg as Chief Crandall came out on the porch of the lodge, his hands in the air, followed by three troopers, their arms full of cigarette cartons. He nodded at Borg.

Running Bear, after the scuffle, held up his handcuffs, posing for Evelyn Clear Creek. Bear obviously could have put several of troopers out of commission, especially the smallest one by his side. He put on his fiercest face for Evelyn.

"We'll book the Bear for resisting arrest or something and let him go," said the Colonel, anticipating Borg's question. "The others, too. No harm, no foul."

"The way you like it," said Borg. The Colonel volunteered a thin smile, and left Borg to amble toward the Bear, said a few words, and the big Quonset nodded and got into one of the patrol cars.

Within minutes the raid was history, the state police caravan roaring out of the reservation, carrying enough cigarettes to poison any wayward smokers left in the state. Chief Crandall and Evelyn Clear Creek came over to Borg.

"What's this all about?" Borg asked. "Colonel says the Governor ordered it."

"Yup," said the Chief. A walking, talking, living cliché, he looked just like Tonto in the old *Lone Ranger* TV and movie series, proving once again that life copies art. His Indian name was Strong Bull but a lot of people, even in his own tribe, called him Tonto. He hated that.

"They want to make sure we don't establish the kind of sovereignty that would help us build a casino," said Evelyn.

"And there's the election," said Borg.

"And there's the election," said the Chief.

"Well, nobody got hurt . . ." Borg began.

"The Colonel and the Chief saw to that," said Evelyn.

"And you've got one helluva story for the next issue," said Borg. "With pictures."

"And we lost one more little bit of our independence and sovereignty," said the Chief. He glanced at Evelyn, who was checking her camera to make sure the pictures were preserved. His shoulders drooped, his lips pressed hard together, he folded his arms.

"Let's get the hell out of here," said Borg. "I'll buy lunch and I'll drive you back here afterwards."

The Chief got into the passenger seat of the Caprice Classic and Evelyn into the back. Borg hated what he had just seen. The farcical nature of the confrontation, the cynicism, the awful ordinariness of it all. He had a feeling that this was the way liberties are eroded and the world accepts the small changes until large losses are inevitable and acceptance goes without quarrel. He also knew he had the ability to dramatize, to see more in situations than actually existed, to romanticize and build drama from chopsticks. Still, here was the Chief alongside him, quiet and grim.

Evelyn leaned into the front seat between Borg and the Chief, who leaned toward the window.

"There's a new restaurant on Route 1. He's taken out some advertising so I'd like to eat there and we can say hello to the owner."

"Good," said Borg. "Is the food any good?"

"We'll find out," said Evelyn as she put on her coat. The Chief looked at her and she withdrew to the back seat. Evelyn was a big, graceful woman with short curly brown hair, a kewpie face, and beautiful brown eyes in a face of burnt mahogony. Her other name was Evelyn Greeley but she used Clear Creek more and more. She acted a little bit silly at times, was just the opposite at her job. Instead, fiercely efficient, one of those women in their forties who return to the workplace and are hard to beat. They could tell the difference between wheat and chaff, could separate the two and make sure the good stuff was saved. Maybe even turned into pastry. Whether she was a good Quonset Indian she and Chief Crandall would have to work out.

The Chief hadn't said anything yet, just nodding at Borg about the restaurant. He'd say something when he had something to say. Or maybe not. Now he looked glum, heavy eyebrows accenting his black eyes, broad shoulders slumped in a denim jacket that had seen better days.

"We're having some trouble with the local weekly," Evelyn said to Borg once they were on the road. "Since they were bought out by that chain they've been cutting ad rates, even below ours. It doesn't make sense. Lots of things they're doing don't make sense. Our salespeople are screaming."

"You suggesting cutting our rates?"

"I just wanted to raise the question."

"It would be tough. We just gave the salespeople a new bonus schedule and the health insurance has gone up another twenty five percent. I'm not sure what we can manage."

"Well, think about it anyway. You know salespeople. They scream when a squirrel squeaks. I'll have a better idea of where we are after they finish selling for the spring special."

"Is this it?" asked Borg as Evelyn pointed to a stucco building. "Is it called 'Elmo's?' I never heard of a restaurant called Elmo's before. It's got to be the name of the owner, right?"

"You got it. Elmo Rosensteiter. And he specializes in Italian food."

Borg laughed. Then he laughed harder. Finally he was bent over the steering wheel of the Caprice Classic. Better than crying. He let it out. What a damned silly world he lived in. Actually a couple of silly worlds. He had just chatted with the Portuguese fisherman who was dating a Perry, watched the state police raid an Indian reservation, was about to break bread with an Indian Chief and eat spaghetti from a German chef.

"Better now than when you meet Elmo," said Evelyn as she watched Borg wipe his eyes. "He takes his meatballs very seriously."

The restaurant had a warm and welcoming reception area. The proprietor was standing behind the pretty blonde at the front desk. He was big and burly and had a walrus moustache and very blue eyes to go with his rosy cheeks. Elmo Rosensteiter looked like the perfect host—for a ski lodge.

"Forgive me, but I have to ask," said Borg as Evelyn gave him a questioning look. "How did someone who looks like you and has a name like Rosensteiter decide to start an Italian restaurant?"

Rosensteiter laughed. He laughed big. Almost as big as his moustache. "My mother was Italian, my father was Austrian. They met at a Chinese restaurant in New York. Now will you have anything to drink? We have a nice pinot grigio and an Austrian red you might like."

The spaghetti and meatballs were almost perfect, not cooked too much, juicy and tasty. He sipped a very good Austrian red, and turned to Evelyn Clear Creek and Chief Crandall to talk about their paper.

Evelyn took a small notebook from her purse, placed it on the table alongside her knife. She played with the tableware for a moment, long, blunt fingers moving the spoon and the fork.

"I don't think we're getting the delivery service we should," she said, pressing her lips together. "It's altogether too careless. Maybe we have to go back to the post office delivering them."

"Getting complaints?" Borg asked. "I mean even more than usual?"

"I've checked some of these out myself. The papers are all over the place and some are being blown around on the streets. At some point, the police are going to ask us to cut it out."

"I'll talk to Cliff," referring to Cliff Mondslaw, who was supposed to be delivering the Indian paper to mailboxes or onto the steps of houses.

"Matt, have you ever thought of us hiring our own guys to do it, maybe buying a used post office vehicle, you know, one of those small trucks with the driver's wheel on the right hand side to make deliveries easy? The government sells them off once in a while. I could check it out if you'd like."

"Do it, and thanks. I'm not committing to anything, though," said Borg. "You know we got out of the delivery business because it was just too much trouble keeping vans on the road. We paid high insurance rates and kept finding drivers who were cowboys and wrecked our vehicles."

"Well, I can promise we wouldn't use any cowboys." The Chief spoke for the first time and smiled as he did. "As Evelyn says, at least get on Cliff about it."

"I will and I'll also talk to him about looking into those post office trucks. I'll ask him to check with you. They make sense as delivery vehicles. I know he'll tell me that the post office pretty much uses them up before they're sold. You know, it's a funny thing, I ran into a guy out in Little Bay who has a used post office truck. He's got it all painted blue. Looks pretty good too."

"I'd like yellow for ours," said Evelyn. "Not red." She looked at the Chief.

"Knock it off, Evelyn." Borg laughed. Even the Chief smiled. When he saw that, Borg took a chance.

"Chief, I wonder if we could talk about your casino a little."

"Sure," said Crandall. "I hope you connect the raid today to the casino in your stories. Maybe separate stories in our next issue. We have suggested plans for the place and can get you interviews with the Vegas people with the money. I'd also like you to write it if you can." Borg shrugged, twisted his lips in question. At least the Chief was looking forward, shaking off the raid and its humiliation. Good.

"You've got the background on the area and the people," said the Chief to Borg. "One of your young reporters or one of our people just couldn't do the job we need. Your name on the story doesn't hurt either."

"You know I'd write it straight with quotes from the opposition?"

"We know," said the Chief. "We just want to make sure our side gets a hearing in our own paper."

"Fair enough," said Borg. "I'll find the time."

"One more thing," said the Chief. "Do you think we'll ever make any money on this paper?"

"I don't think so," said Borg. "Too much competition, not enough advertising base. All you can expect is what we talked about when we started it, a voice. If you get a casino, though, the paper will take off."

He didn't add that so long as the dream of a casino dominated the tribe, the newspaper would never get the support or focus it needed. He knew that at its best the paper couldn't match the profits of a single slot machine. So did anyone else who thought about it.

"I guess that has to be enough, then," said the Chief. "And while we're talking newspapers, is there anything new on Perry?"

"Not a thing," said Borg. "You hear anything?"

"Like you, I hear *The Bulletin* will be sold," said the Chief. "Soon."

"Where'd you hear that?"

"You know our backer for the casino is from Vegas," said the Chief. "They have connections in Oklahoma. They tell us the big Tulsa newspaper group is negotiating."

"Well, maybe you'll get a better hearing from them," said Borg.

"Maybe," said the Chief. He didn't sound hopeful. He had ordered ziti and spooned it. Borg wrapped his spaghetti around a fork as carefully as he could. An occasional spot of red sauce escaped anyway. Evelyn ate her eggplant lasagna in small bites, as careful as a good editor should be. Or a croupier.

The rest of the lunch was spent talking about salespeople and why they never managed to get their ads in on time and when they did they had the information wrong. Borg provided a shoulder for Evelyn to cry on. After venting, she would feel better about some problems—like the salespeople—which couldn't ever be solved and he would feel better about helping her get through the day.

Finally, Evelyn asked the waitress to put her remaining eggplant in a doggie bag. "How's the murder investigation going?" she asked as she stirred one spoonful of sugar into her coffee.

"I've been thinking about it driving here," Borg answered. "Basically, we've got two deaths. And we've got two couples, both may be playing around, and a ton of money and a ton of jealousy."

"Sounds easy," said Evelyn.

"Except the cops can't prove murder in either case." Borg took a sip of coffee. As good as the meatballs. "At least they can't prove anything yet. And the couples are tough to understand. At least for me."

"Most are," said Evelyn and turned to the Chief, sitting alongside her. "What do you think, Chief? You've looked into some crimes on the reservation."

Chief Crandall didn't answer at once, looked into Borg's eye in a searching way very few people did, like a hawk, his nose large and sharp as a knife, his cheek bones sharply etched in copper.

"Find the strongest emotions. Like in a stream. Which are the deepest, which flow fastest. Which have been flowing longest. Which will flow over its banks?"

Borg almost laughed. Didn't. Evelyn must have seen him twitch, though.

"Come on, Chief," Borg said. "That sounds like something out of a damn movie or a Buddhist monastery. Or from a medicine man . . ."

"Chief Crandall is also our medicine man," said Evelyn. She didn't laugh. Nor did she smile.

The Chief withdrew into silence. All three of them sipped their coffee. Evelyn and Borg exchanged small talk. She would send her notes to him and pictures as well for his story. The AP would pick that up. Borg was surprised no other news people had been present. Wondered why the Governor hadn't alerted everybody. Maybe he got cold feet at the last minute. Finally the discomfort ended and all three returned to the Caprice Classic for a quiet ride back to the reservation.

On his way back north, Borg regretted what he had said. Would he never learn to keep his mouth shut and his sense of humor to himself? He had known the Chief for several years and it seemed as though he had grown quieter year by year. Sadder too, maybe. Borg didn't think the casino had a chance in the world. The Indians, as usual, were outgunned and outnumbered.

And maybe the Chief was right. Maybe all Borg and Donna had to do was find the fastest flowing stream of emotion.

CHAPTER 43

There was a long, low whistle as Lieutenant Donna Pacheco of the State Police stepped inside the cavernous building that housed the new German presses. She was used to it. No short skirt this afternoon, though. Pants suit. Because she was visiting the production plant of *The Bulletin*, the brand new facility located on the fringe of the capital city.

Huge presses dominated the room, rows of them, standing quiet now. Looming powerful, powerful enough to spit out millions of copies of a newspaper in a single night. Donna had read about them in the special section of *The Bulletin* all about the new plant.

Power to put color on every page, she had read. Power to influence a state, to elect governors and senators. That she knew. Not that these presses would have to print a million. A couple of hundred thousand copies would do. The extra capacity was there if it was needed though. It meant the paper could expand, could print a dozen sections at once, could avoid the strain of printing to capacity every night, something many newspapers had to do. Actually, the stories in the special section of *The Bulletin* had told her more than she wanted to know. Still, it helped, she guessed. Better to know more than less.

"Can I help you?" It was one of the pressmen. If the presses looked different the pressmen who served them still looked the same as the ones she had seen at *The Arctic Valley Daily Times*. One of them, in light blue shirt and dark blue trousers, came walking over from a control panel to where Donna stood. He was a little bit taller than Donna, wiry with pepper and salt hair cut short and a smile that crinkled. He obviously knew about the charm of his crinkle. He was wiping his hands on a rag that was once white. Behind him in the presses Donna could see other pressmen in the shadows of the machines they served trying to look as though they were working. Near the door she had entered was a black Lincoln town car. Next to it was an old red Jaguar.

"I'm looking for Bill Hasner," she said.

"You won't find him down here. Except maybe for a tour. He's in the offices upstairs. You came in the wrong door."

She knew that but she wanted to see the place where Jim Gleason had died. She started to turn.

"Wait a minute. You can get upstairs to Hasner's office through here if you know the way. There's a door behind the presses. I'll show you."

Donna was used to having men do her favors. It helped. Even when she was investigating what might be a double murder case. She gave the pressman a big smile and introduced herself.

"I'm also looking for a Mike Doyle," she added. She offered her hand.

"I'm Mike Doyle," he said and held her hand a little too long. "I'm a foreman here. My brother Pat told me you're investigating the deaths of the publisher and our pressman, right?"

"Investigating may be too strong a word, Mr. Doyle. I'm just making sure we're not overlooking anything. You talked to Matt Borg about it, didn't you?"

"My brother did. Pat's the union secretary. Borg's a pain in the ass, if you'll excuse the expression, but a straight shooter. And not afraid of anybody. Call me Mike, by the way."

"So you think that Jimmy Gleason didn't just fall into the press?"

"A guy who's been around presses all his life? Come on."

"And he couldn't have killed himself?"

"Getting ground up by one of these presses is not a way anyone would want to go. Let me show you where Gleason fell from . . ."

"I was going to ask . . ."

"It's on the way. The city cops took their tape off yesterday."

They had been walking along the row of presses that stood almost fifteen feet high. Now they turned right and made their way between two of the units. Doyle pointed overhead to a catwalk.

"That extends over the presses. It isn't used for much except to check once in a while if something doesn't sound right. Most of the work has to be done right down here."

"Then what was Gleason doing up there?"

"He was a funny guy. Liked to be by himself, you know. The guys on his shift told me he went up there once in a while. Might've stolen a smoke."

"Where was the rest of the crew?"

"I'll be honest with you, these new presses are so computerized you don't need many people to run them, just men to keep an eye on things. If you've got one man at the control panel, you hardly need much more."

"And the others?"

"Well, they might be on a bathroom or coffee break in the locker room, but they would be available if anything went wrong."

Donna recognized a union boondoggle when she saw one. The shift was probably in the locker room playing cards or watching TV. She didn't say anything, however. She also knew these men would gradually be squeezed out by a management team with vice presidents who got paid a lot more and contributed less.

"So no one saw anything?" she asked.

"No. Anyone could sneak in at night. We're not security people. The doors are locked and there's a security guard at the front desk."

"And the back door, the one I came in, is kept locked? No one has a key?"

"Oh, some of us do. I do, for instance, and the three foreman and a couple of drivers. Once in a while a truck will be brought right in here or a company car. That one by the door was Mr. Perry's. Perry used it to have Frankie drive him over here from downtown. The Jag belongs to Hasner. There's a big door that slides up right alongside the one you came in."

"Yes, I saw that," said Donna. "Is this the ladder that goes up to the catwalk?"

"That's it. You can see that it's out of the way here. If you didn't know about it you wouldn't think of looking here for it. And here's the door to the reception area. The stairs there go right up one flight to Hasner's office and there's an elevator if you need it."

"Thanks," she said. "And thanks for the tour. I think I'll just climb up here and take a look." She didn't ask permission.

"Be careful," said Mike Doyle. "Why don't I just follow you to make sure you're all right?"

Mike Doyle, no fool, followed Donna up the ladder, enjoying the view as they went. Like his brother, a junior hound. Donna gave him a look when he joined her on the catwalk.

"Now exactly where did Gleason fall from?" she asked. Go over it and go over it again. Police procedure.

"Right along here," said Doyle. "We're not sure exactly. Probably around here, about twenty feet along the walk. It's where he used to stand when he was up here."

"You saw him?"

"Not that night, but other times," said Doyle. "He'd be here maybe smoking and just watchin' the presses as they ran."

"Solitary man."

"You got that right."

"The rail here is about waist high. Not much chance of slipping and falling."

"You got that right, too," said Mike Doyle.

"I'll hold you if you'd like to lean over." Doyle reached toward her.

"Thanks for your help." Donna pulled away. They climbed down, Donna first.

"Anything else I can do to help, anything at all, just call. Here, let me give you my card."

And Mike Doyle also gave her his crinkled grin. Donna had to admit the smile had its charm. As did his brother, Pat's. As did Borg's crooked grin. Why she would think of him right now she couldn't imagine. She wondered if there were any more Doyles at home, practicing their smiles.

CHAPTER 44

"**N**ice office," Donna said even though it was a lot smaller than she expected. No receptionist on this narrow second floor of the production plant. No room for one. Just a hallway and several doors all on one side hanging over the press room. Donna could see the presses through the big window behind the only desk in the office.

Bill Hasner pointed to a modest wooden chair facing the desk he sat at and Donna settled into it, taking out a pad and her ball point pen.

"Actually, it's not my office," said Hasner. "It's Ron's. He only used it when he was over here and I shared it. The other offices here are for the two top production guys."

"Tight operation," said Donna.

"And secure," said Hasner with a smile. "We built this with the memory of what the pressmen did to *The Washington Post* fresh in our minds."

"What was that again?"

"Sorry," said Hasner, smiled. "I'm used to talking to other newspaper people. The pressmen destroyed the presses down there. The backlash ruined the union."

"Thanks. You don't even have any windows," she said. "It's like a fort."

"No windows looking in anyway," said Hasner. He smiled again. The smile was beginning to annoy Donna. "We don't think of it as a fort, however. Just a secure operation."

"So the night that Jim Gleason died you had a pretty good idea of who was here?"

"Probably. I'm sure you know more about security than I do, Lieutenant. You must know that no facility is absolutely secure. Copies of keys are made, which is why we change locks regularly. Actually, anyone could get in if they really wanted to go to enough trouble. Our security keeps out most people and we have a pretty good idea of who's in here. If we ever had to shut everyone out, we could. At least I hope we could."

Donna glanced out the big window into the press room. She could see the catwalk and the place where Jimmy Gleason fell from. Did Hasner ever look out and wonder about the accident and if it was one?

"You've got some pretty impressive presses down there, impressive even to someone who doesn't know anything about them," she finally said.

"We could probably print every damn newspaper in New England if we had to," said Hasner. "Unfortunately we don't have to."

"You don't sound very enthusiastic," said Donna.

"I'm not and never have been. They were Ron's idea, his toy. No rational explanation, really. We could print millions of copies. We don't need to now and we never will. This business is contracting, not expanding. This place is a vault, a mortuary, a temple to a business that's dying. Everyone but Ron knew that. It's why more of the family were questioning what he was doing with this operation."

"The presses must have added to the value of The Bulletin Company?"

"Good question, Lieutenant. Actually, they might have to the right buyer. Someone with other newspapers nearby could use these presses to print. Every time you consolidate a printing operation you save money, lots of money."

"Sounds like maybe Perry knew what he was doing."

"I can't agree with you and I didn't agree with Ron. We could have bought a small TV station or two or a small network of radio stations or a cable station or more for the same price as these presses. And get a much greater return. You can see the presses sitting idle right now, can't you? That means they're not making any money. A radio or TV station is always on the air, always making money. One more thing, while I'm at it. We wouldn't be printing any other publications because other publications are shrinking, too. No one needs more printing capacity."

"Mr. Hasner, do you think this company will be sold, now that Ron Perry is dead?"

"You are blunt, aren't you?" said Hasner. His pouty lips pressed together, lines appeared across his high forehead. Donna imagined that his next move would be to steeple his fingers in front of him. Hasner didn't assume that thoughtful pose. Instead he chuckled.

"Why should we beat around the bush?" he said finally. And then he did steeple his fingers. "You can find out easily enough, if you haven't already, that I have suggested we can get an awfully good price for this company right now. Not for very long, though, not for very long. Newspapers are not going to increase in value. I believe a majority of the family agrees with me."

"How about Mrs. Perry?"

"Louise is on the fence. I think she'll come around. Her daughters aren't interested in the business and neither is she. She has a sentimental attachment, I'm sure, but remember she isn't a Perry. And if the Perrys want to sell, why should she hold them back?"

"Sounds as though you've got it all figured out?"

"That's my job, isn't it? Looking out for the interests of ownership."

"And you'll come out of it very well, I imagine?"

"Blunt, blunt, Lieutenant. Yes, I probably will. Not as well as the Perry family. Which is how it should be, as I see it."

"One way or another there'll be big changes here, I guess."

"You guess right. Ron was a dear man and a dear friend. He was also a sentimental fool devoted to noblesse oblige. As though anyone cares anymore. He was going to have to cut a lot of jobs as it was, probably right after Christmas, because of the cost of his presses. I think he had even told some of the people already. That Lincoln down in the press area will go. I can drive my own car."

"So Frankie Levesque would be fired?"

"Of course. He was kept on as a gesture by Ron. He was supposed to tell Frankie the day before he was killed."

"Did he?"

"I really don't know. It's not important. We'll deal with it soon enough."

"One last thing," said Donna as she rose to leave and Hasner rose with her. "How close were you, are you, to Louise Perry?"

"What the hell do you mean by that?" Hasner said. His face turned red right up to his ears. He clenched his right fist. Blue eyes could turn from cordial to cold. Fast.

"Just a question," said Donna. "You were out at the house, played tennis with Mrs. Perry. Took a boat trip too."

"I resent the goddamn implication. Louise Perry is a good woman, something you might not be able to understand. If you start implying otherwise, I promise you'll be sorry."

"I don't think you have any idea what I can understand, Mr. Hasner, you better not think you can," said Donna. "I'll let that pass. I think I've learned what I needed to know."

Hasner had not gotten where he was by giving vent to his emotions. In a moment, he was under control again.

"I'm sorry, Lieutenant," he said. "I didn't mean that. I know your job is to conduct your investigation and I think you've done a good job of not spreading invidious rumors. Can't it be that both these deaths were simply the accidents they seem to be? Maybe just a coincidence or two thrown in?" He smiled again. Donna could see that the effort cost him.

"You may be right, Mr. Hasner. By the way, I'd like to come by here tonight and see the presses running and go up where Gleason was before he fell. Just to get a better idea of what happened."

"Haven't you just been there?"

"I'd like to see the presses running. You don't mind?"

"Of course not. I'll let security and the press crew know you'll be coming. I'm busy, or I'd join you. Anything else I can do for you? Aside from keeping my temper under control?"

"What do you think of Louise Perry's idea that the mob killed her husband?"

"I don't want to contradict Louise. I think she's certainly entitled to her opinion and *The Bulletin* will aggressively pursue that lead if it seems plausible."

"You're not sure it is?"

"It doesn't seem completely reasonable. Anything else I can do for you?"

"Just to remind myself, you were all alone on Sunday morning when Ron Perry was killed. Where were you again last Friday night?"

"All alone again I'm afraid. Which probably proves I didn't kill anyone, if that's what you're hinting at. I'd surely have an alibi if I were going to commit murder. Anything else?"

"Not a thing. You've been most helpful. And maybe, as you say, these were just accidents."

Believe that and you'll sell me this building, Donna thought to herself. And throw the presses in to seal the deal.

CHAPTER 45

"**N**ice view," said Donna as Louise Perry led her into the living room of a townhouse in Providence. Standing on College Hill, the house had a view through the large picture window of the river below and across the city the downtown headquarters of The Bulletin Company. The Perrys seemed to have nice views wherever they lived.

"Thank you," said Perry. "Ron loved it. I guess deep down he thought of this as his city. You know, the merchants and ship captains lived up on this hill. His ancestors. They could be close to the port and keep an eye on things. They made their first fortune from the ships that left from the river to ports around the world."

From the slaves you packed into those ships, Donna thought to herself. She bit her tongue. She didn't know much history but she knew about slaves, probably from some TV program. Funny that most everyone involved in this case seemed to be keeping an eye on something, the Perrys on 'their city' and its ships, Bill Hasner on *The Bulletin* and its possible sale, Pat Doyle on his pressroom and its pressmen, Big Nan on the town of Little Bay, the Don on his Hill. Even Borg on her hometown paper.

Louise Perry took a chair and Donna settled onto a couch facing the big window. Louise folded her hands on her lap, looking a little like a schoolgirl in the Catholic school Donna had attended. Her feet set squarely on the floor. It was a pose she adopted naturally. Behind her was the window. She was framed, part of the picture of the city her husband thought was his own. It should belong to everyone who lived here. People like the Perrys had held it longest. And would probably still be around when the others were a memory, or a footnote in future histories that would be written by the Perrys or their friends.

"Mrs. Perry, I've got some questions to ask," Donna began.

"Should I have my lawyer present?" Louise asked and smiled. Comfortable and secure. Donna resented the smug attitude, felt patronized. She would not let Louise Perry dominate this little show. Donna's back was up.

"Up to you. My job is to get to the bottom of these deaths. That's what I intend to do. I hope you'll help."

Louise Perry turned to look out the window. Beautiful profile, thought Donna. Classic nose sharply outlined as was the chin beneath it. Maybe a little too perfect. Like a statue. She crossed her right leg over the left. Her foot trembled, then stopped.

"I'll try my best to be patient," said Louise Perry, finally.

"Good," said Donna. "First of all, we know that you and your husband were separated for almost a year," said Donna.

"True," said Perry. "Everyone knows that, I guess." She sighed.

"What about other men in your life, Mrs. Perry, other women in your husband's?"

"I find that rather presumptuous, Lieutenant. However, I'll continue. There has never been anyone but Ron in my life."

"You play a lot of tennis with Bill Hasner."

"And that's all the playing that goes on, I promise you."

"We have witnesses who saw you hugging Bill Hasner."

Louise Perry looked down at her hands. Her face remained almost immobile, but her lips tightened just a little bit. Always the lips, Donna noticed. There was a time, years ago, as Donna began her police career, when she would have been less than comfortable in this particular house talking to a Perry. Less so now. Donna had seen too many important people squirm in uncomfortable positions themselves. Still, a little bit of the mill mentality lingered in her attitude, the owner against the laborer. She fought it.

"Donna, let me talk to you as a woman." Louise leaned forward, her clasped hands rising to her chin. "Somehow I believe I can trust you. I guess that helps you in your job. Anyway, sex, to me, is not the most important thing in the world. Never has been. Certainly I enjoy it, but it is not foremost. One thing is for certain: I have always, was always, faithful to my husband. If anyone says anything different they are lying and I would like to confront them."

"You seem very sure of yourself."

"About some things I am."

"What about Ron? He faithful?"

"I suppose you know about Ron and the woman he was seeing while we were separated, so your question is really whether I knew about it or not."

"Did you?"

"Of course I knew about it, Donna. I'm not a complete fool. Still, I guess I'm hopelessly old fashioned about some things. Marriage is one of them."

"Which means?"

"I decided it was more important to preserve our marriage and all that it entailed than to hold Ron's infidelity against him," she said. "After all, maybe it was my fault. And maybe my mistake wasn't his fault."

"How was it your fault?"

"Let me try to explain what Ron and I had together."

"Please . . ."

"First of all, ours was a very fortuitous marriage for all concerned: family, business, friends. We were a great match. We fit together. In public we looked exactly as we should have. Our children are what they should be. And there's much to be said for that."

"So?"

"So sometimes people get in the way of plans. They mess up plans. I'm not sure Ron and I ever loved each other very much in the usual sense of passion and all of that. I can say that now, though I'll deny it later if you repeat it. We were very polite to each other, I respected deeply what he was trying to do with *The Bulletin*. I know that we didn't have a perfect relationship in a lot of ways. In its own way, though, it was deep and, I believe, lasting."

There was another pause. Louise Perry looked down at her hands, dropped them to her lap. In the pause, Donna thought about her own marriage, of her feelings for Al. The trouble with listening to a lot of other people's problems is that they reminded you of your own.

Louise was going on: "There may have been ways in which I didn't satisfy Ron . . . ."

"Was that the reason for the separation?"

"That and a number of other little, silly things which maybe revealed deeper problems. I'm not a psychologist. What matters is that finally we decided, resolved I guess is the best way to put it, that all of the other things in our marriage were more important than the problems. We decided that what we had was deeper, more important, than what we didn't."

"You weren't going to let passion get in the way?"

"That's an unkind way to put it. I would answer that our passion for what we cared about was just as important and perhaps more lasting than any sexual passion we may not have had."

"Anyway you got back together?"

"Yes we did, and I think we were happier than we had been. We both tried to be more understanding of each other. Which is a lot harder to do than say. I'm a traditional woman, Lieutenant. I believe you have to work at a marriage. I was trying and so was Ron. That's why I feel so cheated now."

"What about Bill Hasner and you?"

This time Louise Perry laughed. "What about him? You don't think I could be seriously involved with Bill over a period of time? If I were ever to be tempted by anyone it wouldn't be a Bill Hasner. Would you be?"

"I don't go for corporate types. Did your husband know you were hugging Hasner on your tennis court?"

"Let's get something straight," said Louise. "People hug after a tennis match. They even kiss. It doesn't mean anything except that they may be friends. But they may not even be that. If we hugged it wouldn't mean a thing. Ron knew I couldn't be serious about a Bill Hasner. By the way, I have every reason to believe that Ron had given up the woman he was seeing."

"I think so, too," said Donna, letting up a little. "Listen, I think you've been honest with me. I promise that most of what you've said will remain in this room. One more thing. Do you still think the mob killed your husband?"

"Absolutely. I think those people hate us. I wouldn't put anything past them. Ron's paper has always been against them and they know it."

"If not them, who?"

"If you pressed me—and I guess you are—I would say someone at the paper. His employees really didn't like Ron much and he was in the process of making changes, changes that would cost some their jobs. People at newspapers hate change even though they encourage it everywhere else. When changes affect jobs, they like the changes even less."

"Anyone especially?"

"I wouldn't know. You might talk to Frankie the driver. He isn't very bright, but he seems to know everything about everybody."

Just like his mother, Big Nan, thought Donna.

"What will you do now, Mrs. Perry, if I may ask?"

"I'm not sure. Probably go someplace else. This is a big small town, really, and there are too many memories here, a lot of them not very pleasant."

"Good luck. Thank you for being honest."

"Thank you for being such a good listener. I guess it's part of your job and you do it very well. I haven't talked like this to anyone else and I actually feel better."

Too much, thought Donna, just a little too much. But nice try. Louise walked Donna out and as Donna opened her car door she looked up at the brick house and wondered what would become of it and the woman in it and her two daughters. An old saying came to mind: Whether you're rich or poor it's good to have money. Louise Perry had money. Donna shook herself and focused on the case at hand as she wheeled her orange Datsun up the street. She felt sticky. She needed a shower.

CHAPTER 46

The telephone was ringing when Matt Borg started up from the garage to the first floor of his townhouse so he took two steps at a time, his knees paying the price. He made it on the fourth ring, just one before the answering service kicked in.

"It's Angela Rosso," said the voice. "I heard Lieutenant Pacheco was talking to my husband."

It took Borg a minute to catch his breath and put Angela in place. The voice helped. It was husky, breathy. Sounded like someone you would want to talk to in person even though he knew from experience voices could be deceiving. And he had never met Angela Rosso so he was being as unfair as hell. So what's new?

"So why are you calling me, Mrs. Rosso?" Not very polite. Borg was tired.

"You sound out of breath. Am I catching you at a bad time?" She made it sound as though he might have been doing a lot of very naughty things.

"Just running up the stairs," he said.

"Jerry Zampato called me and said Lieutenant Pacheco stopped by his place and saw my husband," she said. Borg waited.

"Jerry said it might be of some help to me and to Ralph if I talked to you. He said otherwise you and Donna might be stirring Ralph up, maybe getting him into trouble. You might be writing something, for instance."

"Donna Pacheco and I aren't partners, Mrs. Rosso . . ."

"I know that." Breathy. "But you are both looking into Ron Perry's death, aren't you?" She made it seem indecent.

"I guess. And I'm looking into the death of Jimmy Gleason, too, for some of his friends. Let's get it straight, though. I'm not trying to cause any trouble for you or your husband or anyone else if I can help it. Not if you don't deserve it, that is. I don't think Lieutenant Pacheco is either, but I can't speak for her."

"Do you think there's some connection between Gleason's death and what happened to Ron Perry?"

"I don't know but it's possible. Why do you ask?"

"I'd like to see whoever killed Ron pay for it," she said. "I talked to Lieutenant Pacheco and I think she's a square shooter. Zampato says you're OK."

Does everyone know everything in this small state? Or, thought Borg, do they just think they do? More important, did he know the difference?

"Listen, Mrs. Rosso, I'm writing about Perry and Gleason in my paper and your husband's name may come up but I'm not looking to stir up any muck if I can help it," Borg said. "You think he was murdered?"

"You don't? Listen, everyone knows the wound was on the back of his head. Ron was on his way up the hill. How does he fall backward and kill himself if he was leaning forward on the bike?"

He tried hard not to show any opinion about Perry's death in his voice. "Who do you think did it?"

"I don't know. I do know who didn't. It wasn't one of our people. Ralph may be crazy but he's not going to kill a newspaper publisher even if he thinks we had a relationship."

"Are you sure about that? I wouldn't bet on it."

"I would. I'm even more sure that Ralph would never have hit him from the back. He would have gone at him straight on. Ralph is a lot of things. He's not a wimp. I was in love with Ron Perry. Maybe he was with me. I don't know. And everybody knew about us including that prissy wife of his. When Ron went back to her I couldn't believe it was over between us, believe me. I still don't."

Borg thought it was. Still, it was interesting that Angela didn't. Or said she didn't. Who really knew?

"Again, Mrs. Rosso, if Ron was murdered, who do you think could have done it?"

"I think it was someone connected to the newspaper or someone in his personal life. Or both."

"What makes you think that?"

"That new production plant of *The Bulletin* gives me the creeps."

"So you've been there?"

"A few times, actually, when they were building it. At night mostly. When Ron would pick me up for dinner or something. He'd want to stop by there to see how things were going. They were usually going pretty bad, if you ask me."

"You could tell?"

"Didn't take a rocket scientist. Sometimes Ron would get real angry, would get into a shouting match with a union boss over there, a guy called Patsy something or other, a real wise guy, if you ask me."

"Why do you say that?"

"One time I get out of the car. Ron didn't like me to, you know. But I was getting fanny fatigue, just sitting there so I get out for just a minute to stretch my legs and this Patsy is standing there talking to Ron and, you know, he looks me over, if you know what I mean."

"I'm not sure."

"Well, most guys will look you over and don't tell me they don't. Even Frankie the driver does." She laughed. "He thinks I don't see it. A guy like this Pat undresses you, if you know what I mean. Looks you up and down fast and gives you the going over. I don't mind too much, usually. I know what I've got, after all. But this guy was too much. Especially in front of his boss and all. If it had been up on The Hill, someone might have slapped him around. Then he has the nerve to say, "hello." Introduces himself. Calls me later, for God's sake. Wiseass."

"Ron must have been pretty angry."

"I'll say. He was having so much trouble with the presses and the union he said he couldn't do anything. And this guy's brother is a foreman or something. Ron said he'd take care of it later, after the plant was up and running."

"Did you have a feeling he would?"

"Ron was funny that way. Do I think he would? Damn right. I know he would. Like the Kennedys, he didn't get mad, he just got even. He didn't let much get by him even though he didn't do much right away."

"He didn't say anything more about Pat?"

"He did to Frankie the driver."

"So you talked to Frankie?"

"A lot. When he would give me a ride home. Or when Ron would go into the office and I would wait. He's a very sweet guy, was always doing little things for me. Like I said, I knew he looked over my legs when he helped me out of the car, tried to get a quick peek up the skirt, if you know what I mean. You goddamn men. Probably he even had a little crush on me."

"Did he ever say anything, do anything?"

"Not a word. Nope. He's a simple guy, a little retarded I think. His job was everything to him. Except for his mother. He worshipped her."

"He loved Ron Perry, did he?"

"He loved the job. He was so proud of never having an accident and keeping the Town Car all shiny and he always had on those pressed pants and a sharp shirt."

"Ever meet his mother, Big Nan?"

"I'll say. Looked right down her nose at me. Ron was taking me to the vineyard out near Little Bay and we stopped at Big Nan's for gas and she came out and gave me a dirty look and then perked up as much as she could for Ron. Frankie told me later when we were alone how his father had died and how his mother hated the Perrys and all the other Yankee bosses. Whoever said that fat people are happy?"

"If it's not your husband, who do you think murdered Ron?"

"I think it was that goddamn wife of his or his assistant, that Bill whatever . . ."

"Hasner, actually. Why do you say that?"

"Because I know Ron would have come back to me sooner or later and I know that Ron was getting more and more fed up with Bill, felt he was going behind his back to get the company sold."

"Ron talked to you about that?"

"Just bits and pieces. I put it together. Just because I'm a hairdresser doesn't mean I haven't got a brain, Mr. Borg. Don't kid yourself. And hairdressers are some of the best listeners you'll ever find."

"I'm sorry if I sounded patronizing," said Borg. "I do think you have a brain and I think you've been a very big help."

"So lay off my husband, will you? We might be getting back together."

Now that Ron Perry is gone, thought Borg. "Let me ask you one more question: Do you know if your husband sent a couple of guys to scare me?"

There was a moment's hesitation. Maybe more than a moment.

"I might have heard something about that."

"Why would he do that? To protect you?"

Hesitation again. Then, "I'll tell you because I guess you'll find this out anyway. And it has nothing to do with this case. I met Ralph when I was doing some modeling. Some nude modeling toward the end. It paid good and, frankly, it turned me on a little. Maybe that's why I was good at it. One of the photographers was after me to make some soft core porn movies and that's how I met Ralph. He was into that business. The nude pictures may still be around. They're pretty good if I say so myself. Ralph has tried to destroy all of them. He's sensitive about it and is worried about the porn stuff the Clinton cops were making. He's afraid something might come up about him or me. So he wanted you to stay away from me."

"Did he really think that would work?"

"Ralph isn't the sharpest knife in the drawer, Mr. Borg. But he never killed anyone."

As far as you know, thought Borg. What he said was, "Well, I appreciate what you've told me. You realize I have to share most of it with Lieutenant Pacheco?"

"I guess so. Can we keep most of it between us, OK?"

"I'll do what I can."

As soon as he hung up the phone, he thought he'd better call Donna Pacheco and bring her up to date. The line was busy. He poured himself a glass of red wine and sat down to sip it and look out on Narragansett Bay. He'd call her again later.

CHAPTER 47

Donna Pacheco let the hot water run over her, down her back, down the drain. Too hot, really. Still, it felt good. Wash the troubles of the day away. Not this day, though. Not all the troubles.

She was taking a shower before going back to the production plant of *The Bulletin* this evening. She had sat down to dinner with Al and the kids for a few minutes first. Taking care of family business. She had to watch Sarah, who was fifteen and headstrong and beautiful. She looked every bit of eighteen just as Donna had at her age. Sarah wanted to date a high school football player, a senior and eighteen. Al being the good guy, Donna played the enforcer. Dating had to wait for sixteen, Donna insisted. Sulking the result. Al Junior, the wise guy, was not living up to his potential in school. Threats of no TV. She hoped it worked. Thank goodness for Mary. Not as smart as the other two. Like her father, sweet and amiable and easy.

"Like the stew?" Al had asked. What could she say?

"Real good," she answered, thought of something to add. "The dumplings were great."

"Making them a new way," he said, beaming.

Same old, same old, thought Donna, restless. Not with her job. She loved solving cases, digging clues out that others missed. Showing off maybe, the smart little girl from the Valley with the funny accent who could outperform those college guys with the fancy talk. Meeting people she never would have in her hometown of Arctic.

"My mom and dad would like us for Sunday dinner," Al continued.

"Sure," said Donna. Watching football afterward. Yawn.

Now that she had reached her job as State Police Lieutenant, head of the homicide squad at thirty eight, she wondered if all this was enough. Was this all there was? She loved Al, or thought she did. Still, she had to admit that at times, increasingly, she found him boring. Was she experiencing a seventeen-year itch? Maybe. She had been exposed to a lot of lives very different from those of this mill town. Donna stepped out of the shower, grabbed a towel, and shook it all off. It could wait.

She drove her thoughts back to Louise Perry. Capable of killing her husband? Absolutely. Bill Hasner? Certainly. Ralph Rosso was capable of anything and so was his wife, in spite of the fact that Donna liked her. She had liked several people she had put behind bars. What about the rest of the suspects? The Doyle brothers were into everything including the troubled presses. Big Nan and Frankie Levesque festered at the side. On the other hand, old Cy Bitgood was a peach. So was Constable Fred Glasgow. She pulled on her panties, wrapped herself in a towel, and placed a call to him.

"Little Bay Police, Chief Glasgow speaking." What was good about a small town police force was that you didn't have an awful lot of people to go through to get to the boss.

"Hi, it's Donna. I thought it might be a good idea to check in after my visit to your town."

"Hello there. If I had anything important you know I would have called you.

"Not much new at your end?"

"Not much. I've been thinking, though, that maybe we should have spent more time with old Cy Bitgood. He's a lot smarter than you might think."

"Oh, I think he's pretty smart, believe me. Think I should come down tomorrow?"

"Don't think you need to do that. You might call him. I think he likes you and I know he doesn't like me much on account of my having to stop him from burning leaves and all that."

"You haven't got his number, do you?"

"Right here as a matter of fact. Just don't tell him I suggested you call or you won't get much of anything." He gave her the number and she dialed it, thinking all the while how silly she felt, sitting on her bed in a towel doing police business. She could see herself in a mirror on the facing wall and pulled her shoulders back and her stomach in.

"Yep," came the voice on the other end of the line and Donna smiled to herself. Exactly what she would have expected from Cy Bitgood.

"Mr. Bitgood, it's Lieutenant Donna Pacheco. Have you got a few minutes?"

"Guess so. Just finished eatin'. Always got time for a pretty gal."

The old scamp was flirting, Donna thought, and smiled. She liked him. You'd never have to worry about him going on about himself like some men, she thought, and almost broke out laughing. She covered the mouthpiece just in case.

"I was trying to go over the morning that Ron Perry was found. I thought you might help me," she said.

"All I can." said Bitgood.

"I remember you said you didn't hear anything that morning. Do I remember that later you said you might have heard a noise? Nothing unusual, though. Am I wrong?"

"Didn't hear a car was what I said."

"I guess that's right. You heard some birds, jays and doves, I think."

"Warblers and finches. Big difference, even for a city gal like yourself."

"You've got me there, Mr. Bitgood. Think you just might have heard something else?"

"Funny you should ask. I been thinkin' about it and then I heard the same kind of sound just yesterday."

"And what was it?"

"I'm not sayin' anything less you call me Cy," said Bitgood.

Men, thought Donna, they never quit.

"All right, Cy, what was it you remember?"

"Well, as I told you I didn't hear a car so I didn't mislead you on that. Yesterday I heard the same sound, as I say, and it was more like an old truck."

"Kind of rough sounding?"

"Didn't say that. Smooth actually. You don't hear many sounds down this way so you get to tellin' them apart. Sort of like doves and warblers. This was an old engine, kind of throbbin' but it was in good shape. Smooth. Not a car though."

"Could you recognize it?"

"Can't say for sure and wouldn't want to say at all if I'm not sure."

"Have you heard it before?"

"Ayeh. Think so. I ain't sayin' for certain 'till I'm certain. Even for you."

"Will you let me know as soon as you can?"

"I'll do that."

Which ended the conversation. Donna dropped the towel, took a quick look at herself in the full-length bathroom mirror, pulled in her stomach again, and finished dressing. Time for one more check of her messages. Before she could return Matt Borg's call he was on the line to her.

CHAPTER 48

"**C**atch you at a bad time?"

"Not really," she said. "I'm getting ready to go over to *The Bulletin* production plant."

"What are you doing that for?"

"To see what the place is like with the presses running and who's there."

"Recreating the crime?"

"Sort of. Anything new on your end?"

Borg could hear the impatience in Donna's voice, so he quickly filled her in on the conversation with Angela Rosso. She told him about her talks with Bill Hasner, Mike Doyle, and Louise Perry.

"You saying they all could be suspects?" He remembered the Chief and what he said about a river of emotion. "Any of them have enough passion, you think?"

"I'm not sure. Just doesn't seem like it. Louise had her man back, Ralph Rosso thought his wife had ended the affair, Angela Rosso seems to be going on with her life."

There was a pause. Donna wanted to get out and see the production plant and get home again, but she didn't want to brush Borg off. She'd give him one more minute.

"That leaves Bill Hasner," said Borg. "He could end up with control of the company, a lot of money, and Louise."

"He doesn't seem like a passionate man to me, if that's what you're thinking," said Donna. Then she remembered Hasner's outburst at her. "Well, maybe. Hasner doesn't have an alibi for either death and, don't forget, his pen was found on the catwalk."

"Just because he wasn't involved in a passionate relationship doesn't mean he wasn't passionate," Borg said. "Maybe he's passionate about other things . . ."

"Like money?"

"Like money," Borg shot back. "And Hasner does drive a Jag with the wheel on the right."

"Absolutely. The better to hit Perry on the head."

"There's not one shred of evidence." Borg waited.

"Doesn't mean there won't be," said Donna. "I'll have our lab boys take a close look at his car and if I see him at the production plant tonight I'll ask more about where he was the night Gleason died. Now I've got to go."

Borg had stretched the call. Not like him. Was it because he had a sense of foreboding about Donna visiting the production plant of *The Bulletin*? He admitted it to himself, admitted also it was silly. Of all the strong women around him, Donna might be the toughest.

"Be careful," he said. She didn't give him a chance to say anything else.

"Always."

CHAPTER 49

T he huge block dark building that housed *The Bulletin* presses looked ominous to Donna Pacheco. Almost frightening. She admitted that to herself. Few who knew her would have guessed she was afraid of anything. The Lieutenant had learned to deal with her fear, to put it in its place, lock that place up, and go on.

Donna had begun that process as a kid growing up in Arctic, the only Portuguese kid in a school largely French. Short and different and feeling terribly out of place. A tough girl called Madeline Monsaratt was her special tormentor. Monsaratt was tough enough to be the catcher when the boys played baseball, squatting behind the plate and shrugging off foul tips that stubbed her fingers. She had a face like a raccoon, with big black eyebrows and a pointy grin. So it was funny that "Coon" was what she called Donna and worse, pushing her or giving her an elbow when they passed in the school hall or played basketball, which Donna tried to avoid as much as she could.

Even now the specter of Madeline Monsaratt lingered. Donna

learned way back then, in grammar school, that she had to get by Madeline Monsaratt. And all the Madeline Monsaratts of the world. She wished she could recall a triumph, even a minor one, but that wasn't the way most of life or her memory worked. Instead, Donna had gone at Madeline with better grades, much better actually. And tried to ignore her.

Then, overnight it seemed, Donna had filled out into a pretty good athlete. And a cutie, as her family called her. Captain of the cheerleaders in Arctic High, the highest peak a girl could reach in the town. Girfriend of football captain Al Pacheco. Madeline Monsaratt disappeared from her life. Donna didn't even remember what happened. Did Madeline move or go to another school? She didn't remember. What she did know is that she herself grew up and grew out and learned to treat the Monsaratts of the world with indifference. Fewer and fewer could stand up to her cold stare and, she had to admit, the position she held. Al had done all right, too. Even though he didn't go to junior college like her. He wanted to go right to work and make some money. Now he had a good, steady job with the state. Until he could get his pension, as he reminded her often enough.

The big dark building was yet another Madeline Monsaratt to be dealt with. Lights overhanging the roof cast few shadows on the facility's blank walls, built to withstand a strike or even a siege. She parked in front, hers the only car on the street, walked to the double door and pressed a button. Through the obviously reinforced glass she could see the security guard at his desk as he buzzed the door open.

"I'm Lieutenant Pacheco," she said.

"Yep, I was told you'd be coming in," he said, all red face with a fringe of white hair, blue eyes, white uniform shirt with some sort of badge. He didn't get up. "Sign the sheet and I'll buzz you into the pressroom." She did. He did.

Donna had heard the roar of the presses even before she saw them, even before she opened the door. Inside their room the noise was almost deafening. She had heard these new presses were a lot quieter than the old ones. She couldn't imagine the noise the old ones must have made. Halfway down the row of press units was the control panel. A pressman sat at it keeping an eye on the gauges before him. Further down the room by its back wall were a line of delivery trucks and one blue truck standing by the garage doors. Had to be Frankie's.

She tapped the pressman at the controls to get his attention. He was wearing ear muffs or something that looked a lot like them.

"Heard you were coming by," he shouted. "We're printing the early sections for tomorrow's paper. Food and Style. Want me to get Mike? He's with the crew in the locker room. They're taking a break. He'll be back soon."

"Don't bother," Donna shouted back. "I want to go up on that catwalk. You know, the one that Jimmy Gleason fell from."

"Be careful. That walk shakes pretty good when the press speeds up or when it slows down. Matter of fact, it's pretty shaky almost all the time. Let me give you a pair of these muffs. The noise will make you deaf if you don't wear 'em."

"OK." She smiled and put the ear muffs on. They were bigger than the ones that kept out the cold and they did make a difference, keeping out a lot of the noise. She began her walk through the press units that were printing recipes and fashions by the ton. There wasn't an awful lot of room between the units and here there were shadows in spite of the bright lights from the ceiling. The whole place seemed to be pulsating as she made her way to the ladder that would take her up to the catwalk.

It was steel, she supposed, like a lot of other ladders she had seen, extending up to the catwalk, perhaps fifteen feet above her. She was glad she had worn practical clothes, black blouse and slacks and black running shoes. Even her sweater, tied over her shoulders now, was black.

This was the ladder, these the steps that Jimmy Gleason had climbed just a few short nights ago, steps she could feel trembling through the rubber soles of her sneakers as she climbed them, counting as she went. Twenty-six there were, twenty-six including the very last one that put her on the walk itself. Now she was at the top, she stopped to take a breath. The physical exertion hadn't cost her. No, it was the tension, her nerves that shortened her breath.

Why was she here anyway? She wasn't certain. She was sure that she should be. Donna wasn't one of those people who believed there was something that lingered at the scene of a murder. Some investigators thought so, that there was an aura remaining, that walls could speak if you remained quiet or receptive enough to hear them. For Donna that amounted to a belief in ghosts and she didn't believe in them, either.

Yet here she was after 9:00 in the evening, holding onto the handrails of a catwalk some two feet wide of corrugated steel, a catwalk that trembled and was causing her to tremble a little herself. Maybe she should have asked for Mike Doyle after all. Then she got hold of herself. She was Lieutenant Donna Pacheco, after all, star investigator of the State Police. She had handled tough assignments before this. She was a compact 110 pounds—though she wouldn't admit it—and while some of the pressmen or even construction workers gave her a whistle, she knew she could take any of them out. She was an expert in martial arts and a crack shot. And damned good looking as well, she told herself.

She sensed a tremor up her spine as she walked along the walk. Looking for what? Maybe an inkling, a clue as to what happened to Jimmy Gleason on this walk. Step by step she made her way. The walk seemed to end at the very end of the building, at the wall where that blue truck was parked below. What was the truck doing there anyway? She should have asked. She'd find out when she got down.

The railing she tried to grip was waist high on her. She tried to remember Jimmy Gleason. She believed he was about six feet. If he was as tall as that, he would have had more trouble gripping the railing than she did. She'd check his exact height later.

Even at a slow pace, she was finally reaching the end of the walk. Here was a platform, about six-by-six, with a few tools, a heavy wrench or two, attached to the wall itself. She wondered if the city police or her people had tested them for blood or hair samples. They should have, but you never know. She'd have that done tomorrow.

The presses were still roaring as she started back along the walk step by trembling step, until she reached what seemed like a central point. She believed this was the spot where Jimmy Gleason had fallen. There was a strip of leftover yellow police tape sticking to the rail. Donna stopped and paused, looking down at the presses. From here she couldn't see the control panel or the man at it. She couldn't see much of anything, as a matter of fact. Just the presses. And no one could see her. Just as no one had seen Jim Gleason. A great place to sneak a smoke. Below her were huge cylinders turning against each other and squeezing pages out between them. She couldn't imagine anyone jumping into that machinery. No matter how desperate or sick.

No, the Gleason death wasn't a suicide. And she couldn't imagine it as an accident. Anyone standing here would be careful. It was too dangerous to be otherwise. A pressman would know that. Anyone would. She gripped the rail to lean over.

As she looked down, she felt hands on her back, pushing her, pushing her hard, toward those very cylinders.

CHAPTER 50

The murderer had watched Donna Pacheco, as she came into the pressroom. She was pretty. And she looked sexy in that black outfit, as pretty as Angela. He stopped himself. His Mom didn't like him thinking like that. It was dirty.

Donna was like all the rest, his Mom said. She hurt people, she hurt families. She did the dirty work for people who owned the presses and the buildings. They did bad things to good people like the Cranstons and the Levesques. It had always been like that. His Mom told him that. He trusted his Mom. Maybe she was the only one he really trusted.

Since he was a kid, his Mom had told him stories. Even when she peeled him an apple. The skin was no good for you, Mom said. She told him Levesque and Cranston family stories as she read him school lessons. None of the kids from school who picked on him ever came close to his house. They were afraid of his Mom.

His Mom would show him pictures of his great grandfather, with his whiskers. He owned the biggest store in town. You could buy anything at Cranston's, clothes or dishes or even a hammer. A general store was what it was. His Grandpa, Isaiah Cranston, was a big man in town. In the county. Even the Governor stopped by when he was in town. The Governor was a Big Man, his Mom said. He and his Grandpa were Masons, his Mom said. He wasn't sure what that was. It was Grandpa who built the store and it was Grandpa who owned all the land by the shore. It was like a summer place. His Mom said in the old days your buggy would take you to your summer place in less than an hour.

Grandpa took his pals to The Camp by the water. They went fishing and hunting. Mom said they just drank and told stories. His Mom said that some of them might have been true. Then she laughed. Frankie didn't see what was funny, but he laughed too. The Camp had gardens that Grandpa had planted. Grandpa loved wild flowers. Big rhody dendroms, some so big they formed a tent he played in. Laurels, too. A few bushes were still there. His Mom's stories made it sound like a fairy land.

His Mom told him stories about playing inside the rhody dendroms as though they were a fort or castle. Bad things happened after that. New roads took people to the city and bigger stores. Cranston's Store got empty. Its wooden floors weren't oiled shiny any more. Its big cash registers didn't ring as much. No young people shopped there. The store died, his Mom said. Land had to be sold. The Camp, too. His Mom still had one of the store's cash registers at the gas station.

His Mom married a poor Frenchman. His Grandpa almost died. Daddy was a mill worker Mom met when her car stalled in the City. Daddy fixed it. Mom said Daddy was like a buccaneer. His Mom said she loved him even though he was a something his Mom called a Catholic. Grandpa stayed mad.

His Mom said that she had murder deep in her heart. Frankie didn't understand that. Wouldn't that kill her heart? He didn't ask any questions when his Mom talked like that. He knew his

Mom hated the people who bought the Cranston land, little piece by little piece. His Mom hated them.

Mom told him the stories. She loved her Frenchman. Even when he drank himself to death. She hated the Mill Owners. They moved the mills away. The Frenchman had been a Foreman, his Mom said. Then he was nothing. He went to the Franco-American Club all the time.

"You were his gift to me," his Mom told Frankie. Frankie loved his Mom so much. When the kids at school picked on him she hugged him and kissed him. When the teachers said anything bad, his Mom came to school and told them off. They didn't say much back to his Mom. Nobody did.

His Mom started telling him the stories about the family when he was a baby. She told him about the days when the Cranstons were like princes in a fairy land called Little Bay. He loved the stories. He hated the people who took it all away.

His Mom told him it was good to work for Mister Perry. They would get a chance sometime to pay back what the Perrys did to the Cranstons.

Frankie felt like he was going to die when Mister Perry told him he was fired. Laid off, he called it. So what if he never had an accident. So what if the car was always shiny. So what if Frankie smiled and said nothing when he saw how his Boss treated Angela, pretty Angela who cried sometimes when he drove her home or back to her shop, Angela who he liked to touch when he helped her out of the car. He remembered once she fell against him. He had felt her right boobie against him. He still remembered that feeling. He didn't tell Mom about it.

He felt bad that day Mister Perry yelled at Angela, told her to leave him alone. His Mom told Frankie that's what Bosses did. His Mom said his Boss would toss Angela away like an oily rag they used at the gas station.

It was a bad day. Not as bad as the day he drove his Boss home and his Boss told him he was fired. He couldn't believe it. He never had an accident. He had the car ready anytime. It was always clean and shiny even after the Boss took his daughters to a movie and they left candy and chewing gum wrappers in the back. Frankie had a little vacuum cleaner he used. The Boss said the company was cutting back. Cutting back sounded like it would hurt just as much as it did. His Boss told him to leave the car when they got to the summer house in Little Bay and he could walk home. He did. He cried all the way.

His Mom was waiting. His Mom was always waiting. He had never seen her so mad. She used words he had never heard from her before. "That bastard," she said about his Boss. "He's like all the rest," she said. "They squeeze you dry and toss you aside," she said. "They make believe they care, but all they care about is themselves and their money." She held him in her arms and said that the Boss should pay for this. She said he wouldn't get away with it.

His Mom worked it out. He would use his old mail truck, with the steering wheel on the right. He had an old baseball bat. His father used it when he played for the Franco-American Club. Frankie and his Mom knew exactly where his Boss cycled every Sunday. Frankie would come up behind his Boss and whack him as hard as he could. He would show his Boss you couldn't keep hurting people like his Mom and him.

It had been easy. Like his Mom said. The door of the mail truck was open so it was easy to swing the bat. His Boss didn't hear a thing. Frankie put the bat out the window when he got close to his Boss. He steered with his knees. Then he swung with all his might. His Boss tried to turn but Frankie caught him good. His Boss fell like a sack of garbage. Frankie circled back to the garage. He cut up the bat and his Mom fed it into the wood stove.

"There goes the evidence," his Mom said and smiled. He was happy even though he wasn't sure what she meant. He didn't feel bad about the Boss. He was a mean man and had hurt people like Angela and him.

His Mom told him to go back to the Perry house and clean the Town Car. Just like nothing happened. He did. He saw Mrs. Perry. She was pretty, too. Frankie liked her in her tennis clothes. The next day she called and she asked him if he would get some groceries. He said he would. Just like Mom said.

Jimmy Gleason hurt people, too. Him and his family. Mom said that after he told her what happened the morning after the Boss's accident. That's what his Mom said to call it. Frankie had been fishing with Jimmy Gleason. Jimmy Gleason was about the only one he talked to besides his Mom. They had been talking about the Boss and casting out over the waves. Jimmy Gleason and Frankie talked when they fished. Frankie said the Boss was not a good man. Jimmy Gleason agreed. He said the Boss's family hurt his family. So he told Jimmy Gleason about being fired and about how the Boss treated Angela. Jimmy Gleason listened and listened and had looked at him. Jimmy Gleason asked him about where he was on Sunday. Frankie kept his mouth shut. Just like his Mom told him to do.

Jimmy didn't say much. Just smiled. "Driving your truck around on Sunday morning, were you, Frankie?" Jimmy Gleason asked finally. And looked at Frankie funny.

Real funny, he told his Mom. She didn't say much for a while. Then she told him about the bad things the Gleasons had done when they were big shots, like she called it, when they had the trolley line and a mill and a newspaper.

After she gave him his second favorite food, baked beans and hot dogs with corn bread, his Mom said that they would have to do something about Jimmy Gleason. He didn't understand. Jimmy Gleason never hurt him. His Mom said that Jimmy Gleason and his family were too big for their britches. She said they were shanty Irish making believe they were lace curtain Irish. He didn't understand. And Mom called them dirty Micks with their trolley lines and newspaper. He didn't understand that, either. His Mom said they had put on airs, which he didn't understand. Did they fill balloons up with air and put them on their heads? She said that Jimmy Gleason was a bad man and she held Frankie in her arms and said he would have to do something. His Mom knew.

His Mom told him to watch Jimmy Gleason, to see where he went, to see when he could be paid back for all the bad things the Gleason's had done to his Mom and the Cranstons. So he followed Jimmy Gleason. It was easy. No one paid any attention to Frankie. They were used to him being around. Even in the garage. He was like the Shadow or someone like that. They were used to the old mail truck painted blue. They didn't know he was fired. He still had his keys to open the doors at the plant.

"Poor guy," they said when they thought he couldn't hear. "He's like a dog, waiting for his master." Even the pressmen would give him a pat on the back when they went by. Frankie didn't like that much.

Friday night at ten o'clock the pressroom was empty except for the man at the panel. Jimmy Gleason, too. The man at the panel couldn't hear or see anything but the panel. The panel made the press go. The other men were in the locker room. "Taking a break" they called it. That's when Gleason climbed up to the walk to sneak a cigarette. Frankie left the blue truck by the big doors. He climbed the stairs after Jimmy Gleason. He stopped with his eyes up over the catwalk. Jimmy Gleason stopped to light a cigarette. He shouldn't be doing that. Then Jimmy Gleason leaned over the rail and looked at the presses. It was easy for Frankie to sneak up on him and push him over. Jimmy Gleason hardly screamed. Just went right into the presses. Frankie dropped one of Mr. Hasner's pens on the catwalk.

When the pressmen came back and found the mess, Frankie made believe he was cleaning his blue truck. No one noticed. Then he drove home and told his Mom. She went over his story twice and then she smiled. She held him in her arms and told him she was very proud. She even made him his favorite johnnycakes and creamy oyster sauce to pour over them. It was the best thing he ever ate. Even better than hot dogs and beans.

Now he was here again, watching Donna Pacheco. She had a pretty backside, as she climbed the ladder to the catwalk. He liked to watch pretty ladies in tight pants. It was too bad she had to go into the press. But Mom had said she had to.

Mom had said Donna Pacheco was a servant of the Bosses. That she was bad. Mom said she was snooping and would hurt Frankie and Mom. Mom said Donna Pacheco was asking about the blue truck and Frankie being fired. She was the worst kind, Mom said. She acted nice and was pretty and could hurt people really bad. Mom said Donna Pacheco was not pretty inside.

So Mom told him to play a game tonight. He had heard from the pressmen that Donna Pacheco would be in the pressroom. "Prying," his Mom said. So his Mom told him to sneak upstairs and get another pen from the office of Mister Hasner. Hold it with your hankie, Mom said. Don't touch it with your fingers. Drop it on the catwalk after you push Donna Pacheco off. Mom said it was a game only she and Frankie would know about.

It was easy get the pen. No one was in the office. Frankie giggled to himself when he took it. Mom would be so proud. He held it in his hankie in his hand just like Mom said as he followed Donna Pacheco up the ladder. He stayed on the ladder with his head down so she couldn't see him. Then, it was easy to sneak up behind her. First he dropped the pen on the catwalk. He put the hankie back in his pocket just like Mom said. She would be proud.

What was Donna Pacheco looking for? Like Jimmy Gleason looking at the presses? Frankie got closer. He was quiet as he could be even though he knew no one could hear him. Step by step he sneaked up on her. The game was fun. He was almost behind her. He drew himself up. And lunged.

CHAPTER 51

Joe Smollens—the pressman at the control panel—later said
he heard the scream above the roar of the presses, through
the earmuffs and even through the eardrums that had been
permanently damaged by twenty-eight years in the pressroom.
Others found it hard to believe. Not that it mattered.

Joe Smollens had been in a kind of trance. Not asleep, mind
you, sort of tuned out. It was a condition he found comfortable
when he manned the panel for an hour or more, just watching
the instrument panel filled with dials. He had learned most of
the dials didn't mean a thing. One or two meant everything. So
he focused on them and thought about his family and about
his eldest son who was in the Army and in harm's way. Smollens was worried, plain and simple.

But the scream—or something, it couldn't have been a
bump—yanked him out of the trance and he lunged forward
and pressed the red button that stopped the presses. Joe Smollens knew that, in spite of what you saw in the movies, nobody
stopped the presses without an awfully good reason. He had

only seen an editor do it once. But a scream was worth a stop and Joe Smollens didn't hesitate. A siren went off, the presses screeched to a stop and all hell broke loose.

First of all, the pressmen on the shift came pounding out of their locker room, sounding like a herd of horses in their heavy work shoes.

"What the hell is it?" shouted Mike Doyle, leading the herd of a dozen or more, the last one fresh from the bathroom and fastening his pants.

"Heard a scream," said Joe.

"Better be a good one," said Doyle, "or it'll be you screamin' if that press got damaged. Or the paper is screwed up."

"I thought this press was supposed to be fool proof to fast stops," said a pressman behind Doyle.

"That's what they say," snorted Doyle. "They'll blame it on us if anything is screwed up. Now, where did you hear the scream from?" he asked Smollens.

"Damned if I know," said Smollens. "I sure as hell heard a scream." And now he was sure as hell hoping that he had.

"Well, let's take a look," said Doyle.

They didn't have to. Because with that, Donna Pacheco and Matt Borg came out from between the press units.

Both looked as though they'd seen a ghost, whether they believed in them or not.

"What happened?" Mike Doyle roared even though the big room was silent now and his voice echoed against the walls.

"Frankie Levesque is dead," Donna said. "You'd better go and look at the presses back there." And she pointed.

In a moment Doyle was back, his face ashen.

"Jesus Christ," he said. "What the hell do we do now?"

"First of all I've got to get the medical examiner and a team over here,' said Donna.

"We can't do that," said Doyle. "We'll be holding up the First Edition. I've got to clean up that unit."

"It'll have to wait," said Donna.

"It'll give the news guys a chance to get a story written about this," said one of the pressmen, a grizzled runt with a fringe of orange hair topping a pale, round face. He spat out, "We'll have to re-plate the front page at least."

"I'll have to reconfigure the press," said Doyle, gathering himself. "We'll print around that unit."

"You damn well better," said Donna. It was the first time Borg had heard her swear.

CHAPTER 52

"So, now that we have a minute, tell me how did you figure out that Frankie was the killer?" Donna and Matt Borg were at the Rue de L'Homme in Providence when he looked up and asked the question.

It was ten o'clock the morning after *The Bulletin* presses had swallowed Frankie Levesque. Donna was attacking an omelet with tomato and spinach and mushrooms and Borg was digging into a stack of buttermilk pancakes with a side of sausages. Both were guzzling coffee. They had been up all night, she completing her investigation. He had been a witness and then had used a desk in *The Bulletin* newsroom to write a story and send it down to *The Arctic Valley Times*. Managing Editor Aimee Solante pumped him for as much additional information as she could before giving up to lay out her front page.

"I should have figured it out sooner," Donna told Borg. "Now it seems obvious."

"What tipped you off, ace detective?" Borg stopped working on his pancakes and sausage and rested his knife and fork on the plate in front of him. Just for a minute.

"Some detective. I almost got sucked into one of those presses myself. The presses really were at the middle of everything, weren't they? The presses and the history of this place. Anyway, I should have paid more attention to Big Nan right from the start. She knew a lot and she and her son were connected to everything and everyone. But the newspaper took over. More attention-getting, I guess. The spotlight was on *The Bulletin*, never on her."

"There didn't seem like any reason to focus on her or Frankie," said Borg, adding syrup to what was left of his pancakes. "The infidelities were more fun. The Levesques were the kind of secondary witnesses I guess you find in any crime investigation. Jimmy Gleason seemed to lead away from them, if anything. Hasner had a great motive. So did Louise, it seemed to me. A woman wronged and all that stuff."

"You really believed she might have done it?" asked Donna. She put jam on a last piece of whole wheat toast, her omelet long gone.

"I thought she was a serious suspect," said Borg, wondering how a small package like Donna could consume so much food and still remain trim. "Big money involved and another woman. Pretty good motives on the face of it. She was strong, a good athlete, a tennis player. She could have swung a club to kill her husband."

"I didn't think that, especially after talking to her . . ."

"Woman's intuition?"

"Maybe. I'm not ashamed of that. I had a feeling Mrs. Perry had settled for what she already had in her life. Hasner looked better to me, driving that convertible. His Jaguar so old it had its steering wheel on the right. It would have given him room to swing the club. And if he didn't have something going with Louise Perry, he wanted to. The big money he figures to gain from the sale. I'll bet that goes through, by the way. After I talked to her I realized she really didn't care about Ron Perry much. I had a hunch she was a straight shooter. Then again, Big Nan fooled me."

"She fooled me too," said Borg. "Maybe *fooled* is the wrong word. I just overlooked her, I guess. All that mill stuff and resentment. I've heard it so many times in Rhode Island, I figured it was just more of the same. So I looked past her. And her son, with that silly grin, seemed harmless."

"Some harmless," she said. "He almost killed me."

"What happened up there on the catwalk? I just got to the bottom of the steps when I heard the scream. That wasn't you, was it?"

"Sure was. Poor old Frankie really wasn't a match. Somehow I sensed or maybe heard him reaching toward me. Maybe it was his tread on the catwalk. I dropped to my knees and let him go right over me, screaming like crazy. I couldn't grab him in time and he went right over the rail. Then there you were, just a little late to save me."

"Story of my life. You saved yourself."

She put her fork down. "Now I guess I can ask: How come you came over to the production plant?"

"Funny thing. I wasn't even thinking of the case. When I was down in South County talking to the folks at the Indian paper, the editor suggested we buy an old mail truck to deliver the free papers. You know, so the drive would be on the right side to throw them out. And the Chief said something about passion and how deep it could be.

"When I got home Frankie's mail truck with its steering wheel on the right wouldn't go away. Then there was Frankie and his mother not saying anything about Frankie being fired. Most of all I remembered how emotional Big Nan had been about The Perrys. How vicious really. The most passionate anyone had been about anything. And then when you told me you were going to the production plant I thought maybe Frankie might be there. I got an awful bad feeling . . ."

"Male intuition?"

"Maybe. Anyway, I tried to get the plant on the phone but I couldn't so I hopped in my car and arrived in time to see you handle the whole thing yourself."

"I saw that mail truck myself when I got to the plant. Should have put two and two together then, but I was never sharp at math." She cackled, finished her orange juice, and went on.

"When Cy Bitgood told me earlier in the evening that he had heard the smooth sound of a motor, I should have thought that if there was anyone with a smooth sounding car or truck it would be someone at a garage. Bingo! Big Nan's. I had even heard the sound when Frankie drove away from the garage after I questioned him and his mother. I took a close look at the truck tonight. A big scratch on the right side like a bike would make, maybe the handlebars. I made a note to have the lab boys look it over . . ."

"So Cy and a scratch did it?"

"More than that. Something bothered me about Big Nan. How she knew about Perry's death so fast. How she kept calling me 'sleuth' and asking if I was any good. Like baiting me to see how much I knew. Kind of funny. She wouldn't let me talk to Frankie much . . ."

"You'd have to think she might be wanting to protect the boy, though, wouldn't you? He was obviously not all there."

"Maybe. But it all started to add up. It seemed like she was hiding something. She also knew about Perry's wound on the back of his head. A lot of stuff. Not much of it definite. But it began to add up. And then there was the passion the Indian Chief talked to you about."

"What passion?" Borg looked at her, questioning.

"Maybe not passion. I'm not as good with words as you are. But love, deep love. The love of Big Nan for her husband and father, the deep love of Nan for Frankie and the love that would make her son kill for her."

Borg sighed. Maybe not a woman's intuition. But almost. Maybe just smarts and knowing people better than any kid from Arctic should.

"What happens to Nan now?"

"Who knows? No question that she put her son up to kill Perry and Gleason. Maybe we could build a case. But I think we'd have a hard time convincing a jury that she should be put away. She lost her son, after all, and who's to testify as to what she made him do?"

"You've got to feel a little bit sorry for her. She lost her husband and now her son pretty horribly."

"Yeah," said Donna. "Meanwhile she was responsible for the murder of Ron Perry and, think what you like about him, he leaves two children and a widow. And Jimmy Gleason never did anything to hurt anyone."

"Except maybe a few presses."

"No one would sentence you to death for that."

"If you were in the newspaper business you might." He smiled. "They were all killed by ghosts, weren't they, ghosts and memories and the resentment that lingers from the mill years. You'd think it would all be gone by now, but it lingers on."

"Listen, I've got to get home and see my family and then hit the sack." She smiled at him, reached across the table to pat his hand, hold it briefly and then slide her own away.

"Well, I've got to get to my paper. Make sure it's OK. I wish I could sleep during the day. Just can't do it."

"You would if you had three kids on top of your full-time job."

"Maybe."

"Count on it."

Donna Pacheco. Always got the last word. He was getting used to it.

ACKNOWLEDGMENTS

So many helped me in writing and producing this book that, like the recipients of Academy Awards, I know I will leave some out. But best to begin with my mother, who inspired and encouraged me to read from the very beginning and, without reading there can be no writing. Noreen Wald got me started with the basics of mystery writing. Thanks to the patience and generosity of the fellow members of our little writing workshop that kept the flame alive, Helen Schwartz, Mary Nelson, Sylvia Straub, Carolyn Mulford, and Mary Ann Corrigan. Larry Sasso encouraged me to publish the book and John Woodrum jumped in at the last minute with an informational life-saver. The inimitable f-stop fitzgerald and designers, Gabe Stuart and Maria Fernandez, made it happen. Ingrid and Erik were always there. Then there is, of course, my severest critic and heartiest booster, my wife, Susan Bokern.

ABOUT THE AUTHOR

During his time as an award-winning newspaper columnist, Ted Holmberg enjoyed a liquid lunch with Richard Burton and more serious meals with Walt Disney and Ronald Reagan. He also took a dip in the pool with Lloyd Bridges of *Sea Hunt* fame.

After decades in the newspaper business he turned to his first love, writing, and began a mystery series exploring the social and sexual mores of New England as well as its colorful history.

During a convoluted career that began as a teenage sports columnist for a weekly newspaper in Brooklyn, he played basketball in Madison Square Garden and served in the U.S. Army as a military policeman as well as editor of a base newspaper.

After Columbia Graduate School of Journalism, he joined the *Providence Journal* as a reporter and went on to write about television, movies, and the arts, before leaving the newspaper as deputy executive editor to buy a Rhode Island daily newspaper with considerable help from his friends. This led to his partnership with a New Zealand company to form the Independent News Corp. of which he was president. Eventually INC owned newspapers in Texas and California as well as Rhode Island.

He also led one of the first delegations of journalists to the Soviet Union as President of the New England Society of Newspaper Editors.

Ted Holmberg has three children. He and his wife, Mary Susan Bokern, divide their time between Rhode Island and Maryland.

THE ART OF MURDER

THE NEXT LT. DONNA PACHECO CASE

by TED HOLMBERG

CHAPTER 1

"**I**s it true that he has a hair piece for every occasion?" asked Carolyn Perry, of the newspaper Perrys, spiffy in her black sheath dress. Above the knee, as always.

"What do you have in mind?" Matt Borg raised an eyebrow, smirked, then answered his own question, something he did more than he should. "Trysting, maybe? I wouldn't be surprised. He's always prepared for anything."

"A trysting toupee," said Carolyn, laughing. "Only you would think of that. You haven't changed."

"Expect me to?"

"Not really," said Carolyn. "Still hiding behind jokes and banter. Still trying to save the world, one mill village at a time . . . except, of course, the mills have left."

She had nailed him. She always had been able to do that. One of their problems. That they knew each other too well. Even before he owned the smallest daily newspaper in the smallest state in the union and spent his days scrambling to keep it alive. Trying, at the same time, to be fair. Finding that harder to do all the time.

"You haven't changed either," he finally answered. "Still analyzing, still reading more into things than there is . . ."

"Maybe," said Carolyn. "But I still think of you as fighting the good fight, and losing, an ink-stained wretch or knight riding your dinky press . . ."

"Cut it out, Carolyn. I do what I do because I can't do anything else . . ."

"Or won't," she said. "Still hate talking about yourself?"

"Not much to say about not much."

"Still haunted?"

"Boo," said Borg. "Back to the mayor . . ."

Mayor Joseph 'Toby' Fragnoli wore the best hairpieces in New England. Even his enemies admitted that. Tonight at the Arts Club, Fragnoli would debate columnist Benjamin J. Couzens. The subject was bias in the press. Cuz countered his own disappearing hairline by artfully distributing his few remaining strands over his increasingly bald head. Only in Rhode Island and Providence Plantations would the mayor of the biggest city debate a newspaperman in a club more ancient than the Republic. Here, everyone knew everyone else. Or so it seemed.

"I hear that he tried a sprinkling of white, like yours, in his newest wig then gave it up," said Carolyn. "Chose youth over dignity—or reality."

"A wise choice," said Borg. "If I was faced with that decision. I know what I'd choose."

"Me too," said Carolyn. "Except not so black. Think he'll be indicted?'

"Sooner or later," said Borg. "He's got big guns against him."

"They'll take away his hairpiece in prison . . ."

"Without question," said Borg. "Otherwise, he might use it to escape. Remember, he has one for every occasion."

Borg and Carolyn chatted during the cocktail hour before the debate in the large second-floor gallery of the club in Providence. A couple of hundred people had gathered, anticipating verbal fireworks. The crowd knew that Toby and Cuz hated each other. Most members of the club didn't like either one, holding in equal contempt journalists and politicians, other than Republicans of course. Men wore blazers and sports coats and an occasional suit; women favored Talbot's though a few dared a Ferragamo shoe.

Years before, Borg and Carolyn had been lovers. Briefly. Ardently. When he was a poor cub reporter and she was vested in position and wealth. They had pretended otherwise at her family's country house in Padanarum before reality and her parents set in. Now, he was still poor but a publisher. She was, two husbands later, still rich. Somehow, their friendship persisted. Intermittently.

"Why in the world are you moderating this silly thing?" Carolyn looked over her glass of pinot gris at Borg. Still knew how to use her blue eyes.

"Damned if I know," said Borg. "It might be fun. I'll get out of the way once they get started."

"Watch out you don't get caught in the cross-fire," said Carolyn. "You usually do."

Borg left her to climb the three steps to the dais at the end of the room where he joined the two speakers. He took his Dewar's with him. Couzens and Fragnoli took seats on either side of him, behind an ancient oak table. Behind them, a large oil painting of an early club president looked down on all three with a sniff of disdain, as though he had just encountered a whiff of bad cheese. After introductions and sparring it didn't take long for the fireworks to begin.

"Voters are fools." Benjamin J. Couzens spit his pronouncement at the mayor.

"For electing me?" Fragnoli, smiled. Everyone expected him to win a third term by a huge margin.

"I didn't say that." Borg knew he meant it. So did everyone else. The political columnist for the statewide *Bulletin* resembled a turtle, bulging eyes behind thick glasses, sparse hair combed forward, strand by strand, a bulbous mouth, petulant and prissy most of the time, trying to smile now. The most potent argument against freedom of the press since William Randolph Hearst started the Spanish-American War.

"You think you're smarter than a majority of the people?" the Mayor asked.

"I hate to see them fooled." Cuz's smile tightened.

Matt Borg's long, lanky body slid lower in his seat, looking even more rumpled than when the debate began, his blazer creased, his tie loose, his chino slacks riding up from his scuffed loafers. The grins depressed him more than the insults.

Borg found it impossible to smile and smile and hurl insults as these guys did. Still, he admired Toby and his sense of humor even as he hated to hear him bash the press. After all, Borg, in his cynical way, still believed in freedom of the press. Still believed that it was the worst system in the world—except for every other. Didn't Churchill say that about democracy? Probably. He had something to say about almost everything. Like most politicians.

A rustle of unease filled the hall as mayor and columnist stared at each other. Borg could sense sentiment turning against Cuz and his solemn self-righteousness. Mayor Fragnoli looked as though he had swallowed the canary and could sing its song. Pleased with himself, his round face wreathed in a moonlike smile sharpened by eyes that shone like dark buttons beneath hooded lids. Even his hairpiece, glistening black, reflected triumph. Borg watched as Fragnoli with an air of amused indifference listened to Cuz go on about freedom of the press.

Borg couldn't keep his own mind from wandering, tired of the same guys saying the same things he had heard over and over again. Most of the audience in the uncomfortable metal chairs studied the paintings on the walls as he did. Some began to whisper. Bill Grunther, his horsy face looking silly, chirped to his wife at the back of the gallery that served as an auditorium for club affairs. Artist Randall Ransom, paying no attention to the debate, chatted with two elderly women who bought his paintings. Carolyn Perry, bemused as always, held a glass of the cold but otherwise unremarkable wine against a cheek and watched Borg squirm.

Now the mayor prepared his final riposte. Borg knew what he'd say. He had heard it before.

Toby paused for effect. "You know, I think if one day I was able to walk across Narragansett Bay, like Jesus himself, the next day *The Bulletin*'s headline would be, 'Mayor Fragnoli Can't Swim.'"

Toby Fragnoli waited for the laughter to die down.

"What have you got against me?" the mayor asked Cuz, feigning innocence.

"I hate corruption in government," said Cuz. "And I don't like crooks."

"You're not calling me a crook, are you, Mr. Couzens?" The mayor's smile froze in place. A momentary look of pure hatred flashed across his flushed face. It shocked Borg.

"I didn't say that."

"I guess I'll accept that as an apology," said the mayor. Borg didn't wait another minute.

"A good time to end this lively debate," Borg interjected as he rose to add his thanks to the mayor, the writer, and the audience.

He plunged off the dais and toward the bar, grabbed a fresh Dewar's and water. The Club Manager, Joe Medeiros, was behind the bar. A waiter mustn't have shown up. Borg was disappointed that the press had lost another argument. On the other hand, he liked Toby a lot more than he liked Cuz. Though he probably trusted Cuz more by a margin too thin to measure. Figure that out.

"I need a drink as much as you do." Standing behind Borg was Ace Adams, publisher of *The Bulletin* and once Borg's boss.

"Think Cuz did a pretty good job standing up for our free press?" said Borg as they shook hands, as friendly as most publishers, especially competitors, pretended to be.

"Hate both the bastards," growled Adams as he charged to the bar. Even as Borg turned away, Cuz collided with him and Borg lost some of his Scotch.

"What's the damn hurry?" said Borg, wiping the alcohol from his tie. It already had a few stains. One more wouldn't matter.

Borg didn't expect an apology, didn't get one. "On my way to find something out that will set this town and this club on its ear," said Cuz.

"A scoop?" Borg laughed. "You've got to be kidding."

"You'll see," said Cuz. "It's a scoop and a scandal too."

Cuz had worked for Borg at *The Bulletin* years before. Cuz became a star columnist, developing sublime confidence in the process. Borg, on the other hand, with considerable help from a bank and friends, bought a small daily that struggled to stay alive.

Borg watched Cuz leave the gallery and disappear down the stairs. On his way to his scoop? Probably. Borg couldn't help but wonder what Cuz would find at his meeting. And whether the mayor would be involved.

CPSIA information can be obtained at www.ICGtesting.com
Printed in the USA
BVOW070226271112

306571BV00001B/64/P

9 780533 166008